DEATH BY
Dissertation

KELLY BRAKENHOFF

DEATH BY
Dissertation

KELLY BRAKENHOFF

To Mom and Dad and Teri
It's been a long wait

Chapter One

Cassandra Sato cradled her palms around her warm Morton College travel mug, hoping the coffee inside would calm the churning in her stomach. Half anticipation, half impatience at wasting her time, uncertainty was the last thing she needed her boss to see at the start of their probationary coaching meeting. She fixed a serene expression on her face, pretending to admire the view from his picture window, while reviewing her mental list of the issues he might raise. As the youngest person to earn a doctorate in education from the University of Hawai'i at age 28, she had years of practice appearing more mature and confident than she felt. Still, feeling confident in the tropical sunshine of Manoa was much easier than squirming on an antique wooden armchair in Carson, Nebraska—population 8,300—in an office that best resembled a British men's club.

After two months as Student Affairs administrator, the honeymoon period was wearing off. Ten more probation meetings to go until her contract became permanent. She blew out a sigh. *No big deal.* She'd only relocated thousands of miles for this job.

The office door swung open and her boss eased in, a large ceramic platter in his arms. Cassandra stood respectfully. "Good afternoon, Dr. Nielson." She made to help him with the dish, but he waved her off, placing it on his desk.

A moist, yeasty smell of freshly-baked bread tinged with something sour drew her eyes to the pile of baked golden-brown dough rounds. Nielson raised his bushy gray eyebrows and nodded, his eager expression one she would call pride. "My wife home-baked some bierocks. Please, help yourself."

Nebraskans enjoyed sharing homemade food and excess produce just like her co-workers back home, although sampling new dishes at work was often dicey. The snacks resembled manapua, but she doubted his wife made them from scratch.

Although he graciously offered her a napkin, his toothy smile hinted at a dare. "Do Hawaiians eat bierocks, too?"

She swallowed the automatic *I'm-not-Hawaiian* reply that popped into her head. It was too complicated to correct him—again. Native Hawaiian meant a Polynesian descendant, not simply any Hawai'i state resident. Anyone familiar with the islands would never confuse the two. Grinding her back teeth together, she pasted a smile onto her face. "Thank you, Dr. Nielson, I'll try one."

She chose a small piece and bit into the soft, warm crust. Looking away, she tasted hamburger, Swiss cheese, salt, pepper and . . . and . . . *Was he seriously trying to gross her out about food?* Her regular diet included dried seaweed, octopus and taro root. She'd grown up believing Spam was its own food group.

Lightly tanned crow's feet framed his twinkling blue eyes. "Becky's secret ingredient is to mix in a little sauerkraut with the cabbage."

Cassandra's main experience with cabbage was fermented in kimchi, and this was quite different. Not disgusting, but probably an acquired taste. She politely said, "Your wife is an excellent cook, sir."

Hanging his suit jacket on a wooden coat rack, he opened the top button on his blue shirt and tugged his tie an inch looser while seating himself behind the desk. He referred to their meeting agenda. "Are you up to speed on Morton's upcoming capital campaign?"

The armchair creaked as she adjusted her wool pencil skirt and reached for her Moleskine journal on the edge of his desk. "I received the donor analysis and architectural renderings you emailed." She flipped to a blank page and headed it "Probation meeting" with the date.

Reading glasses perched on the end of his nose, he laid a finger on his desk calendar and sighed. "Unfortunately, our Chinese contacts rescheduled my team's cultural exchange trip to conflict with Homecoming next week. I need you to pinch hit for me at the finance committee meeting on Tuesday. One key player is Board President Dr. Schneider. You'll replace me in the Homecoming Parade with Schneider, the grand marshal. Do your homework and get to know him."

Nodding, she noted the meeting, retrieved her travel mug from the floor, and sipped fragrant Kona coffee. Homecoming parades were not her forte, but she welcomed the extra duties. His absence would be an opportunity to practice her management skills at the highest level.

His voice became stern. "In addition, you need to leave the office more. Get out on campus and talk to the constituents. I should invite you to the next dinner reception I host at my house. There are key people you need to talk to and find out their agenda. I need to know you are on my team working to advance Morton College into the future." He wrote a reminder on his agenda about the dinner invitation.

Constituents? *What was wrong with calling them students?* Disciplining undergrads and mentoring thesis candidates comprised a good chunk of Cassandra's daily schedule. Turning a few pages in her journal, she said, "I attended the faculty welcome orientation and luncheon several weeks after I started work in August." His dinner invitation fell in line with the carefully choreographed steps she'd taken since she was twenty years old to get this far. Finally, she was breaking into the old boys' club, meeting decision makers and gaining valuable leadership experience towards her goal of becoming a university president.

"Yes, that's a start, but you need to do more to dispel the stereotype that you're a shy, quiet Oriental." His sudden smile promised a great idea. "Hey, while I'm thinking about it . . . maybe you can give me language tips for how to greet the welcoming group when I arrive in China next week."

Resisting the urge to roll her eyes, she said, "Dr. Nielson, I've never been to China either. I don't speak any Chinese." It wasn't the first time she'd tried to set him straight on her ethnicity and background, but correcting her boss required delicacy. He had a reputation for ping-ponging between creative problem solver and theatrically moody despot with no patience for weakness or indecisiveness. "I was born and raised in Waipahu, Hawai'i where my family has lived for generations—110 years. They originally came from Japan, and most people nowadays call people who look like me Asian." Her grandmother would jump out of her sickbed and slap his ruddy face if she heard him mistake Cassandra for a Chinese girl.

The crease between his brows furrowed for a few seconds, then he shrugged it off. She wanted to believe he meant well, but his ignorance set her on edge sometimes. He thumbed through a folder, handing her the homecoming event flyer. "This is a bad time for me to leave town. You'll need to coordinate with the other administrators to cover events."

Relieved he was on track with the meeting's purpose again, she skimmed the schedule: game night, a carnival, the parade, and Saturday's football game. A sidebar advertised lunch and tours for visiting alumni.

Nielson cleared his throat and puffed out his chest. "Obviously, the staff will take care of logistics, but I expect you to come out of the office and handle your share of hospitality duties."

Welcoming guests with "aloha spirit" was much more Cassandra's comfort zone than parades. She pulled up her phone's calendar app. "Shall I ask Julie to put my name down for the events that remain unfilled?"

He said, "I'm concerned, Dr. Sato, about student and public perceptions when you represent this office. My personal support can't completely overcome negative

episodes like the photo of you and that preacher woman ..."
Shaking his gray-haired head, his lips pursed together in
disapproval.

A warning quiver tiptoed down her spine. Last week
Dr. Nielson had called her into his office, scolding her like
a teenager out past curfew over one photo taken out of
context. His bringing it up again was a bad omen. "I hired
you because of your impressive credentials and journal
articles. The search committee's support of your hiring was
divided because of your limited administrative experience.
I convinced them we needed to bring some diversity to our
campus here in the middle of white America."

Well, he was right about that part. More than 83% of
Morton College's students were Caucasian. "I expected you
to handle committee assignments, teach leadership classes,
and deal with student affairs cases as well as supervise the
team of directors who report to you."

Pulling out a copy of the photo that had gotten her new
job off to a shaky start, he laid it on the desk between them.
Leaning forward and lowering his voice, he counseled, "Use
more discretion about your public appearances. We need
this woman to move on. We don't want you or Morton seen
as a laughingstock."

That bierock now sat more like a rock in her stomach
than a cozy welcome. Cassandra was no expert on social
media, but the photo seemed harmless overall. Ok, probably she shouldn't have stopped to chat with such a memo-
rable figure in the open, but calling her a laughingstock
went too far. She'd written off the inappropriate anonymous

emails she'd received as cranks, but Nielson's disapproval was more serious.

Perfectly timed, a brisk knock sounded on the door. His assistant, Julie, stepped halfway into the office. "Dr. Nielson, uh...excuse me. Campus s-security is on the phone. A body was found at the Edgerton Science building. A d-dead body. What do you want me to t-tell them?"

Cassandra's head jerked around to look into Julie's somber, pale face. Returning her gaze to Dr. Nielson, they stared at each other in momentary disbelief. He said, "We are on our way over."

Chapter Two

They covered the short distance through the green park blanketing the campus quad to the Edgerton Science Center in silence in under five minutes. Cassandra barely noticed the landscaped trees and shrubs that had begun changing colors into soft oranges and reds, instead bracing her uneasy stomach for the coming trial. Two campus security cars were pulled off the drive and an officer wearing a Morton Security baseball cap stood with Campus Security Director Andy Summers blocking the outside staircase. More baby-faced than his job title implied, Summers' calm presence was a welcome sight. Nearby in a small huddle of students, a guy wearing a ripped hoodie held up his phone and snapped a photo of the scene.

Dr. Nielson marched over to the stairs and addressed Summers. "What happened? Do these students need to be so close? Let's get some people to back them up." Raising his hands, Nielson faced the students and told Hoodie to put away his phone. "Let's give the law enforcement some space, folks. Why don't you back up to there?" He pointed to the Media building about 20 feet farther away, and the students reluctantly shuffled over. Cassandra made eye contact with Andy Summers and gave a slight nod, but said nothing. She knew they'd talk later and didn't want to interfere with his work.

Cassandra had seen her share of students with mental health problems, bad grades or family illnesses and deaths; but she'd never dealt with anything like this. Her heart thumped a rapid beat while her mind tried to absorb the growing alarm and activity. Summers reported to Cassandra and Nielson, "Students were playing Frisbee golf and came upon this guy. They said they haven't moved him. We got here about 10 minutes ago. The county sheriff's office has sent someone out, but it could take 30 minutes before they arrive. Don't touch anything."

The three stood on a small concrete area at the bottom of Edgerton's four-story staircase behind yellow crime scene tape. Cassandra's eyes were riveted to the form sprawled over the top edge of the lowest flight of stairs, shoulders and head canted down. The young man wore jeans, Adidas sneakers, and a navy Morton Maples t-shirt. His left arm was partially under his upturned body, and his right hand rested on his hip. There was something familiar . . . but she couldn't say what it was.

Nielson's neck craned up. "Are we sure it's too late?"

Summers adjusted the plastic ear piece wire that snaked over the collar of his thick navy uniform shirt and fit into his right ear. His lips formed a flat line, and he nodded.

Cassandra surveyed the scene, ignoring a lightheaded wooziness. No obvious blood from a knife or gunshot stained the steps. Studying his clothes, she noted the torn knees on his jeans. His left arm had cuts and scrapes and the right hand ... Was it odd to rest like that on his hip? A deep gash marred the right side of his forehead, crusting dried blood on his temple and hair. Despite the purplish skin undertone, she recognized that bruised, bloody face. Her vision blurred. *How would she tell his roommate, Lance, when she could hardly believe her own eyes?*

A catch grew in her throat, but dissolved into impatience that his broken body had just laid there on the open steps for who-knows-how-long alone and undiscovered. Cassandra checked her watch: 3:20 on a Friday afternoon. He'd obviously fallen, but whether tripped, jumped or shoved, she wasn't trained to recognize. She tamped down an impulse to cover him up, protect his now unnecessary dignity. Not used to feeling helpless, Cassandra leaned closer to Summers. "How far away was the fire station?"

Before he had time to answer, an ambulance pulled up, a couple of EMTs jumped out and retrieved their stretcher from the back of the unit. One paramedic climbed the stairs, assessed the student, and spoke into his radio. Nielson broke off from Cassandra to confer in low tones with the remaining medic near the truck.

Summers told her, "We have a volunteer fire department and paramedics. The dispatcher alerts the guys on duty, who drop what they're doing—even if they're at the store with a cart full of groceries—and meet at the station on Main Street before heading to the call." His matter-of-fact acceptance of the delay snapped her out of her emotional paralysis, and Cassandra made a mental note: avoid personal medical catastrophes for the near future.

Classes were dismissing for the afternoon; some students wandered over toward the commotion. Everyone turned as a dusty white county sheriff cruiser stopped at the curb and a large man wearing wraparound sunglasses got out. After updates and an introduction to Cassandra, Sheriff Hart instructed the Morton officer to keep onlookers completely away from the buildings.

The Frisbee players were called to the Edgerton side of the walkway and clustered around Sheriff Hart and Dr. Nielson. "Which one of you guys found him first?" he asked.

A lanky upperclassman wearing a tri-Chi sweatshirt slowly raised a hand. "I-I did."

"What's your name?"

"Evan Hall, sir."

Hart raised the sunglasses onto his combed back, peppered gray hair and nodded once. "Can you tell me what happened?"

Evan's explanation tumbled out loudly. "Um...none of us had afternoon classes, so we came out to play Frolf." Gesturing near the staircase to a metal pole with an attached wire basket, he held up a small plastic disc. "We got to that pole for the 4th hole, and Dan's team behind us threw a wild disc over our heads. It hit the side of Edgerton and landed behind the bush." He walked a few steps and pointed towards the lilac shrub near the building. "I reached in, got Dan's disc, and when I stood up I noticed that shape up there. It looked like a pile of clothes or garbage so I took a second look, and that's when I realized..."

The Sheriff asked, "Did you go up there and touch him? Did you move him or see if he was hurt or breathing?"

"I ran up the steps, and got close to his face, but...he wasn't breathing at all," Evan reported. "We called 911, and...yeah."

Sheriff Hart's hand rested on his thick black leather utility belt. "Can anyone identify the student?"

Evan said, "I've seen him on campus, but I dunno his name. He's a sophomore or junior." The others nodded, but no one volunteered a name.

Cassandra looked right and left in surprise. Morton was so small, Cassandra had just assumed others recognized him, too. "I know him. I'm pretty sure that's Austin." Saying his name out loud had made it real. "His roommate, Lance, is a work-study student in my office. He's deaf...both of them are," she added.

Loud voices drew Cassandra's attention to the far end of the two-story Media Center where a small crowd had gathered. A wide sidewalk, bordered by shrubs and ornamental trees, connected it to the Edgerton Center. Even 20 yards away they chattered animatedly, but one student wearing a knitted hat was more agitated, pointing at the staircase and yelling.

Cassandra looked back over her shoulder at Austin's body. As bad as she felt for him, he was the police's responsibility now. Her job was with the students. No one covered *this* in New Student Orientation. Frowning, she moved towards them and noticed Dr. Nielson doing the same thing. When she came close enough, Cassandra heard shouting. "My lab's in there! I need to check the rats! Who is that?"

They wouldn't be able to disclose Austin's name until his family had been notified. She answered, "No one is allowed in Edgerton until the police are finished."

But the kid wouldn't take no for an answer, and he pushed against Nielson. Nielson held his hands out towards the student's shoulders to restrain him. "What's your name, son?"

"Let me go! What the hell is happening?" he shouted.

Cassandra stepped back to avoid getting hurt if this thing came to fists. "We can't help you until you calm down. Please stay back and listen," she urged.

Momentarily they were joined by Andy Summers, Sheriff Hart, and the brown-shirted deputy. More than a head taller than the freaked-out student, the Sheriff bent over and spoke close to his ear for long seconds. Once he seemed to regain self-control, the deputy led Knitted Hat to his county car and opened the back door.

Cassandra's eyes followed the cruiser as it eased from the curb and drove away. Tempting as it was to call a lawyer for Knitted Hat, she had to follow federal privacy laws.

Sheriff Hart told Summers, "The deputy will bring him into the office as a person of interest. Let's organize the Frisbee players to get their statements." He walked to the staircase holding his shoulder radio up to his mouth.

These students were all adults with the right to give a statement without their parents' knowledge or consent, although back home they would certainly have asked an elder for advice. Mainland students were much more independent. Cassandra told Nielson, "We should get back to the office."

His lined face looked older, tired. "You can help me make some calls."

"Sure, go ahead," Summers said. "After the students' statements, we have to wait for the forensics team from Lincoln, and then the coroner."

Nielson headed back toward the quad, but Cassandra felt a gentle touch on her arm from Summers. Nielson didn't notice her absence, so she paused.

Summers' forehead leaned close enough to Cassandra that she could see perspiration forming along his buzz cut hairline. He said quietly, "Do you know if Austin did drugs? He had some bruising and old needle marks on his arms. Mostly his left arm, but there's a couple on the right side, too."

Meaning he suspected a drug-related accident or overdose? "What, er . . . ah, I don't really know. I've never heard his roommate say anything like that." She wouldn't be the first person Lance would tell anyway. People assumed she was the one who suspended or dismissed students from school.

One question lingered. She hesitated but decided to ask anyway. "Could you send me a couple of photos of Austin after you're done here?"

Summers' light brown eyes sharpened. "That would be totally out of line. I used to work for the sheriff's office. You should know I can't do that."

She hadn't realized her request would be unwelcome, but she really wanted a photo from the scene. She needed to figure out what was familiar about the way Austin's body had landed, and her memory wasn't enough. She held her breath, calculating how far off the mark she'd missed. "I just want to check out a question I had about Austin. If I'm right, I'd let you know immediately. If I'm totally off-base, I don't want to waste your time."

Arms crossed in front of his chest, Summers gave her a long, appraising look. "I can *show* you a couple of photos. Unofficially. But you can't keep them."

Chapter Three

Cassandra's trademark clear thinking failed her. Normally, her airy office with its soft, tranquil gray painted walls freed her mind to focus on important tasks. Instead, her three framed degrees, all from the University of Hawai'i, hanging in the narrow space between two large bookshelves seemed inadequate training for handling the death of a student.

Her planner lay open on her desktop, and she penciled in follow-up questions as they popped into her head. "Call Austin's parents." She hoped Nielson was able to contact them immediately. "Tell Lance, student workers, directors."

Poking her head around the doorway she called, "Annie, can you text all the work-study students from our office? We're meeting here ASAP. Lance is still in class, but anyone who's available should come over now."

She gathered a few files and walked them to the outer office. Placing them in the To Be Filed bin, she retrieved the plastic watering can she kept behind a cabinet door. She wrote, "Fell down stairs, jumped, or pushed?" She drifted out to the hallway water fountain to fill the can. "Were security cameras on the floor where he worked?" Each time she passed through the outer office, she overheard three student workers bantering among each other, their ordinary conversation a soothing balm to her frayed nerves.

"I should've never let my grandpa friend me on Facebook. Now he comments on every photo someone posts of me. The old people shouldn't know so much about us. If I don't respond, he emails me to tell me he commented. I'm gonna block him."

"My grandma likes to watch cat videos on YouTube. Worst thing is when she sends them to me. I don't know how to tell her. Just. Stop."

Cassandra balanced the full watering can and dutifully fed her college-issued large palm tree. The leaves' edges had already turned crispy brown from neglect. Apparently, these needed water more than once a month.

Annie told Cassandra, "The gang's on the way, boss."

Good. Once she got confirmation that next of kin had been notified, she could make it official to the students.

Devon held up his phone, "What's going on over at Edgerton? Is some class filming a project for YouTube?" Annie and Bridget checked their phones for more details.

Cassandra slowed to glance at Annie's phone while she held up a photo from the Edgerton scene. *Crap! News was already getting out to the students!*

"Maybe my Anthropology professor is doing another YouTube tutorial, I watch those multiple times. He's easy on the eyes," said Bridget.

Annie said, "You mean Professor Hottie? Um, what's his real name again?"

Cassandra carried a medium-sized postal box with brochures for a national committee she was working on and placed it in the outgoing mail pile. She half-listened to snippets of their conversation while she went back to her office.

Bridget laughed, "Isn't that the name on his birth certificate? Professor Jason Hottie?" Cassandra recalled his wire rimmed glasses and Indiana Jones wardrobe. Yeah, he was hot by any standards.

But Devon scoffed, "Oh, give it up. He's married and has little kids."

"Still hot," insisted Annie.

"No one's answering my texts about Edgerton. I can't tell if it's real or a class," said Devon.

"Who's not hot?" Annie pointed to the picture. "No-Nonsense Nielson. Kind of a dorky Professor Lupin. Does he even know what YouTube is? He probably has a flip phone."

"Right," Bridget agreed. "What's with those tweed cardigans he wears? They just scream, 'I was bullied as a child.'"

Even as Cassandra chuckled inwardly at the Lupin comparison—she'd thought the same thing—their chatter had probably wasted enough time and crossed several boundaries. Paused in her doorway, arms crossed over her chest, she glared wide-eyed at the three students facing her, chairs together and thumbing through their phones as they talked across each other. Cassandra remained there quietly, her jaw twitching with stifled laughter, allowing the conspicuous silence to stretch.

Annie raised her eyes and didn't turn her head, but said, "He's in our office, isn't he?"

Bingo. Cassandra nodded slowly.

Devon's face reddened. "He's right behind us?"

Normally, this would be hilarious. Not today. Cassandra nodded again. "Probably now would be a good time to email appointment reminders for the next couple of days, Bridget." They dropped their phones and scrambled back to work.

President Gary "No-Nonsense" Nielson stood in the office entrance for about five beats, apparently deliberating whether to dispute the allegations of his nerdiness or to scold them to get back to work. After waiting long enough to make it seem like the incident had never happened, he walked straight through to Cassandra's office door. "Can we talk for a few minutes?"

She was surprised by his ability to ignore their insults. She flipped one of the cushioned student chairs in front of her desk around so it faced the loveseat and large framed Japanese print overhead, opened the mini fridge, and took out two bottles of water. Handing one across to Nielson, she sat in the chair and opened her mouth to apologize for her students' unfortunate remarks.

He held up a hand to quiet her. "I know what they call me, Dr. Sato. If that's the worst they can come up with, I figure it's not worth taking personally."

Nielson looked around her simply furnished office. He'd been there maybe once since Cassandra had started. Nodding at the sea turtle Hawaiian artwork filling the wall space next to her window, he smiled. "Did I mention already that my wife and I celebrated our 10th anniversary in Hawai'i? Beautiful women greeted us with those flower necklaces at the airport, and we stayed in Wah-kiki. We rode a tour bus to the pineapple cannery, the snorkeling bay, and the shopping mall."

She tried not to wince at his mispronunciations. Knowing he was headed out of the country for a week, Cassandra had assumed his unexpected visit had a point. But instead of delegating tasks, he acted vaguely nostalgic.

"My wife drank frou-frou drinks with little paper umbrellas in them and bought me the loudest orange and blue Hawaiian shirt in the store. I've never worn it again. Nowhere here to wear something that bright. Except once when I attended the board president's beach party at the Fremont Lakes." His face relaxed. "Hawai'i truly is paradise. I don't understand how anyone wants to leave that place."

He'd taken the stereotypical Hawaiian vacation to the three or four most famous tourist spots where the couple couldn't have enjoyed the hidden treasures outside the bustling waterfront. She tried to sound polite. "Yes Dr. Nielson, Hawai'i is a lovely place to visit. The people are warm and friendly. It was a wonderful place to grow up and live."

She couldn't resist her memories of bamboo forested hikes up to breathtaking lookouts and local foods the tourists never ate. She missed the beautiful colored muumuu and flowered skirts she had left in her closet back home; the traditional Aloha Friday shirts men wore weekly, tucked in or out depending on the level of formality dictated by their profession; the fragrant flower leis handed out to coworkers and friends for birthdays, promotions or any special occasions.

He said, "The timing of today's incident couldn't be worse. My flight leaves tomorrow morning at 6:00 out of Omaha. I need to get home soon to finish details before the trip."

Cassandra readied her journal list and sipped water from her bottle.

Elbows resting on his knees, he leaned forward but talked as if he had no audience. "From what I saw, it looked like he fell down those stairs. But with no investigation or autopsy yet, we just don't know. The Sheriff said Mr. Price was wearing a science lab key card name tag. I suppose they'll have to start in the lab to back track his activity before the accident."

Nielson was speaking too slowly and carefully, without making direct eye contact. His stalling wasn't like someone in a hurry to get home. "I'm going to need you to take the lead on this problem. Keep me informed. Here's the thing though . . ."

When he inhaled a long breath, she wanted to scream, *get to the point before my hair turns gray!* Nielson said, "Look, you may be unaware of the biology lab's research importance. There are several ongoing studies, but the big one is the NIH cancer study we've arranged with our food services department. This National Institutes of Health grant is a huge feather in our caps. Not only is it research dollars for our college, but we use beef from a nearby farm in all our campus cafeterias and Greek houses."

Cassandra's pen paused on the page. This seemed more like background information than action items. He said, "It's prime meat—very lean and healthy. Even though it's a small pilot project, it's great PR for our school. I've asked Bergstrom to highlight our successes during Homecoming next week when visitors want to see what's new on campus. Do what you can to make sure they don't close the lab or the area around the building to visitors."

She wrote, "Keep lab open—critical."

He stood and planted one foot near the door. "I'll check my email as often as possible, but you'll have to keep this contained. Liaison with the investigation, but focus on college business as usual. A smooth Homecoming Week should be your top priority. Many alumni and benefactors are visiting. It won't do for them to be constantly reminded of this tragedy. Keep it out of the news as much as possible." Without waiting for a response, he yanked the door open and left.

This was not the way she'd planned to start her week as temporary administrator in charge. She added to her list, "contact media relations office," and "keep out of news." He'd hardly given her any details, yet expected her to liaison with police and the media.

She eyed the little Buddha shrine subtly displayed on her credenza under the window. Most visitors looking at the arrangement would think it was a generic Asian display of statue and artifacts. She prayed a quick nembutsu, "Namu Amida Butsu." Her plea was interrupted by the ringing of her desk phone. It was Nielson's assistant, Julie.

"Hello Julie, have you spoken to Dr. Nielson?"

"Yes I have, Dr. Sato. What would you like me to do first?"

Cassandra slipped into administrator mode. Her voice was clear. "Has anyone called Board Chairman Schneider?"

"Dr. Nielson called him after he talked to Austin Price's parents about 20 minutes ago."

She was grateful he'd made those calls, but dismayed he hadn't even mentioned it while in her office. "Good. Can you contact the directors and other administrative staff, please? Anyone who's still in the office today can meet me in your conference room at 5:00."

Chapter Four

Cassandra faced the six student workers gathered in the Student Affairs' front office. Haley perched on the beige metal reception desk where Annie worked, one leg dangling off the edge. Logan and Rachel squished into a wide plush chair, her head resting on Logan's shoulder. Creases lined her face like someone had roused her from a nap to attend the impromptu staff meeting. Devon and Bridget slouched in modern shaped foam chairs thumbing through the apps on their phones and mumbling low to each other.

Rachel whined, "What are we doing here? I need to get ready to go to the Theta Psi formal in a couple hours."

There was no easy way to say it. Cassandra ripped the Band-Aid off quickly. "Have you heard that there was a body found over by the Edgerton building?"

Heads nodded and a couple of the kids gestured towards their phones. "Yeah we heard, but no one knows who or why."

"I wanted you to find out in person. It was Austin Price."

"WHAT!" they shouted in unison.

"I just saw him at breakfast!"

"Does Lance know? They grew up together."

"What happened?"

Cassandra reported, "When I got there he was already gone ... er, dead. He was found on the stairs outside the building. It looked like he'd fallen somehow. I'm sorry I can't tell you more. They'll do an autopsy to find the exact cause of death." When they all just stared at her wide-eyed for a moment, she continued, "Did any of you know him very well? Did Lance tell you anything about Austin that would help us figure out how this happened?"

"We're from the same hometown," said Haley, "but we didn't really hang around together."

Cassandra wondered who were Austin's friends besides Lance. Noting their blank stares, she remembered Summers' concerns. "Was he in trouble? Did he drink or do drugs? Anything would help right now."

They spoke over each other. "His work study is over in the research lab with the rats."

"I just can't believe this."

"I don't think he did drugs."

Annie frowned, "You'd be shocked if you knew what some people do."

Devon bellyached, "Oh man, if my mother hears Morton has a drug problem, she's gonna make me transfer back to community college near home."

Wait. Cassandra had heard little about drug use on campus since her arrival and doubted it was a widespread problem.

"How do you know Austin fell? Were there any witnesses?" Rachel was wide awake now.

"Not that—" Cassandra began but Bridget interrupted.

"What if someone killed him and planted the body . . . like that Netflix series?"

They'd veered off into gossip she didn't have time for now, and Cassandra's head started to ache. She raised her voice to get their attention. "Guys, the sheriff and campus security will figure it out. Don't freak out, it will be ok."

"I am totally freaking out. There's supposed to be a formal tonight." Rachel's hands flailed at her sides and her voice whined. "We're going off campus to eat. Then to the VFW hall for a dance."

Devon warned in a deep voice, "Keep your eyes open for a mysterious stranger hiding behind the VFW."

Logan put an arm around Rachel's shoulder. "Dial down the drama, Rach. Dr. Sato said it was an accident."

Rachel said, "I wonder if they'll cancel."

A formal dance would be a much better distraction than sitting around replaying death scenarios from horror shows. Cassandra put on a reassuring smile. "Give me the dance chairperson's phone number, and I'll encourage them not to cancel. You folks can take off now. I just wanted you to hear the news in person."

Only Annie remained when the students picked up their backpacks and shuffled out of the office because she was still on the clock. She stared at Cassandra a few seconds until the ringing office phone interrupted the quiet. Cassandra blew out a big sigh and took two steps towards her office doorway. Reversing direction, she realized she didn't want to sit in there, alone. She listened until

Annie's phone conversation showed that the call wasn't for Cassandra, then walked downstairs towards the Special Student Services suite.

She knocked once under the "ASL Interpreters" nameplate then slowly opened the door and peeked around. The red-headed woman seated in front of a flat TV monitor next to the desk conversed with a man using American Sign Language, but no voices. She glanced at the doorway and waved Cassandra ahead.

Standing just inside the door, Cassandra waited a few minutes while the Skype-looking screen-within-a-screen conversation continued. A small window dimly lit the cramped space's Spartan decor: two desks, an ugly black metal bookshelf, a printer stand and the table for the 24" TV screen. A large white board with a color-coded schedule filled the available wall.

Margaret Mary O'Brien or "Meg" and Cassandra were co-workers seven years earlier at Oahu State College. Her husband, Connor, had been stationed at Bellows Air Force Base for two years before transferring to the mainland and settling in Connor's home state. Cassandra had contacted Meg when she found out she was a finalist for the Vice President position, even staying with the O'Briens during the interviews. Cassandra had her choice of several Midwestern jobs, but decided on Morton College in part because of the opportunity to reconnect their close friendship.

Meg remoted the screen off, spun around in her chair, and did a little hand salute. "Aloha!"

Meg's cheery smile made Cassandra feel a teensy bit better. Cassandra plopped down in the only empty chair. "Howzit!"

Meg shrugged. "Pretty good. Just setting up interpreters for one of the deaf instructors' night classes next month."

"Wow, your technology has really improved since our old days together."

Meg indicated the screen. "This is my video phone. I use it to talk to students or parents and instructors. Much easier than typing conversations on a TTY keyboard like before. Why are you slumming down here in my little kingdom?"

Meg was taking the afternoon tragedy much better than Cassandra had anticipated. The cheap mismatched rolling chair squeaked as Cassandra leaned back and covered her face with her hands, massaging temples she'd just noticed were throbbing. "Seriously," Cassandra's hometown vernacular came out. "Dis Aloha Friday gone bad, sistah."

Meg was breezy and sarcastic. "Big surprise, Cass. Nielson leaves town for a week and you get to deal with all the Homecoming stuff while he's gone. Has he asked you to water his plants, too? Whose bright idea was it to send that man to another continent anyway? Everyone he meets is going to have a warped idea of Americans in general and Nebraskans in particular. Are they hoping he'll be separated from the tour group and get lost?"

Among all the challenges in moving to Nebraska, Meg's humor and friendship was a beacon of light. However . . . she should've been very upset right now. Cassandra sat up fast, planted her feet on the ground and looked closely at

Meg's face. "Wait . . . haven't you heard what happened this afternoon?"

Meg's hands casually rearranged her long, wavy red hair into a high, messy bun. She expertly twisted, tied and fluffed until only a few stray tendrils framed her freckled face, making her appear younger than her thirty-three years. "Uh, no . . . what are you talking about?" When Cassandra didn't respond right away, Meg's light brown eyes focused, a question on her incongruently dark eyebrows.

Cassandra's eyes welled up. "You know Austin Price? He . . . was found dead a couple hours ago over by the Edgerton Center. I'm hiding from my ringing telephone and trying to regroup . . . How have you not heard about this?"

Meg's face paled and her mouth formed a silent Oh! "I was in a Chem Lab all afternoon; I had no idea. I'm sorry I was so sarcastic just now." She frowned and shook her head in disbelief, "Why didn't you text me? You can't be right. I just interpreted a Geography class for him this morning."

Regret swamped Cassandra for not thinking of Meg right away. She said, "I've been a little busy . . . Well the sheriff is going to want to speak to you, too. They're trying to go over everything that happened today to figure out the time of death."

Meg was one of the last people to see Austin alive. Her voice broke, "I don't even know what to say. That never happens." Cassandra watched helplessly as Meg's eyes filled with tears. "I've only known him a little over a year but . . . wow. What happened?"

Seeing Meg's reaction released the floodgates Cassandra had held back. Her eyes spilled over too, wetting her cheeks. Cassandra said, "I don't know. It looked like he fell down the stairs, somehow. There wasn't a lot of blood. I'm waiting to hear more from the sheriff."

Cassandra leaned forward and fiddled with her necklace. "When I left, they were waiting for Lincoln's forensic team to arrive. Dr. Nielson contacted Austin's family. You had him in Geography. Did he seem ok this morning?"

Meg groped around in a desk drawer until she came up with a box of tissues. They both mopped up their cheeks and eyes. "We just had a short review and a quiz in Geography this morning. We left class early. Austin barely said anything to me. He'd showered before class—his hair was wet—and he walked in with a cardboard coffee cup from the cafeteria. I told him have a good weekend as we walked out of class, and he said you too. That was about 12:30. I never saw him after that."

Your basic college student's Friday morning. Cassandra wiped her runny nose. "Did he normally talk to you much?"

Meg dabbed at her eyes. "Not more than politely nodding hello and goodbye to me. He avoided calling extra attention to himself. Some deaf kids like him would rather just be an anonymous face in a lecture hall. Hard to fade into the crowd when everyone in class notices your sign language interpreter on the first day, standing in front of the room by the professor, every word and facial expression played out on her hands and face." Meg shrugged. "Usually the other students lose interest by the third class, but it's still hard to blend in when you converse in sign before class starts or to participate in discussion."

She'd never thought about that. A twinge of guilt pricked Cassandra's chest as she realized how little she knew about Meg's job and the deaf students' experiences. "I just assumed a close relationship develops because of how much time you spend with the deaf students."

Meg wiped the mascara that had smudged under her eyes. "It's hard enough to be 20, away from home, and navigating the emotional rollercoaster college scene. Others stare in fascination at a language they've rarely seen, and a person they are uncomfortable communicating with directly. I let the students lead the way on how close-by they want me. I don't want them to feel harassed." Cassandra scooted her chair nearer, reached around and squeezed Meg's shoulders in a consoling hug.

It was time to get back to work. Cassandra checked her watch: 4:45 p.m. "I already met with the student workers that were still on campus, but next I'm meeting with the admin staff. Can you stick around and interpret for Lance Erickson? He's in class until 5:30 and might not know about Austin yet."

Meg's video phone flashed to signal an incoming call, and a phone number and name appeared on the screen. Meg wiped her nose one more time and turned toward her desk. "I'd better answer this. Should we walk to the AOO house and talk to Lance there? I'll hang out here until you're done with the directors." She thumbed a remote and a face popped onto the screen. Meg waved goodbye while Cassandra returned to her wing.

* * *

Half an hour later, Meg joined Cassandra in the administrative board room as the staff filed out. "Hey, Meg. Good timing."

Cassandra, Cinda Weller, the Counseling Center director, and Marcus Fischer, the Housing director, were still seated at the table after the meeting. Cassandra picked up her phone to leave but paused. Cinda and Fischer were the two directors closest to her own age among the administrative staff.

Cinda Weller and Cassandra had hit it off quickly. Cassandra liked Cinda's quirky sense of humor, no-drama personality, and willingness to reveal the unwritten rules of Morton's academic climate. Also, she had great hair. Cassandra's hair was nearly black and stick straight. Cinda's was so blond, her thick, bouncy curls glowed white in the sunshine.

Fischer's quiet presence was versatile: from ironing out roommate conflicts to putting away equipment and cleaning up housing emergencies. She admired his habit of showing up to meetings with a brief report ready to go. None of the meandering recaps that less prepared members inflicted on the team.

Cinda turned to Cassandra and Fischer, scrunching up her nose. "That went well."

Cassandra noticed Meg gave Fischer a slow, appreciative look from shoes to hair before she sat quietly next to him. Cassandra had heard other women comment that his wavy dark hair, and trimmed beard were hot. She wasn't blind. But clearly her time in Nebraska was temporary, and she had enough complications to worry about without staring at his translucent baby blues all day.

Cassandra still had a lot of work left in her Friday. She sighed at the growing to-do list in her Moleskine journal. "I wanted to tell the staff in person and get our facts straight." Using her mechanical pencil, she added another note while talking. "Thanks for jumping in and reminding them to focus on the students, Cinda."

Cinda put her notepad into a leather portfolio and zipped it up. "Professors Gregory and Young can be such condescending chauvinists." She held up a finger, "As though number one, you magically know what exactly happened, given that they just found Austin's body a couple hours ago; and number two, you're in some way responsible for a random event on campus. They look for any excuse to treat you like a twenty-year-old undergrad."

Cassandra still worried that the tragedy could have been prevented. She rubbed her temple; the ibuprofen she'd taken earlier hadn't worked. "I get that administration is worried about public relations, but I'm worried about Austin's friends and family. I want to know what caused this horrible thing."

Sitting forward in his chair with one arm resting on the conference table, Fischer looked ready for action. Once by mistake, she'd turned her swivel chair before a staff meeting and clipped her travel mug with her elbow, nearly knocking it to the floor. His quick reflexes had him leaning over, scooping it up, and refilling the (thankfully) empty cup from a nearby coffee carafe. For just a nanosecond, she'd lost herself in the reflection of those clear blue eyes. Then President Nielson had begun the meeting's agenda, and the earth resumed spinning on its axis. Moment over.

Fischer said, "We should send a reminder email telling students that areas of campus may be off-limits while the police work. I talked to Andy Summers earlier, and he's called in some extra off-duty deputies. He wants them to patrol the campus and be available to walk students to their housing units or the parking lots if needed."

Cassandra asked, "Is it normal for a college security director to be so involved with the local law enforcement? Shouldn't we just let them handle everything?"

Cinda laughed, "This isn't the big city with hundreds of police officers. Carson shares the deputies and sheriff with everyone in the county. Andy Summers actually worked there before he took his job at Morton, so he has a good relationship with their office."

"I worked at Oahu State College for four years. We had a couple of suicides and some assaults, but no random dead bodies." There were so many differences between Honolulu and Carson. Cassandra stood, gathering her journal and mug while everyone else headed for the door. "I'll look up his course schedule. The more we can help the police, the faster they'll finish the investigation."

She'd have to delegate more of her list to get it all done tonight. She asked Fischer, "Can you find out more about Austin and his friends?"

Fischer's lean, athletic frame filled the doorway. He was more than a head taller than her. "Sure, I'll check around. When the police have taken what they need from Austin's room, I can send in a couple guys from my office to box up his personal effects for his family. We'll probably need his roommate's assistance in figuring out who belongs to which items."

Cassandra said, "Hopefully the extra security will help students feel calm until we have more news. However sad they might be, it is a Friday night."

When Fischer had left the conference room, Cinda fanned her face and blew a sigh at Meg. Like seventh grade. Cinda's head tilted towards the now vacant hall. "If I wasn't married, I'd let Fischer move into my office—for security, you know. That's the way to go, Cassandra."

Meg sputtered a laugh at the random comment. Cinda had a gift for breaking tension, but Cassandra's face flushed. "Shh...I can imagine the HR harassment complaint already. I don't need a wingman, Cinda. I need to do a good job."

"Yessir, Ma'am. All business, fine. I'm going to meet with my staff and set up the grief counselors in the Student Center. I'll put a message on social media about the hours available tonight and tomorrow." Cinda gave a mock salute and turned away towards her office.

Meg followed Cassandra down the hall. "It's cooling off outside. You might need a sweater on the way to the fraternity."

Chapter Five

Local Nebraskans apparently prepared for drastic temperature shifts by keeping multiple clothing layers handy. The lowering sun gave the bands of clouds an orange glow as Cassandra shivered in the twilight and groused, "I should have asked the actual temperature instead of just grabbing my sweater like you advised. I need a parka, not this flimsy little cardigan."

Meg nodded sympathetically, "Stick around here long enough, and your warm blood will get used to it."

She couldn't imagine how long would be "long enough" for that. Fallen amber leaves crunched under Cassandra's 3-inch heels as she and Meg walked toward the Alpha Omicron Omicron house. While some older students lived off campus, most of the 4,000 Morton College undergrads lived on school grounds. Cassandra focused on the unpleasant task at hand. "Tell me more about Lance and Austin. Lance works in my office part-time, but I don't know much about him personally. We only really talk when you're there to interpret."

"They went to high school together at a residential school for deaf students in Council Bluffs, Iowa. They're both sophomores: Austin was majoring in Psychology and Lance in Computer Science."

Turning between two brick buildings and crossing the street onto Greek Row, Cassandra gestured towards the stately, ivy-covered structures where small groups of students lounged outside on balconies and front porches. "I'm impressed by their bravery coming to Morton and joining a fraternity." Mainland students were much more independent than young adults in Hawai'i who lived with their parents into their 30s. Moving hundreds of miles from home to sleep in a fancy dorm and doing their own laundry would be a completely foreign thought. "It can't be easy for the deaf guys."

"It was a bit rough their first year with only twenty deaf students on campus, but the fraternity guys have figured out how to communicate with them by gesturing, texting and writing notes. We send interpreters for the weekly house meetings, but most of the time they're on their own. Lance is probably more studious; Austin was better at flirting with the girls." Meg's voice caught. "They were a good team. Lance is going to be devastated when he finds out."

Home to 30 young men, AOO was the oldest fraternity on campus. Its whitewashed picket fence bordered a lush, green front lawn with clusters of switchgrass, Russian sage and orange coneflower along the sidewalk and identical manicured boxwoods under symmetrical white windows. The ladies turned up the front walkway to the recently swept brick steps leading to the wooden front door. An eager member opened it promptly upon Cassandra's knock, said good evening and ushered them inside. "Who can I get for you?" he asked.

Cassandra glanced around the community room full of overstuffed, brown leather couches and coffee tables arranged in conversational groupings adjacent to a dark brick fireplace. "We're here for Lance Erickson, please."

Handsomely framed composite photos of the Alpha Omicron Omicron brothers by year lined the walls. On the left side, a large wooden staircase wound towards the second floor. On the far right, a hallway led towards the back of the house where clinking dishware indicated the direction of the kitchen and dining areas.

The underclassman nervously looked behind his shoulder. "I'm afraid he's already meeting with some, ah . . . um, people right now."

At that moment, a group stomped heavily down an unseen staircase and a strained voice yelled, "Wait, I'm going! Stop pushing,"

Although the words weren't clearly spoken, Cassandra and Meg could overhear. "Wait a minute. That sounded like Lance Erickson!" Cassandra exclaimed and hurried down the hallway towards the kitchen with Meg close behind.

The doorman objected, "Stop, you can't go back there!" But they ignored him.

They pulled up short in the doorway at the sight of two brown-shirted deputies coming down a wooden stairway each holding an arm of a 6'2", athletically-built young man who was visibly upset but not struggling.

A tray of freshly baked cinnamon rolls cooling on the center island counter top filled the commercial sized kitchen with a sweet cozy smell, and the plump cook turned from stirring a pot of chili, her ladle frozen in mid-air as she watched the unexpected commotion.

Cassandra recognized Lance Erickson, hands cuffed behind his back, his cheeks splotchy red. Trailing several steps behind was a frowning woman who locked eyes with Meg as if to say, "Do something, please!"

Meg subtly leaned into Cassandra's ear and whispered, "she's Nancy Ellis, a licensed sign language interpreter from Omaha."

Alarm tightened her chest. "Officers, I'm Cassandra Sato, Vice President of Student Affairs. Why have you hand-cuffed this student, and where are you taking him?"

The senior looking partner went about 240 pounds, presumably spent a lot of time behind a desk or a steering wheel, and still had his standard issue Marine haircut, now graying. "Ma'am, I'm Deputy Kobza. We're here to secure Austin Price's room and talk to his roommate. Campus Security told us both boys are hearing impaired so we called this translator. She arrived about five minutes ago, but by then Mr. Erickson was already very agitated and started shoving Deputy Tate. We had to cuff him. We're taking him out back." Kobza jerked his chin towards two sets of large French doors that opened onto a landscaped courtyard and patio. Deputy Tate appeared only a few years older than Lance and was built like a football lineman.

Meg signed as she spoke. "Let me make sure I under-stand you correctly? You two walked into a deaf student's room without warning, looked through his roommate's things and questioned him without an interpreter present?"

The older man nodded. "We knocked first, but there was no answer, so we went inside."

Cassandra could feel tension in the air around Meg. "Did you write down on a piece of paper who you are? Did you show him your badges and tell him why you were here?" She persisted in a quiet, slow voice, "Did you stop for a minute to think how it would feel if police poked around your bedroom with no introductions or explanations and you couldn't hear what they were saying?"

"We told him why we were there," Deputy Kobza said warily.

Meg stopped speaking and signed to him, "Yes . . . but if he couldn't understand your English like you can't understand American Sign Language then it wasn't an effective way to communicate, was it?"

The officers exchanged confused looks then turned back to Meg. "What did you say?"

"I signed clearly. Didn't you understand?" she spoke and signed.

Tate shrugged and Kobza shook his head no. "Of course not."

Cassandra saw them struggle to get the point. "Well . . . how did that feel?" Meg prompted.

Lance had cooled down while watching Meg confront them. His lips fluttered into a smirk that disappeared as quickly as it appeared. The Omaha interpreter coughed into her hand and looked away.

The cook was still staring at them. Maybe they needed more privacy. Cassandra suggested, "Sir, why don't we go out on the back patio, sit down, and calmly talk about this. The interpreter is here, now. Please remove those handcuffs, so the student can communicate."

Kobza shrugged, "Once he started shoving, we had to stop him."

She could also understand it from their perspective. Cassandra look pointedly at Lance. "Well you can see he's fine now, right? And he won't touch you again . . . right?" The interpreter had been signing everything they were saying, and he nodded.

They gathered around the table and chairs on the concrete pad outside the back door under a bright overhead light among the gathering dusk. The officers guided the student into a chair and removed the cuffs. Lance rubbed the red welts on his wrists to restore blood flow to his fingers.

"What's going on?" Lance signed and said out loud. His voice was deep and he didn't pronounce every single letter like a person who hears might say it, but they all understood him.

Loud Friday night voices burst from a group of young ladies wearing formal dresses and photo-ready makeup parading through the adjacent parking lot towards the fraternity house next door. They stared at the patio tableau, but Cassandra's grim face and slowly shaking head discouraged them from getting closer.

Once they had passed by Deputy Kobza cleared his throat, "Like we said before, I'm sorry to be the one to tell you this, son, but your roommate, Austin Price, was found dead a few hours ago."

Lance's eyebrows arched towards his hairline, his face blanched and his mouth formed a *what*? "Austin?? A few hours ago! I don't understand."

Kobza faced Lance, one arm on the patio table, their knees nearly touching. "Mr. Erickson, Austin was found at the bottom of the outdoor staircase near the science center. Can you tell me the last time you saw him?"

There was a pause while Lance looked around in bewilderment. When he signed, the interpreter spoke his signs in English. "He was asleep in his bed when I went down to eat breakfast. When I came back to the room, he was gone. I think he was in the shower. Then I left for my 9:30 History class before he came back to the room." His eyebrows wrinkled in concern and confusion. "The last time I saw him was around 8:30. What happened? I can't believe this. He's . . . gone?" Lance's eyes welled up with tears and he put his head down. He composed himself after a bit and looked up again.

Cassandra stood quietly a few yards away from the interview and looked at Meg. Arms crossed over a long black sweater and feet planted shoulder width apart, Meg nodded slightly, her face a grim mask.

Deputy Kobza took notes on a small pad. "What did Austin do last night? Were you with him?"

Lance's face looked angry. "I'm not his mother; I don't know what he does every minute." After a big breath he signed, "I was studying in the house library until about 9:00 for my History test this morning. He came home around

10 but he didn't tell me where he'd been and I didn't ask. He sometimes has a study group at the library. Or he works in the biology lab too. We just chatted about this weekend for a few minutes. I don't know."

"Was he in any trouble? Did he do drugs? Or sell them? Is anyone mad at him that you know of? Anyone want to harm him?"

Cassandra wanted to believe Austin accidentally fell down the stairs. But Kobza's questions showed the police were checking every possibility. That vague familiarity she'd felt when she saw his body still eluded her. She'd think about it later when she had time alone.

They all waited while the interpreter relayed the questions in ASL, the deputy's large Timex ticking off the seconds. Lance looked down, considering. Cassandra tried to read his expression for clues. *He's taking a long time to answer.* Part of her itched to tell him to wait and call his parents, but she shouldn't disrupt them.

Lance wiped his eyes with both index fingers, straightened and answered again, more controlled this time. "I don't know. He was my roommate. He always kinda did his own thing though. We had different schedules. I never saw him do anything illegal." One shoulder twitched in a shrug.

Kobza flipped a page. "Did you and he argue recently?"

"What? Of course we argue. We're friends and roommates. We've known each other since fourth grade; he's like my brother. What a stupid question. Us arguing and Austin falling down the stairs have no connection. Why are you wasting time here talking to me? Don't you have more important things to check?"

Both lawmen stilled. "I never told you he fell down the stairs. How did you know?"

"You said he was at the bottom of the staircase, right? How else would he get there?"

Kobza referred to his paper again. He looked at the interpreter, "I'm gonna ask my partner something. Hold on a sec'. Don't tell him this," He pointed at Lance, then turned to his right and spoke more quietly to Tate.

Something about that didn't feel right. Cassandra watched the interpreter and listened closely to the deputies. She heard bits, "...holding back...take him in...call Sheriff Hart first—Hey!" Kobza stopped suddenly. The interpreter had been signing everything he'd said.

Kobza frowned at the interpreter. "I told you not to interpret! Why are you still signing?" When she continued signing while he was yelling at her, his face got red.

Meg interjected, signing while she spoke. "That's her job, Deputy Kobza. Interpreters don't pick and choose what to interpret and what to ignore. If she can hear it, she must interpret it. If you want to keep something secret, you should step out of earshot."

He flushed again, but looked more embarrassed than angry. Deputy Tate coughed to get his attention and gestured towards Lance. "Are you telling us everything?"

Lance's eyes were glued to the interpreter and then he shrugged. "I can't tell you what I don't know. You figure it out."

Kobza shifted in his seat. "If you don't cooperate, son, we'll have to bring you over to our office. We need to search

Austin Price's room, and you can't be in there when we do that."

In one quick motion Lance came to his feet, gesturing animatedly, "Cooperate with what? It's my room, too. I haven't done anything wrong. I don't give you permission to look through my stuff. This is bullshit. Leave me alone." He took a step like he was going to walk away.

The deputies moved in unison, grabbing Lance's arms. "First, your house mother is going to search Austin's half of the room to see what's out in the open. In a few hours, we'll be back with a search warrant for the entire room. This will be a lot easier if you tell us what we'll find on your side. Are you hiding something?"

Lance turned his head away and refused to look at the interpreter, dismissing them all. He was done.

Kobza stepped back inside the fraternity leaving Tate with Lance. Cassandra hadn't predicted Lance would be so aggressive. He'd always seemed happy and funny in the office. Nothing about this afternoon was normal though.

Kobza returned after a couple of minutes and said, "Sheriff wants to ask him more questions while we've got the interpreter. I'm not taking any chances that he takes a swing at me on the ride to the station." They cuffed him again—in front of his body this time so he could still use his hands to communicate.

Lance glared at the women as though expecting them to help. Meg took a step towards him but stopped. It seemed unfair to detain him, but Cassandra had to defer to the county authorities. They hadn't arrested him yet, but he wasn't helping himself out either.

Kobza and Tate walked him to their patrol car and put him into the back seat. "Ms. Ellis, could you follow us to the station? We have some more questions for him there."

"Yes, sir." The Omaha interpreter went over to her car.

As soon as they were out of sight, Meg blurted, "Well, shit."

Chapter Six

A trim, 50-ish lady with shoulder length blonde hair met Cassandra and Meg in the fraternity's common room just as they returned inside. "Hello ladies, I'm Laura Graham, the Alpha Omicron Omicron house mother. I saw you outside the back windows with Lance and the police."

Cassandra stuck out her hand as she answered, "Hi, I'm Cassandra Sato, the Vice President for Student Affairs, and you already know Meg O'Brien. I'm really sorry about Austin. Anything you can do to work with the sheriff's office will be helpful."

Wearing black slacks and a royal blue button down shirt with simple, elegant jewelry, the house mother's eyes teared up at the mention of Austin's name. "I'd hoped there was a mistake, but it's true then." They stood awkwardly in the entry for a few seconds while she wiped away tears.

Several young men sprawled on the couches, talking and working their phones. One guy held his overhead. "There's a SnapChat of Austin on the stairs. Gees, the body's not even cold and he's already plastered all over the 'net. That's harsh."

A preppy kid with curly blond hair said, "This isn't gonna look good for us during Homecoming Week. Are the alumni supposed to step over the yellow crime scene tape to get inside? I hoped to have a shot at winning the Greek Cup this year. It's my last chance."

"It didn't happen *here*, you idiot," another guy in a faded t-shirt and a patchy beard retorted. "Our house isn't a crime scene. But maybe his ghost will come back and haunt you until you tell him where you hid his Halo game."

"That's cold, bro." said the blond guy.

"It was just a joke, man. I didn't mean anything by it," Spotty Beard defended himself.

Ms. Graham raised her voice a level, "Gentlemen... please." The guys stood up and shuffled over to the stairs, still talking amongst themselves.

Cassandra said, "More deputies will be back later tonight. Can you keep everyone away from Lance and Austin's room, please?"

"Actually, I was asked to do a quick visual check of Austin's room to make sure there's no immediate crisis. If you have time to stay for a few minutes, I'd feel better if an administrator was with me."

Cassandra answered, "Sure, we can help," and followed her towards the wooden staircase. Unfamiliar responsibilities were coming so fast, her stomach felt jumpy. College students were a strange blend of child and adult. They gave up some rights to privacy by living on campus, but at the same time were treated like adults by the police. Lance would have to call his parents or lawyer if he didn't want to cooperate, but she and Ms. Graham were expected to secure campus property and protect the other students from potential danger at the fraternity.

Halfway down the third-floor wood paneled hallway, Ms. Graham inserted her master key to open a door. All three of them stepped into the 12 by 14-foot room and in a few seconds their eyes adjusted to the dim light from the partially closed blinds. A slightly sour smell filled the air and Cassandra noticed an empty cardboard pizza box sticking out from the full garbage can. Cassandra's nose wrinkled. *That should've been taken out a few days ago.*

Ms. Graham didn't seem surprised by the room's messiness. Cassandra noted the unmade beds, the wrinkled clothes and a small mountain of shoes: dress, athletic and casual Sperrys piled under the clothing racks in side-by-side modular wooden closets. Several half-consumed water bottles littered the desks; fun-size candy wrappers and extra fast food napkins shared space with a Chapter 1 Philosophy review packet. Crammed in the bookshelves above the desks were worn notebooks, 3-ring binders and random pieces of paper.

Over what appeared to be Austin's desk—according to the wooden fraternity plaque leaning against the wall—Cassandra spotted a framed 5x7 photo of two lanky 14-year-old boys: younger versions of Lance and Austin wearing swim trunks standing on a dock in front of a lake, shirtless skinny torsos, happy smiles and messy hair. Seven squirming fish hung from a chain while the boys struggled to hold up each end. The photo's white caption read "Summer Camp 2011." Lance's desk had no photos or personal items.

His open laptop had gone into sleep mode while they'd been downstairs talking and the login page awaited his return.

A monitor screen on top of a little black device rested on a shelf between their desks. Cassandra leaned in to get a closer look at the setup. "Is this some kind of gaming system?" she wondered aloud.

Meg glanced over and responded immediately, "That's their video phone like the one you saw in my office. They can also use it to call people through a relay service using an interpreter."

A video relay service. *Didn't know that was a thing.* Wondering if the video was stored inside like a surveillance camera, Cassandra asked, "Could a person like me call them on this phone, too? Or would I need special equipment?"

The house mother explained, "If you call the phone number, it connects directly to the interpreter service. The guys see the interpreter on the screen, and they sign to her. Then she speaks English back to you."

Meg added, "There's even mobile apps so deaf people can use their cell phones to make calls just like we do."

That only seemed fair. If she were deaf, she would expect phones to be accessible. "I don't like driving out of town without my phone for emergencies. I bet they like being connected, too."

Unfortunately, the video phone wouldn't have any footage of what Austin did earlier that morning. Cassandra concentrated on finding something out of place in the room or a clue to where Austin had been today and yesterday. After several more minutes, she caught Meg's eye and made the palms up "I got nothing" gesture. Meg nodded and tilted her head towards the door. Cassandra said, "I don't see anything here that stands out to me; is there anything else we can do to help you?"

Ms. Graham followed them out the door. "Not right now. Will counseling be available for students who need more help than I can provide?"

"I'll give your contact information to the counseling center and ask Cinda Weller to schedule some time this weekend for his fraternity brothers."

* * *

On the way to the Student Affairs Office Meg said, "I hate that we couldn't do anything directly to help Lance."

Cassandra said, "I wouldn't interfere with police business. You saw Lance. He was pretty uncooperative."

Meg was in protective mama bear mode. "He just found out his roommate died. I hope he doesn't get himself arrested. I get the feeling that without his scholarship he wouldn't be able to afford Morton; he comes from a large family with some deaf people and some that can hear. Lance is a good kid."

Since there were less than 20 deaf students at Morton, Meg knew them pretty well. "What else should I know about Austin?"

Meg thought for a bit. "Austin must've been a good student to get that biology lab job. Those only go to top Biology 2 students who survive a competitive interview process. I've told you this before, but honestly all the deaf kids who succeed in college are smart, determined hard workers."

This was one of Meg's pet topics: advocating for deaf students. "Imagine yourself as a student paying attention to an interpreter signing, the teacher speaking, and his PowerPoint presentation all at once. Plus, there's a worksheet in front of you to fill out during the lecture. Part of your grade is based on participation points. You hope your interpreter is good enough to get all the important keywords and the main point of the lesson into the interpretation. You hope she can keep up with the class discussion so you know what the other kids in class are saying too. If the teacher has a foreign accent or uses lots of jokes and sarcasm, it's easy to confuse which part is the lesson and which part is the joke."

Way more work than she'd had in undergrad. Cassandra hadn't stopped to think about how deaf students learned compared to other students.

They arrived back in the empty Osborne building after 6:30 p.m. Cassandra's head still throbbed. "I'd better check messages. Still need to send few emails before I can go home."

Meg retrieved her lunch bag and purse from a chair in Cassandra's office. "Connor knows I'm running late, but I want to hurry home and hug my son."

Meg and Connor's nine-year-old son, Tony, and their Brittany Spaniel, Burt, had quickly become Cassandra's adopted ohana away from home. Cassandra hugged Meg. "Give them both hugs from me, too. Finding you again has been a gift."

Chapter Seven

Cassandra's brain refused to relax even though she'd been sipping hot chamomile tea in bed. Her nightly professional reading ritual normally grounded and relaxed her within minutes. Tonight she stared at a *Higher Education Administration* community engagement article until the words blurred into a surreal watercolor of print. Visions of Austin and pressure to fill Nielson's shoes—even temporarily—made her wonder if taking this job had been the right move.

President Nielson's call brought her to full attention a little after 10:00 p.m. "What the Hell is going on? I told you to keep this out of the news!"

At what point had the friendly, charming gentleman she'd met during the hiring process evaporated, leaving No-Nonsense Nielson, the scathing critic, behind? She held her phone gingerly, away from her ear.

He said, "I just turned on the Omaha evening news. Not only did they report about our student's death, they invited people to join the Morton community for a candlelight vigil Sunday evening! How is that keeping this quiet and contained?"

She'd learned from her previous photo faux pas that it's better to put the facts out first instead of letting others control the message. Cassandra scowled at Nielson's haole brusqueness. "Some students requested a candlelight vigil outside the chapel." Austin's funeral services would be far away and most wouldn't be able to attend. "Cinda texted me a couple of hours ago asking permission. I didn't see any harm in allowing it."

His voice lowered a notch. "Don't give out details to the media. Stick to the basic facts: student's name, year in school and hometown. 'Our thoughts and prayers are with the family. The police investigation is ongoing.' This is not the kind of publicity we need right now. Didn't I make that clear to you?"

So much for bringing her to Morton for her expertise on gender and leadership style. The proposed visiting professor program for mentoring female grad students and faculty would never happen if he thought she couldn't handle simple press releases. She said, "We've given few details. This is student driven. Austin Price was a fraternity member. His friends and classmates want to gather and honor his memory. Don't we want to encourage their feelings of connection and community? To help them begin the healing process."

Nielson was silent a few seconds, and she realized it had been a long day for him, too. Although he could be a touchy jerk sometimes, he usually made intelligent decisions. Cassandra suspected that's how he'd risen up through the faculty ranks from professor, to department chair, then Dean and now President for the past six years. He warned, "You'd better keep a tight lid on this gathering so it doesn't get bigger than you expect. I'll be traveling all day tomorrow and won't be available to advise you."

When Cassandra pictured a kindly mentor, it was her first boss, Ralph Masato's face who came to mind over Nielson's. As effective with business leaders and state senators as he was with young staff, Ralph never forgot the human side of the academic machine. He found time to sit with struggling students, chat about their Aunties and Grannies, and today's surf on the North Shore. In contrast, this conversation only added to her anxiety.

Nielson's last words were so quiet she had to strain to hear them. "Look, I'm sorry I yelled. I'm worried about our lab's grant funding. I need your help." The phone clicked off as he disconnected without waiting for her reply.

Cassandra felt a jarring uncertainty at his motives for calling her out. The vague reference to the lab's funding and plea for help made it seem like he hoped Austin's death was just an accident. First the police, and now the president had doubts. *If it wasn't an accident, how did it happen?*

Chapter Eight

Early Saturday morning Cassandra padded into the small, outdated kitchen wearing a richly woven, purple silk kimono loosely tied over her pajamas: men's large boxer shorts and a baggy Honolulu Symphony fun run t-shirt. A white headband and high ponytail kept stray pieces of black hair from falling into her eyes. Pressing the brew button on her Keurig, she watched as fragrant Kona dark roast coffee dripped into a delicate china cup that had belonged to her Gran before a series of strokes forced her move to a nursing home in Honolulu. The move had been much harder on the family than on Gran, who had lost a little more of herself with each mini-stroke. No one had expected her to hang on more than a decade, but she was a stubborn old Japanese woman who wasn't going to be told when to die.

Gran would have approved of Cassandra's sparkling clean kitchen, whose cabinets had been painted bright white sometime last century. The vintage 80s appliances were ugly, but functional. *At least there was a dishwasher.* Though she rarely had time to cook, the stainless-steel sink gleamed without one drop of dried water on its surface. A dishcloth and dry towel were draped over the side to wipe up any spills.

Taking the cup over to the gate leg wooden table, she sat in one of her two chairs and sipped contentedly. If she closed her eyes, she could imagine herself back home in the house her grandfather had built, and where she'd lived after undergrad. Her grandfather's house sat abreast a hill with a panoramic view of Oahu's leeward side. Grandpa's pride were the lush tangerine and banana trees, while Gran cultivated colorful orchids. Truthfully, Cassandra's Mom and Dad had taken over watering the garden, house plants, and trimming the small patch of grass for at least five years. Mom stopped by several times a week to work in the garden and leave meals in the fridge for her daughter. Since the Nebraska move, her Mom still made sure everything was cleaned and watered. One simply didn't sell a house that'd been in the family for three generations.

A quick browse online showed no news on the Austin Price investigation. Cinda Weller emailed her about the walk-in counselors' coverage for the day. And Nielson had been distracted enough by his travels to leave her alone. She released a big breath she hadn't realized she was holding. She'd be able to do some housework this morning instead of rushing over to campus.

First on her agenda was a 30-minute *Yoga with Rodney Yee* DVD. She rolled out the green yoga mat onto the middle of the wood floor. If she pushed the coffee table to the side, she could reach around doing the Warrior series and Sun Salutations movements without hitting any walls or furniture. Listening to the ocean surf in the video's background helped focus her mind, while moving through the poses warmed up her muscles and worked out her body's kinks.

Cassandra's grumbling stomach interrupted her Corpse Pose interlude. She rolled up the mat, refilled her coffee, and surveyed the refrigerator contents: wilted bagged salad greens in the crisper drawer, a couple of apples, French vanilla coffee creamer, two eggs and a large container of leftover rice. Reaching into the upper cupboard she found one can of Spam next to a box of raisin bran cereal. She had two go-to breakfasts: mainland or Hawaiian. Which one she ate usually depended on how rushed she felt that morning, and how homesick. She opened the Spam, chopped a third of it into bite sized chunks, and lightly browned them in the pan with the eggs. The familiar aroma grounded her senses. *Ahh . . . the breakfast meat of Hawai'i!* She reheated the rice, refilled her coffee and cleaned up. Sitting down she forked in a mouthful of Spam, eggs, and rice just like she would have eaten at home with her family.

Usually Cassandra talked to her mom every Saturday, but factoring the time difference, she decided to run to the grocery store first. It wouldn't take long to browse every item on the tiny store's one half-aisle where the Asian food shared space with the Mexican food. Dressing in loose fitting "Saturday" tan cotton ankle pants and a flowing dark blue top with lotus flowers embroidered down the front buttonholes, she checked her phone's weather app while shrugging on a thick navy cardigan, warm socks and slip-on blue Toms. Meg teased her about the fall and winter temperatures, but even 60 degrees felt frigid to her thin skin. She'd visited the mainland often enough at various times of the year that she owned a puffy winter coat and hat, gloves, and a scarf. Meg had promised to take her shopping in Lincoln soon to prepare for winter. Part of her was excited to experience snowstorms and curl up under a blanket with a cup of hot cocoa like those people on TV and movies. The cold feet and dry skin, she was not looking forward to. She'd purchased a used Honda Accord when she moved to Nebraska, but she lived only two blocks from campus and four blocks from the grocery store. Most days she got around on foot.

* * *

An hour later, Cassandra juggled keys and two large cloth bags as she stepped into the bungalow's vestibule and heard the laptop noise alerting her to an inbound Skype call in the dining room. Cassandra had eschewed a dining table for an antique wooden library desk with a lamp and printer shelf. Leaving the front door open, she rushed towards the desk and tapped the keyboard to open the call. "Hi Mom!" she yelled, "I'm just back from the market. Let me put away the food."

Michiko Sato's diminutive torso filled Cassandra's laptop screen. She yelled as though she was shouting from 3500 miles away. "Aloha, Cassandra! How are you? Good ting you wen to da market; you don't eat enough. You look thin."

Her mom always said that. Cassandra put away the groceries and spoke into the direction of the laptop moved to her kitchen table. "The market owner remembered me from last time I was there. Said I needed to eat more, too. Sounded like a haole version of you."

The woman's motherly scolding had given Cassandra a homesick longing. She didn't mention the cold stare from the balding old man in the produce aisle while she chose ripe oranges, or that the grizzled deli guy ignored her until everyone else in line had gone first. Cassandra said, "How's dad? And Gran? You're up early, Mom."

"Oh, I woke up at 4:00 and couldn't go back to sleep so I did some laundry and cleaned the house. Your brother's family is coming over this afternoon for Leilani's birthday party, and your father's outside working in the garden. I started roasting the pork this morning so it'll be ready in time for the party. I still need to make da kine, birthday cake. I visited Gran yesterday; she's the same. She knew who I was, but she thought it was 1995." Her mom's head tilted, and her lips met in a silent grimace.

Amazing that the powerful little woman who had ruled their family with an iron fist for 60 years now had the mind of a three-year-old child. Cassandra had helped care for Gran in their home for several years before Michiko finally admitted it was time to move her to a professional nursing home. Her mother asked, "How's your job? Have you seen Meg?"

Cassandra didn't mention Austin's death. Mom would worry. She crossed her fingers that it hadn't made the national news. Her mom wasn't too savvy with the Google searches. She could find MSN headline news but hadn't figured out yet how to access the campus newspaper online. Cassandra hoped she wouldn't find out until next week. Maybe by then she'd have better information. "Yes, Mom. I saw her yesterday. She sends her love. Tony's getting so big. He's in 4th grade this year, and his hair is getting darker. He played flag football but I haven't seen a game yet."

"You need to stop workin all da time. Go enjoy yourself."

If only it were that simple. Cassandra said, "I've a lot to learn still, Mom. I'll watch Tony play soon. If you send me some Japanese candy, he can share it with his football team-mates." Mainland kids rarely got to experience the chewy taffy-like candy that came in an edible wrapper. It would be an exotic treat for them.

"Your sister brought home a nice young man for dinner on Sunday. His name is Rick Tanaka and she met him at the self-defense class she's taking on Tuesday nights. His father passed away, but his mother lives in Hawai'i Kai, and he's a nice Punahou boy. He's quiet, but handsome and he drives an Audi. He let the nephews practice their judo moves on him. You know dey can be a bit . . . da kine . . . rambunctious."

Her 8 and 6-year-old nephews were known to drop to the floor anywhere, even the supermarket checkout line and wrestle like Labrador puppies. Her younger sister Kathy was 27 and had a Master's in social work. She'd dated a guy for four years in college and everyone had thought he was "the One"—except Kathy who had broken up with him last year. The unspoken worry was that Kathy would end up like Cassandra—34 and still alone. Mom thought getting married to your high school or college sweetheart was an item you checked off the list in your early 20s. Then you moved directly on to motherhood, just like she'd done.

The plan allowed no space for unexpected tragedies or boyfriends that didn't live up to husband standards. Try explaining that to a woman who had been happily married for 37 years to the best man/husband/dad ever. On cue, her father appeared on the screen behind her mother. "Hi! Precious." He grinned widely, happy to see his eldest daughter. "It's good to see you. Why you didn't sleep well last night?"

For one thing, she couldn't shake memories of Austin alive and smiling in her office. Mixed with Nielson's marching orders, her legs would not relax. "Just a late night at work, Dad. I'll go to sleep earlier tonight, I promise." Cassandra crossed her heart, but knew it was a fib.

Michiko said, "Helen from my Wednesday Mah Jong group announced that her daughter, Lori, is engaged. Some lawyer from the mainland. He's a haole guy who has no respect for local culture. They're getting married in Santa Monica in May! A mainland wedding...pfff. I told'em you goin teach that leadership class for da new job."

Her mom's Mah Jong group was not just for playing games. Michiko Sato got as much mileage out of her daughter's considerable achievements as her peers would tolerate. The other ladies shared photos and stories of their successful families, too. Cassandra knew the new job would only temporarily postpone the inevitable insinuation. She should find a nice guy from the mainland like her high school friend, Lori. This was the same Lori who stole Frank Silva, her first crush back in Mrs. Yamamoto's sixth grade. *Maybe that mainland lawyer wanted to marry Lori because she let* him *copy her homework, too.*

* * *

Hauling a cleaning carryall from kitchen to bedroom to living room while Cassandra methodically dusted and vacuumed spaces that would already look clean to a casual observer, she stewed over the call with her parents.

Her 1920's bungalow in Carson was far removed from home in many ways. Cassandra had moved her quilted bedding, artwork and a few trinkets to remind her of the islands. In the short time she'd lived there, Meg had been the only visitor. Cassandra was often gone by 6:30 in the morning and didn't return until almost dark. Some nights she attended special events and dinners or sporting contests. She barely had time to water the one special Plumeria plant she'd taken great pains to bring to Nebraska. The cutting had been packed, sealed, stamped and certified by an agriculture inspector before she could board the plane. She hadn't moved thousands of miles and given up her home, her job, and her family, to fail.

Saving the bathroom for last, she cleaned every fixture and gathered the dirty clothes for laundry. The house came with a small stacking washer and dryer in the basement near the furnace. Having never lived in a home with a basement, Cassandra was amazed by how many storage boxes she could keep down there.

Sweat dampened her face and neck like a gym workout, while the cleaning routine had settled her mind. A walk around the neighborhood would've been more pleasant, but when faced with a choice, she'd always choose a sparkling house over exercise. Tepid water sprayed from the recently installed ultra-rain showerhead while she shivered outside the antique clawfoot bathtub waiting for the home's plumbing to catch up to Hawai'i water temperature standards. Her phone chirped and the screen indicated a local call. She missed the caller's first words while she stepped into her bedroom to escape the loud noise in the bathroom. "...not too early to call, I hope?" She recognized Andy Summer's voice while she held the phone an arm's length away and sat on the bed comforter, drawing it around her chilled skin.

Using her professional voice, she assured him, "No, it's not too early. Is something wrong?"

"Nothing's wrong. Just wanted to let you know the sheriff's office is certifying Austin's death as violent. It could be anything from accidental causes to homicide. Probably hit his head when he fell."

"Homicide? ... You mean he was pushed?"

"Violent means unnatural causes. There's any number of ways he could have gotten there. Pushed, tripped... suicidal. Now they'll focus on finding out how by tracing his actions from the lab to the stairs." Cassandra thanked him and numbly ended the call.

Back in the steamy shower, Cassandra briskly massaged coconut scented shampoo into her scalp. Nothing erased the mental image of Austin's lifeless body yesterday afternoon. She struggled to wrap her brain around the H-word. If it wasn't a "natural" incident—medical or otherwise— what made him tumble down those stairs into a broken heap? There were many more questions to answer and it was time to head to campus. If she wanted to fix this during Nielson's absence, she'd need to be completely prepared and in charge.

Chapter Nine

Cassandra carefully placed a bottle of Chateau Ste. Michelle Merlot into a pretty blue paper wine bag with a twine handle. She wrapped matching ribbon around a small box of chocolate covered macadamia nuts that her mother had included in the last care package to thank Meg for inviting her to Saturday dinner.

She plugged Meg's address into the Honda's map program, and crossed her fingers that Google knew more than she did about rural Eastern Nebraska. Probably she didn't deserve a night off, but a girl had to eat, right? Luckily, dinner at the O'Brien's required nothing more fancy than black ankle length pants and a casual tropical patterned fitted tunic that she'd purchased at Macy's in July.

Meg had been after her to buy jeans and more casual shirts lately. "Midwesterners don't dress as formally as people on the coasts," she'd reminded. "Besides, you have a great tiny body underneath those loose pants and shirts. Show off your shape a little bit!"

Cassandra owned one pair of jeans that had probably been her mother's. She wore them when working on a flower garden or cleaning house. Even she knew that mom jeans wouldn't be right for dinner.

Thirty-two minutes later, Cassandra pulled into the long, gravel driveway lined by an evergreen wind break to the O'Briens' acreage off Highway 31. Their large house sat on a spacious yard where their son Tony could run around with the dog and practice throwing a baseball to his dad. Homes and property values in Nebraska were significantly cheaper than in Hawai'i where it wasn't unusual to pay $600,000 for a 1,200-square foot townhouse. Often a young couple lived with their parents during the early years of their marriage to save for a house's down payment.

Cassandra climbed the front porch steps to the open screen door, inhaling the backyard fire pit's burning wood and savory grill scents. The domestic, appealing scene made Cassandra pause a moment to gather herself. She had once dreamed of marrying, buying a home, and filling it with keiki, flowers, and pets. The barking dog startled her out of her reverie. Burt, their 75-pound German shorthair, danced on the other side of the door in guest welcoming glee.

"C'mon inside, Cass!" Meg greeted moving towards her from the kitchen. "Burt, SIT," she commanded, snapping her fingers. And Burt sat by her leg, his whole backside wiggling, while Cassandra removed her shoes by the welcome mat and entered the house. She handed the treats to Meg who admired the pretty wrapping. "I hope that rattling noise is macadamia nuts. God, I miss those."

Connor came forward seconds later holding a beer bottle and smelling of outdoors and charcoal. He set his beer on the entry table, wrapped Cassandra into a big hug, and kissed her cheek. "Aloha! Haven't seen you in more than a month! Glad you could make it tonight."

The dog paced around them bumping her leg for attention. She squatted down and pet his silvery black head, scratching under his ears. "Burt, you good boy. I wouldn't ignore you."

Connor adjusted the red Huskers ball cap on his closely trimmed blond head. "Maybe you should get a guard dog for your house. For company, too."

Connor's solid, muscular build suggested he lifted a lot of weights or did hard labor for his job. In fact, he worked in an office in Ashland at the Nebraska National Guard, but spent a good amount of time keeping in fit military shape should his unit deploy. "My house is plenty safe," Cassandra assured him. "Besides, I barely have time to water my plant, let alone walk a dog every day."

Behind them loud footsteps thundered down the stairs. Connor warned, "Look out! He's coming in hot!"

There was only one person in the house who could make that kind of an entrance. Tony burst into the hall and slid to a stop on the wood floor. "Move it, Patrick, I'm claustrophobic."

Cassandra recognized the line immediately and answered, "What does claustrophobic mean?"

Tony used his best SpongeBob imitation voice. "It means he's afraid of Santa Claus!"

She raised her hands up by her ears, her voice low in her throat. "Ho, ho, ho!"

Tony copied her and flailed his hands, "Stop it, Patrick, you're scaring him!"

They looked at each other for a beat, then burst into giggles.

He said in amazement, "Wow, you said that just like Patrick! Auntie Cass is awesome, Mom!" Then he darted off down the hall.

Who knew her SpongeBob obsession would come in so handy? Cassandra kept smiling. *Kids were so much more fun than adulting.*

Meg shook her head. "Tony's right—you do sound just like Patrick...However odd that is for a thirty-something woman."

Cassandra did palms up by her hips. "Brain breaks in between all of those grad classes. A couple SpongeBob episodes and you forget every stress. I miss those carefree days."

* * *

After burgers with all the toppings and salads, Connor and Tony went upstairs to do the nighttime bath, story, and bed routine while Meg poured Cassandra a second glass of wine and they curled up on opposite ends of the leather couch. Their family room was dark, cozy and comfortable and decorated in the latest casual farmhouse style with gray sectional furniture. Photos and vintage John Wayne movie posters covered the Western themed walls. A leather bridle and horsewhip were tacked above the couch, and locally brewed beer bottles hugged a narrow shelf on the corner wall over the snack area. Burt sat near Meg and leaned his head by her hand.

Cassandra noted that the liquid inside Meg's glass wasn't wine-colored. She frowned. "Water?"

Meg shrugged casually. "Just not in the mood tonight." Cassandra raised an eyebrow, but gave it a pass.

Cassandra sank into the couch. "My mother and I Skyped this morning and she wanted me to tell you 'Aloha.' I feel guilty because I didn't tell them about Austin."

Meg absently scratched behind Burt's ears. "Why not?"

"I didn't want to worry them unnecessarily."

Meg said, "Yeah. I feel guilty, too, like we should have prevented it. It's Catholic guilt. I don't even know exactly what happened yet, but I feel responsible anyway."

"Catholic guilt is nothing compared to the Japanese mother guilt I'm going to get when Mom figures out I knew about this, and didn't tell her right away." Cassandra sipped some wine.

"Are you in touch with Paul's family still?" Meg asked. "Your moms were friends, right?"

"They still treat me like family. And I feel bad for moving away from them, too." She sighed. Even though Meg really understood her well, Cassandra still had trouble talking about Paul with her. "All moms either worry too much, or give us guilt. Not that you'll ever make *your* kids feel guilty for something they didn't do."

Meg's face clouded. "Sometimes I wonder if we'll actually have more than one kid. I've had two miscarriages the last couple of years." She drank some water and hesitated. "Last time was in May. Before you moved."

Cassandra's emotions were already raw from the day before and her eyes teared up. "Oh, Meg! I'm so sorry."

Meg resumed scratching the dog. "I was maybe 10 or 12 weeks along, but we'd already talked about converting the office into a nursery and debated name ideas. The morning sickness was pretty bad, but I was excited because of the little life growing inside me. Once I started spotting, the whole thing ended a few days later. There was nothing the doctor could do. Connor was away on National Guard drill that weekend. The poor man came home on Sunday night to a crying wreck and our confused son. Tony was sweet though. He offered me his favorite stuffed SpongeBob to cheer me up."

Cassandra had wondered why they were waiting so long. "Your family is huge and you've always talked about having lots of keiki. I'm such a dunce not to realize you were having trouble."

Meg shrugged. "They happened before you moved here, and I didn't exactly tell the world. Both times it was before I started showing, so no one really knows."

Cassandra couldn't imagine how hard that would be. She yawned and stretched her arms out. Her full belly and the wine made her sleepy.

Meg hugged a throw pillow, then bluntly asked, "You seem kinda tired."

She'd stayed in the office until almost 9:00 Friday night. Most days started at 6:30, before the phones' ringing and the students' arrival. Cassandra's shoulders sagged. "The hours don't sound too bad until you add them up." Her hand massaged her temple. "I am kinda tired."

"You're running on what ... 5 hours of sleep a night?" Meg held up her palm. "I did that quite a few months after

Tony was born. Wait 'til the weather turns colder, and we're all stuck inside. The students' germs and yours get all mixed up. You'll get sick if you don't take care of yourself."

"Yes, Mother . . ." She'd love to speed past these awkward months of acclimation. "Between office politics and state history, I spend time studying every day. I've been learning the map so I have an idea of distance and size of the students' hometowns."

"People here aren't raised with the Aloha spirit, but they're friendly. You'll feel more settled by the end of the semester."

She hadn't told Meg about the anonymous texts telling her to go home or calling her derogatory names. She wasn't naïve. She knew the middle of the mainland wasn't as diverse as the coasts. Cassandra hesitated, finding a way to describe her feelings. "Everyone here is so . . . white. It's strange going to the market or big meetings where nearly every face I see is European Caucasian. I've never considered myself racist or privileged, but I never realized how most faces at home looked like mine."

Cassandra tucked her legs underneath herself and let her head fall against the back cushion. "I completely underestimated what an impact it'd be to move here. My whole life, when I walked out my door the first thing I did was orient myself to the ocean and the mountains. I took blue skies and salty ocean breezes for granted. Now when I get in my car and drive out of town, all I see for miles and miles is land. Mostly flat, green-turning-brown land. There's no water. It makes me claustrophobic."

Meg sat up straight and smacked the back of the couch with her hand. "HA! That's exactly how I felt living in Hawai'i! Except I'd look at the blue ocean stretching to the horizon and think, 'I'm on a little teeny island in the middle of this humongous ocean. Forty-four miles in diameter, and I'm floating here in the middle. Funny how something so opposite makes you feel the same way I did."

Cassandra met Meg's deep stare for a few beats. Meg said quietly, "I missed you even though we didn't talk as often after I left. It's not many times in your life you find one of those friends where you can—"

"—pick up the conversation where you left off," Cassandra finished for her. They clinked their glasses together in a toast. Connor joined them, settling into the sectional couch near Meg. He casually reached an arm around her back and drew her closer to him.

Meg had found the right guy for her at such a young age. They'd been newlyweds when he was stationed at Ft. Bellows, and they still seemed to get along well even after 10 years of marriage.

Connor put his feet on the ottoman. "Hey, Cass, I met a guy at the National Guard camp last weekend who said he works with you? Marcus Fischer. Morton housing department?"

Cassandra couldn't stop the little flush that crept up her neck at the mention of Fischer's name. Just like being 14 again with a crush on the cutest boy in the 8th grade. Mental eye roll. Luckily the lighting in the family room was pretty low, so she hoped no one noticed. She should've known better.

Meg teased, "Oh, you mean the Fabulous Mr. Fischer? Yes, we know him. Cass is technically his boss; he's in charge of the on-campus student housing. He and his dreamy eyes report to her."

Connor tickled her side. "Dreamy eyes, eh? Are you the only one who's noticed him, or does Cass think he's dreamy, too?"

Totally middle school again. Cassandra sipped some wine, working for a blank, nonchalant expression. "Yes, of course I know who he is. We've attended weekly staff meetings since August. He does a good job with housing. Seems very organized. Neat. He's got that whole military precision thing happening. Like in meetings, he carefully lines up his papers, notepad and pen in front of him on the table and sits as though he's at attention. His clothes are always neatly pressed. He's quiet but seems to take in every detail around him."

Connor's eyebrows went up a bit. "Well, well…you have been watching him, haven't you?"

She lifted a palm up defensively. "You can't help noticing things like that."

His Cheshire cat grin reminded her of her big brother. "Maybe you'd also like to know, that in our Leadership class last weekend I found out quite a bit about your Mr. Fischer. *Lieutenant* Fischer grew up in Denver, but moved to Nebraska for college because that's where his mother is from. He deployed to Iraq during the second Gulf War as a mechanic, then came home and finished college. He's been at Morton since January."

This was embarrassing. She pointed at the couple. "What'd you do? Waterboard the guy to get all that intel out of him? This is not a good time for me. Do not go there."

"Where?" asked Connor innocently. "Where don't you want to go? Kansas City?"

Her eyes narrowed. "You know what I mean."

He goaded just like Keoni would've done over Saturday night drinks at home. "Yes, I do, but I want you to say it out loud."

"Do not set me up with Marcus Fischer."

"Yep, we went there!" Connor crowed.

"C'mon guys, just let me learn how to do my job ... and teach a class ... and lead some grad students ... and figure out what happened to Austin Price before you match me up with every eligible guy within a 30-mile radius."

Connor held out his right hand as if to shake on a deal, "Done! So, that oughta take what—a couple more weeks? Then we can invite you guys out on a double date?"

Cassandra's brown eyes glared and her mouth tightened into a line. Failing to hold a convincing Stink Eye at his smiling face, she gave her head a little shake and stuck with silence as her best response.

* * *

Cassandra arrived home around 11:30 to a dark street and house. The college kids who lived on her street were probably still partying, and the retired couples next door and across the street had long since gone to sleep so they could be up at 5:30 a.m. Cassandra often saw them outside watering the yard or walking on weekday mornings.

Once she parked in the narrow, single-car detached garage set back fifteen feet from the house, she let herself into the bungalow's side entrance. The postage stamp sized landing led either straight down the stairs to the basement or left to the kitchen. She hung her black leather jacket on a coat hook behind the door and took the two steps up into the kitchen using the ambient light that shone through the door's top window to guide her way. Another window on the same wall in the kitchen between the pantry and the stove allowed her to see her pathway through the galley kitchen. She moved deeper into the house towards her bedroom, the only one on the main floor. Upstairs were two more bedrooms she planned to use for guests and extra storage.

Something odd in the living room made her detour that way instead, trying to make out a dark shape on the floor. Slowly she crept up closer, light and shadows from the windows revealing a pattern to the mottled shape on the floor. It didn't move. Her heart pounded, and she reached into her pants pocket for her phone. She had to get up very close to realize the shape was nothing; it was just a lighting trick. Still, the shadow shapes looked strange, so she turned right towards the living room's fireplace wall. In a window beside the fireplace, she saw the slimy mass of a pumpkin's insides still clinging to the window. A startled gasp escaped her lips.

That's what had made the strange pattern on her floor! Her heart and her head both pulsed, though obviously pumpkins weren't dangerous. She turned on an end table lamp and moved to the window for a closer look. Large chunks of orange pumpkin stuck to the window, stringy tendrils and seeds hung further down. Note to self: *next time turn on the kitchen light when you come home late at night.*

She flipped the overhead entryway light and moved to the front door, hitting the porch lights on as she stepped outside. Around the side of the house, a broken pumpkin half lay beneath the azalea hedge under the window. Light spilled into the small side yard that separated her home from the older couple, the Gills, who lived next door. She kept walking around the corner to the back of the house, checking the other windows for more vandalism. Seeing nothing, she returned to the front, her head swiveling up and down the quiet street.

The darkened porch of the house directly across from hers displayed hay bales near the door, corn stalks tied to the porch column, and pumpkins arranged on the steps in a Halloween scene. A straw wreath hung from the front door, and a homemade scarecrow dressed in a plaid shirt, overalls, and a Nebraska Cornhuskers cowboy hat reclined in the chair near the door. Nothing amiss there.

Cassandra returned inside the house, carefully locked both doors and turned off the extra lights. In her bedroom, she changed into boxer shorts and a baggy SpongeBob t-shirt, and crawled under the heavy blanket and quilt. She kept her bedside lamp on, picked up her iPad, and browsed the news headlines. Nothing new on Austin Price, thankfully. No alerts about widespread Halloween vandalism in her area.

If neighborhood kids thought they'd prank the newcomer, she had news for them. Growing up, Cassandra's older brother often tried to scare or trick her and her sisters. They might fall for it, but Cassandra was immune. Not that her stomach didn't clench in surprise, but she wouldn't give him the satisfaction of knowing he'd scared her. One teeny part of her considered calling the police, but that seemed like overkill for a random kids being kids thing. She would clean it up tomorrow and not worry about it. Reaching over to turn out the light, she realized that was easier said than done. She drew back her hand and left the light on. It was just kids being kids, right?

Chapter Ten

Meg's text pinging on her phone served as Cassandra's Sunday morning alarm: "Your place @6:30 tonight before the memorial service?"

Cassandra's warm, lethargic body had slipped between the haze of rest and eyes open since sunrise when bright sunshine had first streamed into the bedroom window. Cassandra longed to sip hot coffee while hiding under the cozy covers, reading the newspaper without actually getting out of bed first. A small Keurig on her nightstand wouldn't be too indulgent, would it?

Cassandra fluffed her pillow and replied: "Did you just invite yourself over for dinner?"

Meg quickly responded: "Too obvious?"

Cassandra smiled at Meg's answer. Cooking for Meg would help Cassandra remember to stop working long enough to eat.

A few hours later, the knock on Cassandra's open office door frame broke her concentration. "Good morning." Andy Summers held up a brown bakery bag in one hand while the other balanced a cardboard tray with two to-go cups. "Cinnamon bagel?"

Summers was early 30s, his left hand bore no wedding ring, and he carried himself like a former athlete, albeit one who had maybe kept eating more than he was currently exercising.

Expecting an empty office, Cassandra had thrown on loose stretchy black pants and an over-sized green University of Hawai'i-Manoa hoodie that dwarfed her petite frame. Her hair was pulled into a high ponytail, and with minimal makeup she looked younger than her 34 years. The oatmeal from barely an hour ago rested comfortably in her belly, yet she smiled. "That's very thoughtful of you, Officer Summers. Mahalo."

A smidge under 6 feet tall with buzzed, dark brown hair and brown eyes, Summers' complexion put him squarely in the Midwestern European culture of many Nebraskans. Hard to identify a second or third generation German, Swede, Brit or Irishman. Plus, in talking to Meg and other haole friends, she'd found that most local people were a combination from several European countries and ethnicities.

Summers' voice was exasperated. "Why don't you ever call me Andy? I've told you at least 10 times."

Cassandra remembered her third day of work when she had arrived at 6:30 a.m. to find the Osborne Administrative Building's main door locked. Her new office key didn't work, so she called campus security.

Andy Summers had quickly arrived to let her in. "You always going to be getting here this early?"

"Most mornings, yes probably."

"Not that I mind leaving my warm coffee cup to run over here and be your doorman, but I'll set your ID card to permit early access to this building."

Usually at work Cassandra was very careful to speak professionally and formally to nearly everyone, but he was surprisingly warm and friendly. She liked bantering with him. "I do like the idea of having my own doorman . . . but I suppose if you're off fighting crime, I don't want to drag you away from the excitement."

He had laughed, "Yeah, 'cause rousting homeless guys from the doorway behind the dining hall and writing reports about the drunk Beta Psi guy who fell asleep in the bushes by the library is so exciting."

She'd known instantly they could be friends. Summers had sent her new ID key card that same afternoon. Since then, he'd escorted her to her car a couple of late nights. Once, when a dinner in the Executive Boardroom dragged past 8:00 p.m. he'd walked the entire two blocks to her home's front door and warned, "Take care to have a buddy at night. We may not be the big city here, but it's a good idea to be safe anyway. Call me any time, and I'll be happy to walk with you, or I'll send someone to escort you if I'm not here."

What was it about her that made guys act like her protective big brother? *Chivalry still existed in the middle of nowhere.*

Summers—correction, Andy—had a point. She appreciated their friendship but treated him like a stranger. "Sorry. You're right. Anyone who brings me coffee and bagels should be on a first name basis. I'll try to remember next time. How'd you know I'd be here?"

Setting the coffee tray on her desk, he passed one cup over to her. "You'd be physically incapable of staying home today. Too much to get squared away for the week."

Her eyes wrinkled and she half-smiled at being so transparent. She placed brown takeout napkins on her mostly cleared off desk while Summers took out a bagel for himself and passed her the bag. They chewed and sipped coffee, enjoying the quiet moment.

She waited for him to speak first; he wouldn't have stopped by without a reason. "The sheriff let Lance Erickson go home yesterday. They couldn't find a reason to hold him. He confirmed that Price didn't do drugs but he gave plasma over at the AlphaBioGlobal Plasma center in town. Lance's parents showed up and demanded they either let him see a lawyer or cut him loose."

She'd have a hard time believing he did anything wrong. Cassandra nodded. "He's a good kid. I was surprised they even took him to their station. Have they questioned others, too?"

Andy wore his casual Sunday outfit, too: sweatpants and flannel button down showing through the top of his jacket. He finished the bagel and slouched into the chair, one running shoe resting on a knee. "They talked to a few other guys from his fraternity and searched his room. Here's the weird thing: Austin's laptop wasn't in his backpack in the lab or in his fraternity room. Neither was his phone."

Cassandra stared out the window towards the Edgerton lab. "What kid doesn't have his phone within an arm's length at all times?"

Andy banked his empty coffee cup in a garbage can free throw. "The sheriff took papers from Austin's fraternity bedroom including a contract between Morton College food service and a local farmer. No idea why he'd have that."

She frowned. "How does a food service contract connect with a student falling down the stairs?"

He gathered their napkins and the bag, swept the bagel crumbs from her desktop and lobbed the balled-up wad over his head—two for two. "I'm not a huge believer in coincidences. I don't know many 20-year-olds who just fall down the stairs."

She met his gaze in the quiet intimacy of her office, wondering for the first time whether their friendship broke any rules. His right hand slowly unzipped his worn Carhart jacket and reached inside, pulling out a large yellow envelope.

Cassandra slid out two photos, silently examined them, and replaced them in the envelope. Andy's chin came up a few degrees. "When you gonna tell me why you needed these?"

She swallowed hard and handed the envelope back. "V-very soon. I've probably seen too many detective shows and don't want to waste anyone's time."

His face returned to his normal, easygoing smile. "I trust your judgment. Just know my patience has limits." He pointed to his freshly shaved chin. "This charming smile doesn't mean I'm a pushover."

Chapter Eleven

Cassandra greeted Meg with a hug promptly at 6:30 Sunday night on her back doorstep.

"Aloha!" Cassandra said, as they stepped up to the kitchen where hearty barbecue smells enveloped the air around a small Crock-Pot on the counter.

Meg inhaled, "Howzit! Smells ono!!"

Cassandra put water on for hot tea, and Meg sat at the table. Cassandra indicated the Crock-Pot while scooping sticky white rice from her steamer into sky blue glazed bowls. "My best attempt at Kalua pig... without the part about digging a backyard hole so it cooks in a pit of coals all day."

Meg took a long drink from the plastic water bottle she'd carried in. "Hope you skipped the part where they leave the head on, too."

Cassandra placed the bowls on the table and handed Meg shiny black chopsticks. "Head wouldn't fit."

"Ahwe, Sistah," Meg exclaimed in creole Hawaiian holding up the utensils. "I'm full haole again. No mo eating everyting wit chopsticks." She positioned them and awkwardly stabbed at the pork and rice a few times until she was able to squeeze enough between the sticks for a full bite. By the fourth scoop, Meg was a seasoned veteran again. "I probably should use these more often. I'd eat less, cause it's so much work."

After dinner, Cassandra fetched shoes and a heavier coat from her bedroom while Meg cleaned up the kitchen. Before they left, Cassandra handed her iPad to Meg. "Andy Summers showed me a couple of photos of the scene where Austin Price died. I remember a kid taking pictures with his smart phone at the scene too. Can you find those pictures online? I want to show you something. You don't have to look if you don't want to, but I'm trying to help the police with leads."

Meg's voice was hesitant. "Isn't this a job for the sheriff? Why would we investigate on our own?"

Cassandra wanted Meg's unbiased perspective. "I know it's unusual, but Nielson told me to liaison with the investigation. He wants it closed quickly." Cassandra unlocked the iPad and watched Meg tapping and swiping the screen rapidly trying different apps and websites.

Shortly Meg found several photos that were too blurry to see much detail beyond grainy shapes when zoomed in. Finally, she found two clear ones.

Cassandra said, "Look carefully. What do you notice?"

The first was a wide shot showing the concrete outdoor staircase of the Edgerton building and Price's body lying on his back, headfirst on the steps. "I've read mystery novels and watched movies, but guessing how this happened isn't so easy."

The next photo was closer, just Price and no background. Maybe it had been taken before the police arrived. His skin color was purplish, and his eyes were closed as though he looked sleeping or unconscious. Meg took a couple big breaths. "Just can't believe he sat in class with me two days ago."

Cassandra waited patiently while Meg studied the close-up. Meg pointed to his arms. "I see the little marks where the police had wondered about the drug use . . . his legs . . . one straight, the other partially tucked under him." Her finger moved over. "His left hand like maybe he tried to catch himself . . . or to sit up. Hard to tell which."

There was another long pause until Meg exclaimed, "His hand! His right hand . . . is that an L?"

She wasn't the only one! Cassandra pointed to the screen excitedly. "You see it too?"

Meg zoomed in even closer. "It could be. A finger-spelled letter L? It could just be the way he fell. But maybe he did it on purpose. It looks like an L!"

If they both saw it, that couldn't be coincidence. Their eyes met. "So . . . is that a clue?"

Meg's shoulders slumped. "Do we tell anyone? What if we get someone in trouble and it's not the right person?"

He could've just randomly fell that way. The pork and rice settled like a fist sized rock in Cassandra's stomach. "But if we don't tell anyone and we're right, then I'd feel horrible later."

Meg set the iPad on the kitchen table and nodded miserably, "So would I."

Cassandra turned it off and zipped up her coat. "Let's think about it tonight and decide tomorrow."

* * *

The Campus Ministry club had planned the candlelight vigil, expecting fewer than a hundred people to show up near the Chapel building. However, before 9:00 p.m., the courtyard was filled. Leaders circulated through the students with boxes of white 6-inch candles stuck into little paper cones to catch the wax. The temperature had dipped into the 50s; most people wore jackets and light scarves. They spoke in hushed tones, waiting.

Meg and Cassandra arrived 30 minutes early so Meg could talk to organizers about interpreting logistics for the deaf students and employees, if they came. Cassandra and Meg approached Lance while he leaned against a stone wall staring vacantly into the crowd. Cassandra had seen deaf people hug in friendly greeting before, and in Hawai'i everyone hugs hello. Usually Cassandra didn't touch students, but she was suddenly overcome with the urge to comfort him.

Before Cassandra moved closer, Meg swooped in and attempted a sloppy bear hug, but Lance's stiff arms made the gesture awkward. Meg stepped back, smiled uncomfortably, and signed, "How are you doing? Everything okay?"

The look on his face clearly showed everything was NOT ok, but he nodded anyway. "I told the cops that Austin didn't do drugs. The needle marks on his arms were from giving plasma. I don't know why he fell, but I doubt it was drugs."

If he gave plasma, they probably drug tested him anyway. Meg signed when Cassandra spoke. "I heard they couldn't find Austin's laptop or phone, huh? That seemed weird. Didn't he always bring them with him?"

Lance held up a finger to hold off friends who were trying to get his attention to join them. "Austin didn't always bring his laptop to classes; sometimes he left it in the room. If the police didn't find it there, who knows what he did with it. The missing phone is weird though." He waved goodbye to the women and joined his friends in the front of the crowd.

Cassandra drifted back to let Meg do her job and watched the crowd. Promptly at 9:00, some students playing acoustic instruments began the service. Next, the kindly, barrel-chested Chaplain ascended the chapel steps and addressed the hundreds of faces illuminated by flickering candles using his loud voice polished by years of sermons. Meg stood several feet away from him and signed his speech. "Today our hearts are heavy because of the sudden loss of sophomore Austin Price. Whether you knew him personally or not, the loss of such a young life creates an empty space on our campus. There's nothing I can say today that will fill that void, that will lift the heaviness of our collective sorrow. We gather here tonight to celebrate his life and to comfort each other. We're filled with questions to which we have few satisfactory answers. Why Austin? What caused such an abrupt ending to a vibrant, young man's life? Although we may not learn the answers for days or weeks, we can trust today in our Lord's mercy and generosity to those who believe in Him. May Austin's soul rest in a place of refreshment, light and peace. Let us use this time together to remember Austin and honor his memory. I'd like to introduce..."

Cassandra tuned out the speakers and focused on the crowd. She noticed a middle-aged couple off to the side surrounded by young people who were shaking their hands and hugging them. *Maybe his parents*, she wondered?

Even with the extra deputies and staff lining the green space, Cassandra didn't notice any disruptions. Students' faces appeared saddened and shocked as they huddled in small groups together. A few snapped photos of the peaceful setting. The small, brick Gothic-style chapel was a beautiful backdrop to the candle-holding crowd. The mournful, haunting music carried clearly in the crisp night air. As people dispersed less than an hour later, she overheard a few students quietly wondering aloud what really happened to Austin.

Afterward, Meg dropped Cassandra at her house. Cassandra said, "Mahalo for the ride and the help tonight."

Meg looked at her watch. "I'd better get home. I'm going to ask Connor about our fingerspelled L idea. Sleep tight."

Cassandra locked the door behind Meg and turned off the outside light. Once in bed, she relaxed by visualizing the warm sun, cool ocean breezes, and the ono smells in her mother's kitchen. Drifting off to sleep, she felt a little zip of anticipation for tomorrow. So many words began with the letter "L."

Chapter Twelve

Before 7:15 Monday morning, Cassandra had already replied to several state and national news agencies who had clogged her email with requests for information. "Morton College has no comment right now. Please respect student and family privacy. Give them time to grieve, and the police time to investigate."

Her phone pinged with a text from Meg: "Connor and I both think we should report about the L. Even if we are wrong it could be a lead. Hugs. Talk to you later."

Starting up the large coffee pot with her own carefully rationed Kona coffee before the rest of the students and staff arrived, Cassandra considered what other background information the investigators could use. She printed the list of AOO fraternity students, added Austin Price's known friends' names, and his class and professor list.

Because Cassandra knew only ASL phrases that a kindergartener could use, she didn't know Austin well. Deeper conversations happened when Meg was in the room to interpret, or when people took the time to pass a notebook back and forth with the deaf students. She should have tried harder to talk to him and Lance.

Austin hadn't died of natural causes. Maybe he'd been bullied, and she hadn't noticed the warning signals. Too many things didn't add up. They still didn't know why his phone and laptop weren't with him in the lab.

When she went into the waiting room to refill her coffee mug, Annie was sitting out front. Cassandra fastened on her best Monday morning smile and said as cheerily as she could manage, "Good morning, how are you?"

The girl was looking down at her iPhone and making a goofy face right at the time Cassandra spoke to her. The startled expression on her face was probably not the one she had intended to capture for the Snapchat she was sending. "Uh, oh . . . Yes, hi!"

The office's administrative assistant of 42 years, Connie McDermott, had retired four weeks after Cassandra had arrived taking with her the institutional memory of every file's home, every professor's name, and those of many students as well. How the Board of Directors had deemed a professional assistant to the Student Affairs VP as "non-essential staff" during the August hiring freeze was beyond comprehension. Cassandra didn't have the power to fight that battle yet.

To put it kindly, things in her office frequently fell through the cracks. Student workers took turns sitting at the front desk, answering the phone, responding to simple emails to send basic information, making student appointments, and relaying information to Cassandra and the various directors who reported to her.

Annie looked up at Cassandra expectantly and said, "Do you need something?"

For starters, Cassandra could use a great new assistant. For this moment, at the very least Annie needed to get busy. "Uh, yes...Are there any phone messages I need to return?"

"Just a few hangups. And one crabby guy with inappropriate language who said something unkind about you. I hung up on him. I don't have to put up with that kind of verbal abuse."

Great. It was bad enough when crank callers made it to Cassandra's direct line. Now they were harassing her students, too. She said, "Right, sorry about that. What about on voicemail?"

Annie slurped from a disposable coffee cup. "Um. See, I don't know how to work the voice mail here. Can't you listen on your office phone?"

Cassandra ground her back teeth together. "Usually someone screens them for me and deals with the people who can be helped without speaking to me. I only return the calls that need to come directly from me."

Annie's eyebrows knitted together. "So how do I know if someone else can help, or if you need to talk to them?"

Cassandra really didn't have time for this today. "If you make a list of the people's names who've left messages, either I or someone in the office can help you decide which ones are important. Sometimes you can tell by the person's job title and whether they say it's urgent I speak to them."

The girl just stared as though if she didn't move, Cassandra would give up and walk away.

She'd been 19 once, too. Cassandra stared back. *Trust me, wahine, I'm more stubborn than you are.*

Finally, Annie opened the desk drawer and found a pad of paper and a pencil. She picked up the phone and looked at the keypad with its many buttons. "Uh...how do I get the messages again? Do I push 9 or something?"

Cassandra figured by the time she explained the whole process, it would be time for Annie to leave for class. She gave up. "Never mind. I'll do it myself today. Why don't you study the phone instructions so you can do it tomorrow? Do you work here tomorrow?"

Annie eyed her like she was considering running over to the Financial Aid office and asking for a better work-study job. "I don't know."

* * *

Cassandra had just completed her critical list consisting of the top three things she needed to accomplish when the intercom buzzed. A voice she assumed was Annie's announced, "Some cop is here."

At the same time, her door opened and Andy Summers entered holding a white paper bag in one hand and his metal travel cup in the other.

A pleasant surprise. Her mouth watered in anticipation of another treat. "Breakfast twice in a row. You spoil me."

He took a couple steps toward her desk. "My sister would punch my arm for saying this out loud, but you look like a strong Nebraska wind would blow you over."

Judging from some of the winds Cassandra had seen so far around here, he could be right. She gestured to the chair in front of her desk. "No offense taken, but I do usually eat at home."

He reached into the bag for a wax paper wrapped chocolate eclair then handed the bag over to her. "I didn't have breakfast, and I don't want to rudely eat in front of you. You're helping me appear civilized."

Cassandra removed a warm glazed donut and bit into the sweet goodness. "Happy to help you out." She handed him a manila folder. "I made you a file on Austin Price. He worked in the Edgerton research lab, and his roommate Lance Erickson works in our office."

He quietly studied the lists for a minute. "Thanks for putting this together. We've already spoken to some of these people. We still don't know where he was between class and the time his body was found at 3:15 p.m."

Andy took another bite and examined her face carefully. Chicken skin raised on her upper arms as she returned his stare. What exactly were his intentions here? He gave off a casual, friendly vibe, but he lingered too long—like a tongue-tied high school senior two weeks before prom. Maybe he was just a slower moving, thoughtful guy, and she was imagining that he was trying to work up the courage to ask her on a date. He was hard to read.

He must've thought the same about her because he said, "Penny for your thoughts?"

"I couldn't sleep much last night for worrying about Austin and whether this was an accident or if there's more to the story."

He finished the eclair and nodded. "Things don't make sense if he just had a medical incident and fell. At first, we'd wondered about him being a drug user. The preliminary autopsy report showed no alcohol or illegal drugs in his system. Complete toxicology results take a couple weeks. I asked some of the guys who knew him, and they mentioned that he sells plasma over at the AlphaBioGlobal (ABG) place in town. That explained the needle marks in his arms."

The last time she'd tried to donate blood, they had looked at her weight and low hemoglobin and politely rejected her. She shivered at the thought of all those needles. "That matches up with what you said yesterday and what his roommate said, too. How often can a person give plasma?"

Andy pulled out his notepad, flipped a few pages and read aloud. "Up to 7 times a month if you eat right, are in good shape, and time the visits. Some students earn up to $300 a month selling plasma. It pays better than minimum wage, and they can study while they sit and wait. It's not for everyone, but ..."

Cassandra said, "Austin made pretty good money, then. Between both jobs."

"Ya know ... some students get into gambling on college or professional sports or at the casinos over in Iowa. Another angle could be if he was behind in paying losses and loans, that's big trouble." Cassandra wrote notes while Andy talked. The investigation was following so many leads, it was hard to know where she could help.

Summers looked up, "Also wanted you to know the state guys found blood and a small puncture on some surgical gloves in the research lab. They suspect Austin stuck himself with a syringe at work. They're comparing his blood tests to the chemicals used in the research lab."

"Could a lab syringe have caused his death? Remember the contract they found in Austin's personal papers with Nielson's name on it?" Nielson's concern about the lab grant funding was intriguing.

Andy said, "This isn't completely my case now. I have to keep the county sheriff and the state patrol informed of anything I learn. Homicides are rare. Lots of eyes involved."

Maybe she should check the school records to see if Austin paid his account on time. Cassandra told Andy about the fingerspelled letter L that she and Meg had both noticed on the photos. Andy wrote it in his book. "Both of you saw it. You might be right about Austin trying to send us a message. We'll keep it in mind, but without a witness it would be hard for us to use that as evidence."

She'd have one less worry on her conscience if it turned out she was right about the photo clue. She flashed him the genuine smile she reserved for friends. "Whatever it takes to get this cleared up."

Summers neatly packed away the donut bag, swept the crumbs off her desk into his hand and dropped it all in the garbage as he walked out of the office. "Talk to you later, Cassandra." His gaze held hers for an extra breath, and then he was gone.

Chapter Thirteen

Cassandra skipped the polite preamble and started the directors meeting with an update on the Price investigation. "The preliminary autopsy report says no drugs or alcohol were found in his system," she read to the others.

A skeleton crew of eight men and four women were seated around the executive office's conference table cluttered with coffee mugs, leather bound notebooks and two large boxes of sprinkled frosted donuts. Eyeing the three grey-beards who'd staked out the prime seats near the door, she wondered who would be first to make a quick escape. She'd seen them rush to the bathroom during previous meetings when their enlarged prostates gave out.

Cassandra continued, "They've certified Austin's death as violent, most likely trauma to his head. There were some shallow cuts on his skull and bruising on his arms and torso. The theory is he fell down the stairs and hit his head on the way down. The needle marks in his arm weren't from taking drugs. He was a frequent donor at the plasma company in town. I heard regulars can make $300 a month there."

Marcus Fischer added, "We've talked to the other fraternity members and there's a whole group of them besides Austin who donated plasma a couple times a week at the ABG place on Main. It's an easy part-time job where they can study or catch up on Netflix."

She looked up from the report. "A couple kids in our office do it, too. I couldn't handle those needles." Cassandra shuddered. "The police are piecing together a timetable of his last 24 hours. Austin worked at the research lab Thursday after classes. According to the grad assistant, the earliest he would've left was 7:30. Between class and work on Friday we don't know his movements, yet. What's still unknown is why he fell. They're investigating like they would a homicide. No one knows who was the last person to see him." It was surreal to discuss death so coolly.

Bob Gregory, VP of the business office, frowned so deep his eyebrows met in one bushy line across his forehead. "You can get as sentimental as you'd like, dear. The way I see it, a homicide would be better than finding the college negligent—for liability purposes."

Big picture budgets notwithstanding, she couldn't hide an instinctive wince. "Likely his family isn't concerned about liability now. They're simply missing their son."

Fischer raised a finger to speak next. "His parents have left a couple messages on my phone, but when I called back I've missed them. You may hear from them at some point, Dr. Sato. They want answers."

Everyone wanted answers, but first Cassandra needed to confirm which director was in charge of each Homecoming event and where they had coverage gaps. Intensely aware of President Nielson's absence and maintaining an excellent Homecoming tradition, she wanted no more surprises. Gregory had volunteered to oversee Tuesday night's Obstacle Course Race where the teams competed while dressed in Halloween costumes. Cassandra had pegged him as most likely to lurch sideways in cardiac arrest from 30-odd years of breakfast donuts instead of unexpectedly leading a silly race.

Hannah Chapman from Marketing said, "This year's theme is 'Zombies Rising.' Anyone feeling energetic, let me know. I'm still recruiting players for the student versus faculty and staff volleyball match Wednesday night." She was Cassandra's age, impeccably dressed and confident. Cinda had already warned her that Hannah was being headhunted by larger institutions.

Papers shuffled as the old-timers avoided eye contact with Hannah. Three hands went up from the younger administrators whose air of anticipation was palpable that one day soon they'd take the reins. After only two months, Cassandra knew how they felt. Morton had so much potential if they could just move this place into the current decade. Thursday was the Alumni Dinner, then Friday the parade and carnival, topped off by the football game vs. Iowa Christian College and the bonfire on Saturday night.

Cinda Weller said, "Thanks to Dr. Sato's new Women of Tomorrow leadership group, we have partnered with the wellness people to promote students having fun without binge-drinking. Student clubs will perform skits all week in the residence halls to advertise the weekend events. We have hired three bands to provide entertainment on Friday night."

The traditional carnival included booths and games lined up all around the center green space. Several popular food trucks from Lincoln and Omaha had been booked for meal times. Alumni, parents and visitors were encouraged to attend the parade, carnival and stay overnight in hotels in the neighboring towns to return on Saturday for the football game and bonfire.

Hannah added, "We have all the signs and posters ready to hang this morning. We're paying some students to Tweet and take event photos to create the buzz."

"Create the buzz?" asked Gregory.

"Spark enthusiasm among students to increase attendance," she clarified. "They won't come if it's not fun. We have to offer a viable alternative to get them on board."

He grumbled, "Why couldn't you just say that? These young pups make up new words every other month. They have the attention span of fleas from their screen addictions."

Cassandra hoped the students' enthusiasm wouldn't be dampened by the previous Friday's events. She crossed her fingers that nothing more would happen to make campus unsafe. "Old business...the Finance Committee meets tomorrow about the physics lab capital improvements. There are some suggested revisions to the architectural designs and then the full Board of Directors votes preliminary approval at their next meeting. We don't get involved until the full Board approves designs."

Professor Mike Bergstrom held up a cautionary hand. "Whoa. The Faculty Senate should be involved in the process too. All this preliminary work has been completed without our input. Once it's approved, it'll steamroll forward and making changes at that juncture will be difficult. What about open dialogue with faculty, staff and students before this moves forward? All the stakeholders should be involved or later there's going to be clashes."

Former Morton President Bergstrom had stepped down seven years earlier to return to his first love—teaching philosophy—and had been around the college longer than anyone else in memory. If he decided something wasn't going through, he knew hundreds of ways to block passage. His appearance and manner was 100% stereotypical college professor from his Einstein-esque wild gray hair and trim beard to the cardigan sweater with leather elbow patches. Before the current no-smoking laws, the upper floor of Bryan Hall where his office and most philosophy classes were held had a perpetual cloud of blue pipe smoke. His love for C.S. Lewis was surpassed only by his love for instilling critical thinking skills in young minds. Rated consistently as one of the best professors on campus, the students flocked to his classes. Cassandra had seen him work the faculty senate meetings where he often sprinkled philosophy-related quotations into his lectures and conversations.

Bob Gregory was only a few years younger than Bergstrom, but grouchier. "What's your resistance really about? We're following procedures."

"Didn't you build a biochemical lab four years ago? Now physics, too." Bergstrom reminded the group. "Just because you can't get a National Institutes of Health grant for studying Thomas Aquinas doesn't mean humanities facilities upgrades should lag behind the physical sciences. What's so glamorous about observing rodents anyway?"

Cassandra followed the old guard's debate like a chess match, recognizing she had lost control of the agenda. In this classic higher ed standoff, her old college was exactly the same as mainland institutions: the antagonism between science and the humanities.

Greg Murray, Faculty Senate Chair and Biology professor, defended his turf. "In order to sit around discussing dusty old men, all you need are desks and chairs. You don't need nano technology, elaborate database server systems, or dry chemical extinguishing agents."

Bergstrom stood so quickly his chair rolled away and hit the wall behind him. His eyes bulged from his face and his mouth spluttered incoherently. "Dusty old—!"

Bob Gregory lectured, "This is the post-secondary environment we live in today, Mike. The research dollars are in the sciences. Young people use free time in their dorm rooms huddled around a white board to brainstorm that patentable Big Idea that will make them the next Bill Gates or Mark Zuckerberg. If students attend here four years without becoming entrepreneurs for the latest sexy new venture, they figure their degree is the consolation prize. Kids today don't want to graduate, get married, get the entry level job, buy the starter home and move up the ladder slowly, methodically like we did in our twenties."

Cassandra was transfixed, along with everyone else in the room.

Gregory pounded the table with a fist. "They talk about Lifestyle design as though you could buy a life. Hell, compared to my college days, they already have it all! They live in fancy suite-style apartments we build them, use top-of-the-line computers, and the latest smartphones. No wonder they don't aspire to a life where the pinnacle of their career is thirty years in the future. This is the way we've brought them up. They knew how to use a computer before they knew how to use the toilet. We have brought this curse upon ourselves."

Bergstrom remained standing letting Gregory rant, eventually folding his arms across his chest and nodding in agreement. When he finished, Bergstrom slowly applauded his sermon. The others looked at each other around the table in bewilderment and politely clapped as well.

Cassandra was torn between admiration of his speech and irritation that these gentlemen were wasting valuable minutes of her very busy day. She checked the clock on the wall, conscious of keeping to the allotted time and the student waiting in the front office for her next appointment. Since her job was Vice President of Student Affairs, she thought the serving students part of it should be the highest priority of her day.

This discussion, while enlightening, was not moving them closer to action on any of her agenda topics. She pasted a chilly, polite smile on her face. "Thank you, gentlemen for your insightful debate on prioritizing spending during these difficult economic times. Can I put both of your names down for the campus task force on strategic planning that meets next month to begin work on the next biennial budget cuts?" She paused just long enough to scribble their names on her paper and continued, "If everyone agrees on their roles for this week's events, I suggest we adjourn this meeting until the next one in November. We'll keep you all informed about developments in the investigation of Mr. Price's death. Thanks for your time, and have a good day."

The table quickly cleared and everyone stood, whipping out their smartphones to check messages and calendars for their next destination. Cassandra chuckled inwardly as she noted old man Gregory was one of the first to become engrossed in his technology, sausage-sized thumbs fumbling over the tiny phone screen as he flipped through his calendar. Ironically, she should be one of those connected 24/7 Millennials, but she had no social media accounts and her Facebook profile picture was the default shadow. She preferred her notebook and pen, and a good yoga workout to wasting time online.

Chapter Fourteen

"This is a long shot because I know you're busy, but Deputy Tate from the sheriff's office and I are going to the plasma place today. I'd like your help." Cassandra had squinted her eyes tight when Andy Summers called her between student appointments. She needed a clone or a magic wand.

She wanted to follow through on her offer to help the investigation, but stepping on jurisdictional toes would not go over well. "What's our role?"

"Morton's research labs work closely with the medical personnel. You could authorize information sharing if needed and eliminate delays."

She consulted her calendar. "I could meet you in 90 minutes after two appointments."

Nielson would be very pleased if she could wrap this up quickly. Plus, seeing the plasma center was a great excuse to become familiar with another aspect of student life. She agreed to meet him later.

"Dr. Sato, a Blake Shelton is on the phone for you." No sooner had Cassandra hung up with Andy when the student receptionist bounced into her office. Cassandra stared an extra few seconds at Bridget.

Cassandra's eyebrows raised, "Did you say Blake Shelton . . . the country singer?"

Bridget's shoulders slumped and her smile vanished. "Oh yeah, so it probably wasn't Blake Shelton then, was it? Maybe he said Blake Sampson. He asked to talk to you."

She really needed to convince Nielson to hire a full-time office assistant. "Did he say where he works or why he wants to talk to me?"

"He might have . . . I can't remember. If you just pick up the phone, you can ask him. That would be easier." She returned to her chair.

Cassandra shook her head and picked up the phone. "Good Morning, this is Dr. Sato, how can I help you?"

The voice was male. "Hello, I'm Derek Swanson calling from the Omaha Daily News. I have some questions about the Morton College student's death, and I'd like to arrange an interview with you tomorrow."

This was exactly the type of calls the front desk should be screening for her so she could call him back with a prepared answer. Caught off guard, she scrambled to say something intelligent. You never knew when or how reporters would use a quote. "I have many meetings tomorrow, Mr. Swanson." She noted his name on the pad of paper in front of her, along with Omaha Daily News reporter and interview. "Perhaps our Media Relations Director can call you back when we've a prepared statement. I don't normally handle press interviews."

"I understand, Dr. Sato," he replied smoothly. "You're in charge of Student Affairs though, right? When I googled you, I couldn't find any social media posts except that photo of you and the street preacher from a few weeks ago. Funny stuff. Otherwise, it's like you hardly exist."

That photo just wouldn't go away. "Well…since you're speaking to me now, you must realize I do exist, Mr. Swanson. You may find it hard to believe, but my days are full of appointments, meetings, and interactions that involve real people," she said. Not at all defensively.

He fished around, "I wonder what you're not posting. I noticed you recently moved to Nebraska from Hawai'i, correct? I can't imagine why a person who lived in paradise would move to this backwater—unless you're hiding something…"

She didn't like his tone or implications. "Was that a question?"

He switched back to rapid-fire inquisition. "Actually, my article focuses on the student angle. Morton College is a tight-knit community. Our readers want to know how students are affected by this tragedy. Are they afraid? What's the school doing to protect students from another attack?"

No one had called it an attack. This wasn't going well. She took a breath and used her stern teacher voice. "Sir, police are still investigating the nature of the death. We're following normal protocol for a serious incident like this, but now is a not a good time."

He wasn't intimidated. "I gotta submit my article day after tomorrow, and if you don't tell me the college's version,

I'll have to print the theories rumbling around campus and online. I'd really appreciate a call back by the end of the day."

She wouldn't be calling him back. Her stomach was in knots. "I'll give your name to the Media Relations Director, and she'll get back to you."

* * *

Shawn McIntosh shuffled into Cassandra's office and slumped into the seat across from her desk.

"Good morning, Mr. McIntosh. You were referred to me because it's now eight weeks into the semester, and your Theatre teacher tells me you've been to class once."

"Theatre? Yeah, I went. She, like, just read off the Power Point. She posts it all on Canvas after class, so I figured, hey why go to class when I can sit at home and read it myself. Don't need to shower, walk across campus. Can play a few more rounds of Halo, right?"

Cassandra wrote "Remember to ask the students later about Halo," on the notepad next to his open file on her desk. Must be a video game, and it didn't sound productive. "Aren't you here at Morton on a Presidential scholarship?" she checked McIntosh's schedule again.

"What? Oh . . . yeah, I think so. I don't know. Whatever the school doesn't cover, my grandma pays for, so I'm cool."

"How are your other classes going?"

He shrugged, "I'm taking Intro to Business and that's pretty easy. Just a few papers, a midterm and final. Statistics. Geology. Just those four. It's not too bad. Way easier than high school," he bragged. "On Fridays I only have one class at 10:30 a.m., and then I'm done for the day. College is great, bro."

Cassandra had attended university for eight years and wrote a 182-page dissertation so she could be called Bro by this pampered 18-year-old. She repeated to herself: *I love students. I love my job.* Keeping the pleasant mask on her face, she said, "I'm glad you are - enjoying - your semester so far. However, Mr. McIntosh, I can assure you that this is the easiest semester you likely will have in your academic career. You're enrolled in freshmen level survey classes where the instructors start off slowly to ensure that all students become acclimated to their new role as full-time college students. As the year continues you'll notice a marked increase in the number and difficulty of assignments. You need to attend class to hear the additional information the instructor uses to supplement her Power Point presentations."

The rumpled young man across her desk gave her a blank, disinterested stare. Cassandra cleared her throat. "Certainly not every class you take will be a favorite. However, you need to do well on them all to maintain your substantial and generous scholarship. Didn't you do well in high school in order to qualify for these funds? Is there anything I can do to help you?"

"I dunno. I didn't really do much in high school. It was pretty easy, and I just handed in what they told me to do. I aced the ACT, but I really don't care about finishing school right away. I'm planning to ski at Breck over fall break. I hope they get some fresh powder by then."

The skiing part perplexed her. "Breck? Where's that? People ski in Nebraska? It's so flat here how would you do that?"

His laugh came out like a grunt, and he shook his head like she was a dimwit. "Bro, the only skiing you can do in Nebraska is cross country, like you see on the Olympics. I'm talking real sick runs in Colorado at Breckenridge. My dad's family goes every Christmas, but my squad's going early this year since we have a free weekend."

She asked skeptically, "Isn't that a pretty far drive? Can you do that in a four-day weekend?"

Another shrug. "Yeah I'll take off the Thursday before and slide it into six days. I won't miss much, and it's no big deal. I'll get the notes from someone. It'll be fine."

This kid reminded her of Gregory's sermon earlier in the morning about entitled brats. Her growing exasperation showed in her voice. "Are you sure you want to be in school, Mr. McIntosh?"

"Why do you care so much? Do you get paid a commission for each student you save?" His eyes darted down at the phone in his hand as though looking for an excuse to leave.

He was inching up to the line in the sand where her patience ended. She raised one eyebrow at him in warning. "Attending classes is a big part of being successful in college. Surely your grandmother who's helping to pay your tuition would be proud of you for doing well here?"

Mentioning his Tutu would alarm most Hawaiian students, but McIntosh was unmoved. "What's it matter to you? It's not your money. My Granny's sweet for helping me. She's loaded."

Her second eye brow went up, but McIntosh didn't realize his mistake and kept talking. "Really, it'll be fine. I think this schedule is going to rock for me. I can get out to the slopes way more than I could in high school. South Dakota is even closer, but those hills kind of suck compared to Summit County, Colorado. The powder there is top, bro."

Well that's about one Bro too many, Cassandra thought. You can take the girl out of Waipahu, but no reason to forget lessons learned growing up in her working class neighborhood. She placed her palms on the desk and said, "Listen up, braddah. You tink you can throw me attitude and I just goin cave in? You got one nother ting coming."

The smirk fell from McIntosh's face. Cassandra dropped her serious, professional persona and continued in her public school-girl accent, "Back home, I took on kids twice as smart as you and I still wen shoot dem down. You no like be here? Den leave."

She jerked her thumb towards the door. "Do me and your grandmaddah da favor. Get plenty other young people out there who would jump at da chance for come to dis great place."

Cassandra stood, pointed directly to his bewildered face and enunciated slowly. "So, you choose: show up fully or exit fully. Aloha, for now. No let da door hit you on da way out."

After two silent beats, McIntosh stood up and loped out of her office, gently closing the door behind him. Cassandra shook her head. No oceans in Nebraska. After years dealing with stoked surfers who cut class for big waves, now she would see a whole new type of slackers. The ski bums. *Oh boy.*

Chapter Fifteen

Cassandra, Andy Summers and Deputy Tate approached the front desk of AlphaBioGlobal Plasma Center's simple, modern lobby. A fresh-faced young woman with blond hair piled on top of her swaying, bouncing head wore white earbuds in her ears and her eyes were focused on the open textbook on the reception desk. Looking up, Ponytail started, removed the headphones, and sized up the uniformed officers with a slightly confused expression on her face. "Can I help you . . . ?"

Deputy Tate read off the small pad he'd pulled out of his shirt pocket. "We're looking for Dr. Arnold Schneider, the Executive Director."

"Sure, ok . . . just a sec," she picked up the phone and started punching numbers. Cassandra did a slow 360 of the place where so many students spent their time. The comfy couches and countertop coffee station stocked with flavored coffees and snacks seemed more inviting than a normal medical clinic. In fact, the large TV playing a Big Bang Theory rerun silently while captions scrolled along the bottom of the screen was nicer than anything in the dorms.

After a few soft words, Ponytail replaced the phone on the receiver and pointed to her left and behind her. "Just go down this hallway. His office is at the end of the hall."

Tate leaned to the right to read the name tag on her shirt. "Thank you . . . Lisa."

She flashed him a smile, and fumbled with the earbuds while she stared back a few extra moments. Cassandra eyed Tate's broad forehead, high cheekbones and strong chin. Sure he was handsome, but weren't they all at work?

A fifty-ish looking man wearing a white lab coat met them halfway down the hallway. Tate stuck his hand out, "Good morning, Dr. Schneider."

Cassandra knew him already, so she waited while the men introduced themselves. "Officer Summers, Deputy . . . nice to meet you both. Dr. Sato, what a pleasant surprise. I haven't seen you since your first campus interview in July; I trust you're all settled in?"

When she nodded, he continued, "What can I do for you today?"

Tate began, "You heard about the death of Austin Price, the Morton College student, on Friday? We're here to ask a couple of questions about him."

"Yes I did hear about that." His thick, slightly gray hair and wire-rimmed glasses framed a self-assured looking face. A wealthy man used to being in charge. "I'm not sure how I can help you, but I'll try."

"Can you please walk us through the process that happens when a person comes into your center? What do you call them—donors? Clients? Patients?"

"Donor is the preferred term in our business. First timer donors spend several hours completing a health history and questionnaire. Do they have tattoos or piercings, where have they traveled, just like regular blood donation protocol. However, since we pay our subjects, we do extra screening on hemoglobin and protein levels, among other things. That whole interview lasts about an hour."

They stood outside a large open room housing eight reclining medical chairs. Cassandra's quick glance showed scrub wearing staff members bent over two different patients. She maneuvered past the doorway, avoiding the view. Schneider said, "Here in the donation area, depending on the speed and how much they can give, it takes anywhere from another 45-60 minutes. Once we have someone in our system and approved, their subsequent donations take slightly more than an hour. One person can donate 7-10 times a month."

Tate followed up, "Do you have trouble getting enough people to donate blood and sell plasma? Where does it go once you've collected it?"

"We're unique because of the size of Carson. Our clinic is actually a satellite for our larger company AlphaBioGlobal in Lincoln. We collect both whole blood and plasma here. The platelets and red and white blood cells are separated from the plasma which is used for manufacturing lifesaving pharmaceutical products. Any unused material goes to the Lincoln or Omaha blood banks for distribution wherever it's most needed."

"Are your donation rates steady or have you noticed any changes?"

Schneider's hands rested casually in his pockets. "There's been a large increase since August and the campus blood drive last month. Plus, we tend to be busier during the school year when the students need extra cash."

Although interesting information, Cassandra couldn't figure out where these questions were leading. Tate didn't hesitate though. "How does the payment part work? How much do the students make each time they donate?"

Dr. Schneider knew all the numbers. "They make $50 for their first donation, $40 for referrals and bonus payments for returning frequently in one calendar month. It varies widely depending how often students come in."

Andy Summers asked. "Austin Price was a frequent plasma donor?"

Schneider considered a few seconds, then shrugged. "Since he's deceased, I guess HIPPA no longer applies. I looked up his name when I heard about his death. Yes, Mr. Price was a donor here, but I don't know any more than that."

Tate looked up from his notes. "I understand you're ABG's liaison to the Morton lab. It appears that Mr. Price stuck himself with a needle. Could that be related to his death?"

Schneider's eyebrows went up, "Stuck himself?" He shifted his weight from one leg to the other and studied the donation room. "Well, there's two groups of rats: one gets a placebo and the other is injected with an enzyme. I can't think of any reason why that would harm Mr. Price."

Tate scribbled notes while Schneider spent a few minutes explaining the science. "We're also following up on the student's missing technology. His laptop and cell phone haven't been located yet."

Schneider frowned slightly. "His laptop? And his phone, too? Hmmm . . . yes that's odd, isn't it?"

Needles made Cassandra's stomach flip. Little perspiration beads formed at her hairline, even standing in the hallway. Tate changed direction: "What effect do frequent donations have on a person's body? Do the arms scar over? Is there a limit to how long a person can donate?"

Any time she'd had blood drawn, a bruise and poke mark remained on her arm for days. Her back spasmed in a shudder. All the riches of Dubai wouldn't convince her to do that several times a month.

Once all their questions about Austin had been answered, Dr. Schneider took them on a brief tour of the medical lab area, but not inside due to sterilization rules. Back in the cool, comfortable lobby, Cassandra's composure returned. Deputy Tate said, "Do you also know Luke Peterson from the Morton biology lab?"

Dr. Schneider smiled broadly, his crystal blue eyes crinkling. "Yes, of course I know him. I serve as an adviser on his doctoral committee. So does my counterpart from Lincoln, Dr. Baral. ABG is proud of our relationship with Morton College. I'm happy we can contribute to the advancement of research."

He became more animated when discussing his role with the college. Cassandra enjoyed teaching graduate students, too. Summers asked, "Can you explain what contributions you mean, Doctor?"

Schneider's hands raised like he held an invisible football. "Sure. They've identified an enzyme that naturally occurs in our bodies called Superoxide dismutase. It's attached to proteins in red blood cells and some people have a higher concentration of SOD enzyme in their blood than other people. Probably this is linked to diet and heredity. Basically, SODs are antioxidants that defend DNA. Luke Peterson's dissertation focuses on SOD's ability to shrink brain cancer tumors in rats. At ABG, we test each donation for a variety of markers and distribute proteins or blood products to various places, as I've already described. We send the blood containing higher concentrations of SOD to the Morton facility to use as one of the control groups in his treatments."

Cassandra usually advised educational administration majors and the lab's research was nowhere close to her specialty. She struggled to grasp the science.

To her surprise, Summers had followed the explanation. "So this enzyme that we all have naturally could treat brain cancer?"

Schneider shook his head. "We're still in the animal testing phase. But that's the crux of the hypothesis."

Summers asked, "Would people who have a naturally high amount of the enzyme be better protected from developing those types of cancer?"

Schneider became the professor again, his hands resting in his pockets. "That's a question for further research, if this is successful. But in essence, that would be our hope. Eventually we could develop an injection or oral supplement. Sadly, most of the patients stricken with this cancer are children under age 14. This is one of many similar tests happening around the world."

Cassandra hadn't heard about the grant during her interview process. Deputy Tate was also impressed. "Fascinating. Pediatric brain cancer!"

Proudly Dr. Schneider agreed, "Exactly! I attended Morton for my undergrad and I'm thrilled to be able to give back to my alma mater by mentoring students and serving on the board. Our synergistic relationship between the private and public sectors is a shining example of how academic and private institutions can benefit the larger community."

They all shook hands, thanked him for the tour and information and left together. Deputy Tate didn't stay to talk.

Cassandra turned to Andy Summers on the sidewalk as they returned to campus, "I see now how Austin got the needle marks on his arms."

"You can find one of these places near lots of college campuses. Poor college students provide a steady supply of blood and plasma to the surrounding community hospitals. It's easy part-time "work" if you don't mind the needles."

Cassandra shuddered. "I prefer waiting tables like I did through college, but to each his own."

Andy's phone buzzed and he checked the message. "The results came back on Austin Price. His blood did show abnormally high levels of the enzyme used in the research lab. Guessing that's what was in the syringe. Assuming he had a reaction to the enzyme, maybe his death wasn't violent. Still, I've hired a few extra off-duty guys this week to watch the Homecoming activities and patrol the campus. Even if there's no danger, it'll help the students feel more safe."

She really wanted it to be an accident. The alternative was scary. "There's probably some explanation for where he left his devices." She couldn't think of one yet. "But if you think the students will feel better, then I agree with your plan."

They arrived at the path where their offices were in different directions. Andy said, "All you need is a couple of wigged out parents to blow everything out of proportion. You have enough to worry about this week."

* * *

She'd barely sat down in her chair twenty minutes later, when Dr. Nielson checked in with an instant message from China. Cassandra calculated the time difference. *Gees, he's awake early.*

Cassandra responded: "Hello! So far we're ok. Do you recall that contract between the farmer Hopkins and the food service department?"

Nielson's message said: "Yes. It's a win-win plan. College uses healthy lean locally produced beef at a fair price. Why do you ask?"

Because somehow Austin Price was interested in that contract, Cassandra thought. She told him: "I don't completely understand the farm contract's connection to the research lab. Police are asking questions and I don't know the answers."

After a few minutes Nielson replied: "Deflect suspicions. Can't afford to lose this contract or the NIH grant. Research dollars are key income for college. I really appreciate your support in my absence. Keep up the great work!"

Cassandra looked at her phone skeptically. *Keep up the great work?* She shook her head. She'd never understand Dr. Nielson.

Chapter Sixteen

Cassandra texted Meg: "Hey. FYI tox report says A had high enzyme levels in blood. Call me."

She'd barely refilled her water cup and returned from a bathroom break when Cassandra's phone chirped with Meg's call. "Austin was sick?"

Cassandra said, "No, I don't think he had been sick. Andy said they tested Austin for other substances because of the needle poke and rash on his hand. The marks on his arms were from plasma donations and the campus blood drive. At the plasma center I learned about the SOD enzyme they use in the science lab. It's interesting, but mostly over my head."

Meg laughed. "Yeah, I remember the campus blood drive. Worst 45 minutes of my month."

Cassandra vaguely recalled notices about the blood drive, but she hadn't paid much attention at the time. Not like she'd be rushing over to be first in line. "Why?"

Meg explained, "I went in to donate and the nurse-tech-vampire-lady couldn't find my vein right away. She dug around in my left arm for like two minutes. Finally, she called her supervisor over. The head nurse switched to my right arm and slid the needle right in. Ten minutes later, the vein just stopped. I hadn't given a whole pint yet, so they stuck me again to fill the rest of the bag. Only good thing about the whole experience was the orange juice and M&M cookies afterward."

Eyeing the faint blue line in her own right arm, Cassandra flinched. "Ouch."

Meg said, "They had a pretty good turnout for the blood drive. Austin helped coordinate it, and he did a good job recruiting people. I remember waiting in a line and it seemed like there were 8 or 10 stations all around the multipurpose room in the Student Center."

Cassandra remembered something she'd overheard. "Oh yeah . . . the student workers in my office said his fraternity won the pizza party prize."

"Right. I interpreted a chapter meeting for Lance and Austin's fraternity a few weeks ago. Austin must've hustled a lot the last week to get so many more registered. Of course, Austin was the Associate Member Educator so he had a ready supply of freshmen to *encourage*. Those guys can be pretty persuasive when they're competing with the other houses on campus."

Alarm bells rang in Cassandra's head. "They aren't hazing those freshmen over there, are they?"

Meg sounded nonchalant. "Not that I've seen. Of course those types of activities are not done—if at all—in front of adults."

Frowning, Cassandra jotted a note to check into possible hazing. Although opening that can of worms now would take up time she didn't have available. "I'll ask Marcus

Fischer who was the judge on that contest. He might know more details." As she ended the call, she fired off a quick email asking what he knew about the blood drive, contest, and potential conduct issues.

One of the student workers peeked her head around the door frame. "Dr. Sato? Are you off the phone? I didn't really mean to eavesdrop, but I heard you talking about the blood drive contest in September?"

Cassandra's eyebrows raised. Had she been speaking loudly? "Yes I was, Haley."

"My dorm floor was mad about that, you know? We were that close to winning the pizza party, but the stupid AOO fraternity won instead. Almost every girl on our floor donated for us, plus our off-campus friends too. Those cheating frat boys get all the fun stuff. Last year at the Spring Fling we had a charity dance marathon. AOO won that, too. Pull—eeze." Haley rolled her eyes and drawled out the word into two long syllables. "They called THAT dancing? Bunch of farm boys shuffling side to side and snapping their fingers for 26 hours. Somehow they find a way to work the system. All those contacts they make."

Why was she still upset about something that'd happened a month earlier? Haley apparently wasn't a fan of the Greek houses. "What makes you think they cheated?"

Haley said, "I don't know . . . how many guys live there? Thirty? I saw Austin talking to the blood drive head guy. I bet he did something."

Cassandra gave her the long, chilly stare that in Hawai'i is called Stink Eye. "Haley you're accusing Austin of something, and he's not around to dispute it. How about we just leave it alone, ok? Next time maybe your floor will win if you keep trying."

Haley said, "Whatever," and disappeared back into the main office.

Cassandra closed her door. Next time she was on a sensitive call, she'd need to be more aware of privacy.

Minutes later, Cassandra's heart made a large *thump* when she saw an email response from Marcus Fischer appear in her inbox. Which was a ridiculous reaction to an everyday business occurrence. Meg and Cinda's teasing had gotten to her more than she'd realized. The email said, "There was a Student Housing Blood Drive in September. The residential hall floor or Greek house with the most pints donated won a pizza party and the winning coordinator got a $500 scholarship. Later, MAF."

Five hundred dollars was a nice-sized scholarship. She'd check on who won that. She also wondered what the A meant in Marcus' initials.

* * *

Cassandra was mid-search trying to find the scholarship winner's name when she heard a knock on her door. Lance poked his head inside and asked, "You have time?" She waved him forward towards the seat in front of her desk.

Placing his backpack on the floor, Lance unzipped the top and started to remove something, but stopped and looked at her uncomfortably. His face reddened slightly, like he struggled to find the best way to start. When he spoke, Cassandra didn't understand him and shrugged in frustration.

Lance held up a finger, bent over, and rooted around in the side pocket. Pulling out his cell phone, he opened an app and scrolled down until he found the right conversation. He handed over his phone and waited for her to read it.

Friday, 1:25 p.m. from Austin: "Hey hide my laptop. Will explain later."

Friday, 1:37 p.m. reply from Me *(Lance)*: "OK. Let me know. L"

Cassandra's jaw hung partially open, and she stared at the screen a few seconds longer. She pointed at Lance and asked, "Austin sent you this text?"

He nodded. She asked, "When?"

He spoke and signed, "The afternoon he died."

Cassandra's eyes widened as the facts slipped into order in her head. Twenty more questions were on the tip of her tongue, but her ASL signing ability was not up to sentences longer than three words. She grabbed a yellow legal pad near her keyboard and flipped a couple pages until she found a blank sheet. Quickly she scratched, "Did you hide it? Where? Did you tell the police that he sent you this text?"

Leaning forward, he read while she scribbled. Lance pointed at the page. "Yeah," he responded, a blush reddening his cheeks. "No. I didn't tell police."

Cassandra stared at him. Her mind reeled. Are you kidding me, she wanted to shout! Austin's laptop hadn't really been missing. All along Lance had it hidden somewhere. She shook her head. He was a smart kid. Working to control her emotions, she wrote, "What's going on?"

He used his own pencil to respond on paper. "Wait. Need to know how he died. Do you know?"

After a few heartbeats, she told him what little she knew. "Died from hitting his head on concrete steps probably. Police told me no drugs or alcohol in his system. Had a rash and needle poke from work? Blood showed elevated level of an enzyme."

She stopped writing and pointed to her first question again. "What's going on?"

Lance's mouth tightened and he wrote, "He asked me to do him a favor. I didn't know why. I just did what he wanted. I thought he would explain to me later, but then . . ."

Cassandra nodded and gave him the keep going gesture. He continued, "I figured out his password. I looked for hidden files or something wrong on his laptop."

She was still mad, but curiosity won out. "What did you find?"

"He used the same password for Gmail and login. I read some emails. He didn't use his calendar to write test and paper due dates. Mostly blank. Except I saw an appointment last month that said Meet in Lincoln @7 p.m. He never told me he went to Lincoln."

There had to be a reason Austin asked Lance to hide the laptop. She signaled him to continue.

He looked like he was debating how much to tell her. "Found a Bitcoin account. Same password. Saw weekly deposits beginning at semester. Six for $100. Not huge. His parents don't send him money. Don't know where from? Selling something??"

Bitcoin . . . the untraceable online payment thing. Tension crept up from her stomach to her shoulders. She wrote, "I'm calling an interpreter. Meg."

He nodded and stood up. "I'm going to get water and to bathroom. Be right back."

She gave him the thumbs up as she waited for Meg to pick up the call. She also texted Fischer thinking he might be a good person to ask for advice on what to do next. If they didn't answer, she'd try Cinda.

Ten minutes later, Lance, Cassandra and Meg sat around the low table in Cassandra's office. While Meg silently read the conversation from Cassandra's legal pad, Fischer knocked and Cassandra invited him to join them.

Fischer's expression was cautious at being summoned for a private meeting. Although technically his boss, Cassandra wasn't involved in daily housing operations. He worked with the Facilities and Maintenance VP more frequently than with her unless there were Code of Conduct issues or budget requests that needed her attention.

He sat in the last open chair, placing his reusable water bottle, black leather notebook and mechanical pencil on the table and waited expectantly. Meg passed him the notepad then Cassandra briefly explained, "Thanks for coming over. We have a student conduct situation here, and I was hoping you could help decide options for our next steps."

He frowned slightly as he read the conversation between Lance and Cassandra. Looking up he asked, "Lance, want to explain to me why you hacked into your roommate's laptop? Wait, why do you even have his laptop at all? I thought police were looking for it. Hasn't it and his phone been missing since Friday?"

Meg spoke while Lance responded in sign, "He texted me on Friday before he died and asked me to hide his laptop. I put it in the trunk of my car, but didn't know why he wanted me to hide it. After I found out he died, I was curious. If his death was an accident, why did he want me to hide the laptop?"

"If his death wasn't an accident, then you know that laptop would be evidence, right?" asked Fischer.

Lance shrugged, "He wanted me to have it for a reason."

Cassandra asked, "What makes you think Austin's death wasn't an accident? Do you know something more than what you've told the police?"

"I don't know for sure. Look, we've been friends since middle school. I just did what he asked me. He's dead now. I don't want his family to worry if he was selling drugs or doing something bad on the side. I don't want people judging him when it doesn't matter now."

Flabbergasted that he'd hidden it, but glad he trusted her enough to tell the truth, Cassandra said, "It might matter if he was involved in something that got him killed. You hid something important, Lance. We can't protect you if the police decide to arrest you."

Lance's signs became more animated. "I didn't know I was doing anything wrong. When your buddy asks you to do him a favor, you do it and ask questions later. I know Austin wasn't the best student. He could be a screw up sometimes. He's struggled in some of his classes. His parents don't give him much money or support. But he's been my friend a long time."

He stood and paced from the window to the door and back. "I remember one time . . . maybe freshman year in high school. We were out at the mall in Omaha with a few friends. Some jerks saw us signing and mimicked us by waving their hands around. When we ignored them, one asshole came up to me and did it to my face. I told him to leave us alone. So he made fun of the way I spoke."

Cassandra's heart ached for those happy, scrawny boys from the photo she'd seen in the fraternity bedroom. Lance shrugged. "As though it was the first time that had happened. Not. Anyway, Austin strutted up and bumped into him and said, 'Back off, prick!' Austin could speak better than I can. When the guy shoved him, Austin hauled off and slugged him right in the nose. Must've broken it. Blood spattered everywhere." Lance smiled at the memory. "It was awesome how he stood up for me and for us."

His eyes glistened with sadness. "Some days you just don't feel like letting it pass, you know? It's like I owed him one."

A hard lump formed in Cassandra's throat.

Fischer's face was kind, but stern. "I'm sorry for your loss, Lance." He waited while Lance composed himself. "Let's focus on trying to figure out what happened to him. Suppose it wasn't an accident?"

Fischer pointed at the yellow papers. "You wrote here that you found an odd appointment and some Bitcoin deposits. Those are clues the police can use to figure out if there were other factors involved in his death. What if he's part of a group involved in some trouble, and he's not the only person being targeted?"

Cassandra had one last suspicion. "Lance, do you know anything about Austin's phone that you haven't told us? Like where it is now?"

Lance shook his head no. Then a bit later added, "He liked privacy. He got texts or calls occasionally at weird times from numbers not in his contact list. Not that I was snooping, but sometimes I'd see his phone message notifications or come into our room and see him FaceTiming with someone. He'd hang up right away."

Lance held out one empty hand as though it cradled a phone aimed at his face like setting up a selfie. His other hand moved close to his face and signed a little. Cassandra imagined how the signed phone conversation worked; she had seen Meg use her phone to talk to deaf people a few times. Lance shrugged, "I just assumed he'd met a girl."

Cassandra picked up her office phone. "So one of Austin's last acts was to text Lance. What else did he do before he died? It's time to call campus security. You're turning that laptop over to the sheriff." She indicated Marcus and herself, "We will meet later and decide what disciplinary action the college will take regarding the student code of conduct."

Lance sat back down in the chair and hung his head. "I understand," he said.

Even as Cassandra made the call, she wondered if he was more involved than he'd admitted. Noting his deflated body language, she kept those suspicions to herself. If Lance didn't have Austin's phone, where was it? Her thoughts were interrupted by a clipped voice, "This is Summers."

Chapter Seventeen

"I thought the Biology lab students and faculty might cooperate more with the investigation if they see you're involved." Andy's manner was professional, but including her in the loop so frequently was unexpected.

Goosebumps covered Cassandra's bare legs making her regret wearing a skirt as she half-jogged with Andy down the path to the Edgerton Center. She needed to re-think her whole wardrobe. "I appreciate the chance to learn more about the lab and the grant." Her breath made a mini cloud in the air around her face.

He sensed she struggled to keep up with his longer strides and slowed to match her pace. His easy grin revealed charming dimples in his flushed cheeks. "I want your input. I haven't forgotten what you told me about Price's photo, and the finger spelled letter 'L' you saw him making. We're keeping it in mind, but first we have a whole lot of solid steps we're following to determine what happened to him."

He was much more willing to work with her than men had been at her former jobs. She couldn't help wondering if he had ulterior motives, especially when he kept bringing her snacks or drinks. She missed her big brother and wanted to make friends, but not lead him on. "I'd feel horrible if I ignored something that later turned out to be important."

He wore a navy windbreaker over his long-sleeved security uniform, but didn't seem cold at all. "The sheriff's office sent the laptop to Lincoln to have the State Patrol people analyze it."

Cassandra's fists were buried in the pockets of her lightweight puffy jacket and she wished she'd worn gloves. "I hope they find useful information." Preferably before Nielson returned from China.

Andy said, "We checked more on ABG and they're owned by an overseas pharmaceutical conglomerate. Basically, Carson's site collects blood and plasma donations for medical testing and treatment. So far, I don't see evidence of a crime related to Austin Price. Unless you count the allegations that he cheated at the blood drive and won extra pizza for his friends. Doesn't appear to be connected to his death, and doesn't help us determine whether his fall was an accident."

They hadn't gone far when they spotted the street preacher lady handing out booklets and talking at the backs of students who hurried to class. She wore her usual outfit: long black dress, matching tights and dusty, worn Birkenstocks.

Turning towards them, a smile of recognition beamed across her face. She held a weathered Bible in one hand and waved at Cassandra with the other. "Good Tuesday Morning!" she exclaimed brightly as they approached her wheeled metal cart. Inside it were small boxes of pamphlets and a couple of plastic garbage bags.

"Hello," they both replied, but the woman's eyes were fixed on Summers. Cassandra eyed him closely. Judging from his expression—part exasperation, part amusement—they'd previously met.

Cassandra wanted to keep walking past, but the preacher lady offered them a small booklet. Her smile was almost smug. "How are you both on this fine fall morning? Was your search yesterday fruitful?"

Summers' dimples disappeared, and he tilted his head warily. "What search yesterday? Why do you ask?"

She didn't seem like the same zealot who usually exhorted the students to *Repent! Forgive others! Love one another.* The hairs on the back of Cassandra's neck lifted at the street preacher's cryptic tone. "I'm out here most every day. I see many things. People don't pay attention to me, but I notice things."

Cassandra raised an eyebrow at Andy, and they stopped walking. "What makes you think we searched for something?" Andy asked the preacher.

Her eyes darkened. "We're all searching, young man. These students are searching for meaning and truth in their lives. They're trying to find the path that God has laid out for them. They don't know the answers yet, because they do not listen to the voice in their hearts. The world is so noisy. It can be hard to hear. You are searching for answers, too." Her wrinkled, crooked index finger gently pressed Andy's jacket near his heart. "Listen, and you will find them." She picked up a small stack of books and walked towards a group of students leaving the dining hall.

Andy called after her. "Listen where? Did you see something?"

She turned back to him, her smile again beaming. "God bless you. He loves all His children."

They walked a few steps. Once they were out of earshot, Andy said, "I've talked to her often since she set up here. I can't figure her out. It's tempting to dismiss her as mentally disturbed, but sometimes I think she's as sane as I am."

Cassandra shook off the willies. "After my first encounter with her, I've managed to avoid a repeat."

Andy smirked. "Oh yes ... your fifteen minutes of fame."

She wondered if that cursed photo with the preacher lady would ever be forgotten. "Totally not my fault!"

During the first week in September, Cassandra had seen the street preacher several days in a row from her window and had passed her a few times crossing campus. Like the students who stared at the ground and scuttled past her, Cassandra also tried to avoid her attention the first few days. Once she realized the woman was going to stay for awhile, she became curious about her lifestyle and mission. One day as Cassandra walked past after lunch, she slowed a bit when she neared the woman. Cassandra made eye contact. That was the only encouragement needed. Immediately the preacher lady stepped forward. "Repent, sinner! The end is near!"

Cassandra had given her friendly, non-threatening smile and said, "Hello, Ma'am. I've seen you here for a few days. Is this your first time at Morton College?"

"We are ALL sinners! Repent for the end is near!"

She guessed the woman was homeless, and this was how she passed her days. Was she paid for her time from a non-profit group, or was she strictly a One-Woman Show? "Do you have a place to sleep nearby? Do you have enough to eat?"

Her deeply lined, tan face and gaunt frame looked weak, although she worked outside all day, every day. "The Lord provides for me. I shall not want."

Cassandra had reached into her bag and pulled out a banana she'd been saving. She offered it to the woman. "For a snack later?"

Her kind smile revealed teeth that had seen few dental visits during her lifetime; they were grayish colored and crooked, with one or two spaces where teeth had once been. "Thank you, child."

She tucked the fruit into her pocket and reached into her cart. She pressed a plain blue booklet with a little golden cross engraved on the front into Cassandra's outstretched hand. "Take this!"

Her soft, warm palms enveloped Cassandra's. "The end is near!"

Cassandra had walked away holding the book, but didn't tell her she wasn't a Christian. Her family practiced Jodo Shinshu Buddhism common among Japanese families who emigrated to Hawai'i and the West coast. The Buddha's teachings weren't so far from Jesus' example of compassion and wisdom.

The next day, a laughing student worker had showed Cassandra the morning newspaper's article with an accompanying photo of Cassandra and the street minister exchanging gifts. Cassandra was accepting the booklet and the woman had wide eyes and that big grin on her face as she handed over the tract.

Cassandra's cheeks flushed warm. The student showed her other photos from social media apps. "You're all over Instagram and Twitter, too! Someone copied the photo from the newspaper and added a caption underneath that said, 'Best meme wins.'"

People had spent the previous 24 hours creating memes that fit the photo. The most popular so far were: "What year student are you here?" and "Helping the less fortunate: VP Sato seeks administration advice from the homeless."

Back with Andy in the present, Cassandra vowed, "I've learned my lesson. I'm careful of what my actions look like to others. Although the idea of being watched all day makes my skin crawl."

When they reached the Edgerton Science Center, the yellow tape and barricades signifying a tragic scene were gone. The tree near the outdoor stairs was covered in orange and green leaves, caught between seasons. A noise rustled in the bushes as they began the climb to the fourth floor, and a brown squirrel erupted out of the bush and scurried up the oak tree's trunk.

Andy noted her quietness. "Are you ok? You don't have to come inside if you'd rather not."

This was her job. She couldn't skip the hard parts. "No, I need to do it. I just can't stop remembering how he looked."

To her relief, he didn't ridicule her. "Funny how sometimes we're so curious to see something, but once you have, it's impossible to turn back the clock. I saw a lot of sad things when I went on a mission trip to Haiti a few years ago."

She said, "So much of life is messy or ugly. Makes me appreciate the beauty of the everyday things even more."

Chapter Eighteen

Leaning over the three-foot-high wall and decorative metal railing that enclosed the 8 by 8-foot platform at the top of the Edgerton center outdoor stairs, Cassandra peeked down to the smaller landing where she'd seen Austin's body four days earlier. Chicken skin crept up her arm at the memory.

Her phone buzzed and she read Meg's text: "Meet us for lunch @ 12:30 The Home Team."

Andy Summers held the door open for Cassandra, and they found Deputy Tate leaning near the hallway door to the lab, head down thumbing through his phone. Oakley sunglasses sat atop wavy blond hair, his radio mic was clipped to a shoulder strap, and his full utility belt included a handgun and baton.

Andy nodded when the deputy looked up. They must've worked together often because they treated each other like equal partners with no hint of rivalry. "Is it locked?"

Tate straightened up to his full, broad shouldered height which was several inches more than Andy and probably 20 pounds more muscle underneath his dark brown uniform shirt. "No, I'm just catching up on some reading."

Deputy would be a good starting job for a small town, baby-faced farm boy. Cassandra asked, "Are you setting up your weekend fantasy football lineup?"

"Reading case law for a Torts class I'm taking for my Legal Studies degree."

Her eyebrows raised up high at the unexpected answer. From his satisfied smirk, she knew she wasn't the first person to make that assumption, although she should've known better than to judge a book by its cover. Still, a master's degree in Legal Studies was pretty impressive.

Tate opened the hallway door and they all filed into the cramped front office space behind a girl rapidly typing on a computer keyboard. A music speaker sitting atop industrial metal shelving blared a synthetic pop dance tune that Cassandra didn't recognize. The girl's eyes widened at the sight of the uniforms, and she jumped out of her seat, saying, "I'll get our grad assistant," over her shoulder.

Outdated machines and extra pieces of equipment were wedged under the desks and countertops in an unsightly hodgepodge. Next to the work area a large garbage can nearly overflowed with takeout pizza containers, candy wrappers and Styrofoam cups. The cleaning crew couldn't have hit this place more than once a week. Even with cleaning and disinfecting, the air held a stench of cedar wood chips mixed with lemon floor cleaner and a primal rodent smell that likely never disappeared.

Shortly the student returned to the lab entry trailed by a thin, 20-something young man wearing jeans and a plaid shirt. The Morton ID badge clipped to his white lab coat's pocket said Luke Peterson. He shook Summers' hand.

"Hello Luke, I'm Andy Summers from campus security, and this is Deputy Tate of the Sheriff's office. We're investigating Austin Price's death, and we'd like to ask you some questions."

"You can come back into the lab, sir," Luke said politely as he led them down a short hallway decorated with faded research poster results. To the left, a door opened into a dark storage room, then they rounded a corner into the main work area. "Austin was one of my work-study students for the last two semesters."

Cassandra recognized Peterson as the freaked-out student with the knit hat who the Sheriff had taken in for questioning Friday afternoon at the scene. Her mouth opened into an Oh! at the same time Andy looked back at her and nodded once.

Tate opened a small investigative pad and asked, "How many hours a week did Austin work here?"

Standing to the side, Cassandra absorbed as many details as possible. This room's sterile cleanliness made the front room even more slovenly by comparison. Shelves lined an entire wall where maybe 150 rat cages were neatly stacked in pods of 9.

Peterson frowned slightly, "Um . . . I already talked to the Sheriff on Friday and answered a bunch of questions for him." Peterson seemed much more calm than before.

Cassandra noticed Tate look over his pad at Andy. "We know. Those were more personal questions. We investigated the scene Friday and Saturday to collect evidence."

"I'm the only assistant here today. I can't really speak for anybody else." He shifted from one foot to the other.

Tate's shoulders lifted in a small shrug. "Today we're here to learn more about the lab itself, but you might need to repeat some things you've already told the sheriff. Now, how many hours?"

Peterson stood behind a stainless steel lab table near an open laptop with a stack of papers and folders nearby. He let out a sigh and looked down at his papers. "Probably 10-15 hours, depending on his classes and homework. We try to be flexible, but we have to follow our feeding and treatment protocols strictly to ensure accurate data. Two other grad assistants run experiments in this lab, and we share six students who cover for each other when someone needs time off. Austin and Mikaela, that girl you saw out front, help me. Without Austin, she's been putting in extra hours until I find someone to fill in for him."

Andy faced Peterson across the table, but he spoke casually like they were just a couple of guys chatting at the bar. "Can you explain what your research project studies?"

Peterson perked up at the interest in his project. "Sure. It's funny you ask because in my doctoral dissertation seminar this week, we practiced our '30-second elevator speech' so we can describe to potential employers and outsiders what we do, and our future plans. Let's see if I can do this now."

He paused and looked up at the ceiling, then took a dramatic breath and launched into a monotone rehearsed explanation. "Basically, we're testing an enzyme called Superoxide dismutase that potentially shrinks cancer tumors in laboratory rats. This study is in cooperation with the AlphaBioGlobal Plasma Center and funded by a grant from the National Institute of Health."

Peterson didn't know where to put his hands. They started on his hips, then one in a lab coat pocket and finally he crossed his arms awkwardly over his chest. "This phase should be done soon, and we hope to have our conclusions by December. That'll give me a few months to analyze the data and write the results in my dissertation by May. After graduation, I hope to do cancer research for a pharmaceutical company."

He ended on a loud exhale and adjusted his wire rimmed glasses. "How was that?"

Cassandra had heard most of the spiel at the plasma center but she still didn't understand how it was all related. Summers encouraged him. "That sounds promising."

Peterson had a captive audience. She doubted most people bothered to listen long. "Of course, I won't be able to make any definitive answers until the study is complete, but the overall results have been positive. The real breakthrough came previously when the team identified SOD's ability to shrink the brain tumors. Now we're gathering more evidence to measure how much improvement occurs and the time frame. We record food intake, liquid intake, appetite notes and weight. We also note any negative side effects to determine if what works on animals could someday be used on humans."

With 150-plus cages, the lab must be a moneymaker. Tate scribbled notes. "Cancer research at Morton?"

"The way this cancer works is that a genetic mutation suppresses the SOD development in children, and they develop tumors. Lab rats are bred with the same genetic mutation. At the end of treatment, the rats are euthanized, brain tissue sections are frozen with liquid nitrogen and examined under a microscope to look for cancer cells."

Thinking about the rats' fate made her squeamish. Cassandra's research area was education, not biology. Peterson gestured at a wall of conference poster boards showing statistical charts. "Our tests have shown the treatment successfully shrinks tumors in the lab rats. We extract the enzyme from donated blood and plasma, and we require a lot of donated material to complete our tests. Ever since we've been working with the college housing department to recruit more students to donate, we've been successful at getting more of the SODs available for our tests. The control group is a placebo."

Cassandra's eyes started glazing over. The research minutia seemed irrelevant to Austin's death.

"If everything goes well, we'll develop a synthetic version of the enzyme with the same chemical makeup as the naturally occurring enzyme. The nice part about the synthetic version is that we won't need human blood products. If the synthetic version is a successful substitute, we could use bacteria to manufacture larger quantities inexpensively and use them in further research."

Cassandra knew it took years to get new medicines approved by the FDA. Summers asked, "Are there any serious side effects?"

Nearly every treatment has some side effects. Peterson said, "We've noticed aggression like biting and hyperactivity."

"Would there be similar side effects in humans?"

"Human trials are a later stage because of their physiological complexity. People could have different symptoms than rats. For now, I just follow the protocols and write up the results. Someone above my pay grade makes decisions about whether to pursue more research grants or focus on other aspects."

Cassandra's attention was drawn to cages where some rats were noisily scurrying from corner to corner in their cages. As she bent over to peer more closely, one little pink-eyed rat was gnawing determinedly at the cage's metal drink dispenser. She couldn't stop a spasm of disgust. "Like those guys? The aggressive behavior you mentioned?"

Peterson gestured to the right third of the wall. "Those cages aren't in my study. That side is from one of the other GA's studies. Sometimes the rats even bite us. Our study only has 30 rats, and is one of many similar studies done around the country. This type of tumor mostly occurs in pediatric cases where the children were diagnosed with tumors that grew very quickly and usually resulted in death within 8-14 months."

Cassandra wanted to prevent senseless diseases from harming children too, but she wondered about the side effects from the enzyme. In addition to preventing cancer, what else would it do to humans?

Peterson smiled, ending his summary on a high note. "Of course, I'd love to be associated in any way with helping cure an aggressive form of childhood cancer."

Tate asked, "Police looked for Austin Price's phone up here last Friday, but never found it. Any ideas what could have happened to it?"

Peterson frowned, like he was surprised at the abrupt change of topic. "Who. Me? I have no idea what happened to his phone. I wasn't even here Friday when he died. Last time I saw him was Thursday night, and I didn't pay attention to where his phone was. The students keep busy here. They come in, do their work and leave. There's no time for playing on phones."

Tate flipped back through his notes. "What was Price working on Thursday night while you were here?"

Peterson stepped over to his work area and glanced down at a log book among the papers. He turned pages until he found Thursday's notes. "He was here late . . . some excuse about a Chem test in the afternoon so he didn't get here until after dinner. I stopped by around 7:30 to lock up and he had twelve syringes ready to go. I remember counting them. According to this, he finished nine."

He stopped talking while he ran his finger down the page again. When his eyes raised to Andy's, he said, "Price didn't write why he only treated nine rats on Thursday. That's somewhat unusual, but as long as he kept the notes straight, he could've caught up Friday. He was scheduled to work at 4:00."

Andy's brows went up and he made eye contact with Tate. Cassandra questioned how well this study was run. It didn't take a biology degree to know that the messy front room and now the lax treatment notes were deficient. Tate said, "He was found dead on the stairs at 3:15 Friday. Would he have come in early?"

Two large red spots colored Peterson's cheeks and his forehead broke out in shiny sweat. His short, light brown beard was thin in spots and he ran a shaky hand over his hair. "Maybe his afternoon class canceled. I don't know."

Andy said, "Did you and he communicate ok? Do you sign, or did you write notes? Could he have misunderstood the treatment process and made a mistake?"

"We understood each other fine. He told me he could read my lips well. We didn't really sign. We just pointed or gestured and wrote if we needed to. We were working on a tight deadline. My preliminary data and reports are due next week. If I turn those in late, my funding could be pulled."

Peterson jabbed the logbook and paper stack for emphasis. "He was a smart kid and he knew what to do. I wouldn't have left him alone with my rats if I thought he'd do something wrong. I can't afford to lose the last six months of work."

Tate looked at his pad for a few seconds. "So if he mistakenly poked himself with one of the treatment syringes, would that have affected him in any way?"

By his stunned expression, Cassandra could tell he didn't know about the bloody glove they'd found. "Poked himself? Um...uh, well, in a healthy adult the natural enzyme shouldn't have adverse side effects." His voice lowered to a mumble. Cassandra had to lean in to hear him. "We haven't tested it on humans, yet."

Chapter Nineteen

Cassandra hurried into the renovated brick building on Main Street that housed The Home Team. Picking her way through the wooden tables, she slid into a red leather booth next to Meg. The only sports-themed grill of three bars in town, by default it was the place to celebrate birthdays, watch professional sports, or Saturday games of the much more famous football team down the road in Lincoln.

Cinda noted the time on her phone. "12:40. Not bad, Dr. Sato. No Hawaiian time today."

"I'm not late, I'm busy." Normally, Cassandra was a homebody who preferred eating stir fry or sandwiches over taking time to go out for meals, but friends were the exception.

Margie Gallagher, a middle-aged woman dressed in a blue Morton polo shirt and khaki pants, deposited a mason jar of water in front of Cassandra. The bar's owner, Margie was married to one of Morton College's professors, and he helped out on weekends. "I'll be back in a few, hon."

The decor was 2/3 local memorabilia from the Carson High School photos and jerseys, or Morton Maples teams' stuff; the final third was dedicated to the Huskers, a statutory requirement of any self-respecting sports bar in Nebraska. The pizza and burgers were decent and Margie was known to make a Reuben sandwich worth driving a good distance to order.

Hungry from her brisk walk to Edgerton and then the bar, Cassandra ordered a bowl of chili and a salad. Meg got a Reuben and fries, and Cinda, a big chicken salad. While waiting for their food, Cinda said, "I want to know who Austin was with after class on Friday. Did he go straight to work?"

Too bad the lab had no video feed so they could replay what happened. "I don't think they know yet," said Cassandra. "Something made him early, though."

Meg said, "Was that surgical glove with blood from Austin or someone else?"

"The autopsy showed he had a poke and rash on his hand, so they believe that was his glove. None of the other workers reported an accident."

Cinda said, "It's hard to believe no one saw him in the building, the lab, or outside."

It didn't matter if it was believable or not. Austin had a rash, there was blood on the glove, somehow he fell down the stairs, and hit his head. The fact was, no one noticed anything wrong with him until it was too late to help him. "Pretty sure Lance's phone showed a text from Austin after 1:00. That's all."

Meg took a short drink. "Do you think people feel comfortable coming forward with information? If he was doing something sketchy, maybe no one wants to tattle."

Cassandra shrugged. "Nielson wants us to keep it quiet. I'm working with our security and the sheriff's office, but they only tell me what I need to know."

Cinda wouldn't let it drop. "It's too bad they couldn't reconstruct the scene and try different scenarios. What if someone else was there and they argued? Like on NCIS."

Watching Andy and Tate the last few days had been pretty educational. Cassandra frowned. "Who has time to watch NCIS?"

Meg laughed and Cinda's eyes twinkled as she teased, "Those of us who don't read journal articles for fun at night before heading for bed."

Meg added, "Sometimes I read People magazine or watch stupid reality shows to unwind. Besides, it helps me know what the students are talking about in class if I follow the latest TV shows and movies."

Cassandra had never thought about Meg's need to keep up on popular culture for work. "That's cool. Your brain is filled with bits from meetings and studying, too."

Meg, tapped her finger to her forehead. "Too bad I can't remember most of it. It's up there somewhere—all the classes and lectures I attend, plus the other things I read. Gives me a good excuse to watch bad TV occasionally. I forget a lot though, unless I hear it repeatedly."

Cinda lowered her voice and leaned towards the center of the table. "Maybe I've watched too many TV shows, but I do think there's something odd about Austin's death. He was an athletic, healthy kid. There must be more to the story."

"Meg and I noticed something in the police photos, but I don't know if anything will come from it." Cassandra scanned the nearby tables to make sure no one was listening. "When Austin died, it looked like his hand was forming a letter 'L' like he was trying to communicate something. We told Andy Summers about it in case it's a clue no one else noticed."

Cinda's eye got wide. "You mean like how victims write the killer's name in blood at the crime scene? Cool. I wonder what the L stands for?"

Cassandra said, "I've been thinking about this a lot. The graduate assistant who was Austin's boss is named Luke. Austin worked in a lab. It could stand for a Greek letter like lambda. Isn't that used in scientific equations?"

Meg shrugged, "I know you want to help the police, Cass, but I think the L won't lead anywhere. Don't you have a student worker in your office named Logan? Besides, Austin's best friend and roommate was Lance. I for one don't want people thinking Lance was involved."

Cassandra didn't know Meg had lost faith in their clue. Her face fell. "But I really thought we were helping the investigation."

"Even if Austin did it on purpose, they can't use a finger-spelled letter as evidence in a death investigation," Meg said with authority. "You need to drop it, Cass, and figure out a better way to help."

Andy Summers had said nearly the same thing, but for some reason it stung more coming from Meg.

She must have realized Cassandra's disappointment, so Meg prompted, "Maybe you should tell Cinda about the laptop and what else the police found."

Cassandra quietly told Cinda about the laptop and the food service purchase contract with the farmer that Austin had saved in his papers.

Cinda hadn't known about the dining hall side of the agreement either. "I eat cafeteria food for lunch every day. Usually I go through the salad bar, but I like the idea of using locally sourced beef and produce. Isn't farm-to-table the latest thing? Who would've pegged No-Nonsense Nielson for being a trend-setter?"

If the cancer research grant and cafeteria food contract was such a point of pride for the college, why hadn't Cinda known about it? Cinda's eyes shifted to over Cassandra's right shoulder.

Cassandra wasn't surprised when she felt a presence near her. "Dr. Sato? I thought that was you."

Recognizing the voice, she thought, *twice in two days.* Maybe Nielson had been right about her getting out of the office more. "Dr. Schneider, good afternoon."

He was fairly handsome in that well-groomed, sharply pressed way of powerful men. His smile framed perfectly straight white teeth. "Good to see you again. I was just leaving when I noticed you here with your colleagues. After you left yesterday, it occurred to me that we should get together in a couple of weeks when President Nielson returns from China, and you have more time. I want to set up some internships for biology or chemistry students. Our clinic is too small, but if the students are willing to live in Lincoln next summer, they could work at our main office. ABG is always looking for new talent, and I want Morton students to have the best opportunities available."

Cassandra imagined Nielson's pleasure at furthering this community relationship. "I'd be happy to talk to you about potential internships. Cinda, here, works with the counseling and career services center. We could both meet with you."

"I'll have my assistant set it up." Schneider paused like he would leave, but changed his mind, "Say, our plasma clinic staff are still upset about that deaf student who died the other day. Is there any news about his accident?"

Not in the past 24 hours. "The campus security and sheriff are still investigating. We don't really know—"

Schneider interrupted, "It was an unfortunate accident. I didn't know him personally, but I remember seeing him at Edgerton a few times. Frankly, I'm not sure he should've been working in a laboratory environment."

He casually shoved a hand in his pants pocket. "Maybe he didn't understand the protocol. How does he get along if he can't hear or speak to people?"

Meg squinted at him. "What do you mean?"

Schneider said, "With his inability to hear, the environment was obviously dangerous for him. Maybe the accident was partially the lab staff's fault for allowing him to work alone. He couldn't call for help when he needed it. The college shouldn't be hiring people unable to work independently. Huge liability. We'd better cross our fingers his parents don't sue."

Meg took a deep breath, and Cassandra came on full alert. This guy had no idea he was drifting into the deep end without a life preserver. Meg's lips barely moved. "Sorry, what?"

"I'm planning to propose this topic at the next Curriculum Committee meeting. We can't allow students in work-study jobs they clearly aren't qualified for. For their own safety."

Cassandra could feel Meg's whole body tense beside her. Schneider added, "The disabled should be encouraged to major in fields that are less dangerous. Like Computer Science or the trades. Something where they don't interact with customers or use the telephone. Wouldn't it be kinder to guide them to careers that better fit their skills?"

And...there he went...he had just sunk completely underwater and would drown in ignorance if someone didn't make him stop talking. Cassandra squeezed Meg's leg in an attempt to restrain her from going over the table at him. Cassandra didn't need to be a sign language expert to know that you can't discriminate against someone because they can't hear. She said, "Morton helps each work-study student with a disability on an individual basis depending on their needs and skills. Naturally, we wouldn't want any student in danger, but we don't make blanket rules."

Meg's hands formed fists on the table top, but she remained seated and silent, much to Cassandra's amazement. Luckily, Mrs. Gallagher arrived at that moment with their food. Noticing the stony faces around the table, she passed out the plates efficiently and left without saying a word.

Schneider said, "Need I remind you with Dr. Nielson gone, I feel especially responsible to ensure there's no negative exposure for the college. I'm doing everything I can to keep our donors happy. The sooner we move on from this incident the better."

Cassandra assured him. "We've assisted the investigation when they've asked for our help."

"Nielson and I would rather you focus on Homecoming and leave the investigating to the sheriff. The less our staff is involved, the better. Good day, ladies."

They stared after his back silently as he pivoted and strode out the front door. Meg scooped up a handful of fries. "What a tool."

Cinda grimaced and said, "He's not the only person I've heard say that before, Meg. Employers do worry about safety and liability. Maybe we should look at our safety policies."

"Wait, you can't agree with that arrogant idiot, Cinda. Deaf people can do any job they want."

Cassandra didn't want to get into a big debate, so she chose her words carefully. "Schneider seems very dedicated to the college. Although he could use some sensitivity training..."

Meg rolled her eyes. "Just speaking the truth."

* * *

Walking back to her office after lunch, Cassandra mentally rehearsed asking for the Finance Committee's approval on the physics lab design. Dr. Nielson had told her she needed to report on his behalf. She wanted to appear knowledgeable and authoritative without coming off as bossy. Pausing in the office doorway, she saw three students hunched over the large, expensive color copier. Devon yanked out the paper tray, removed the paper and banged the edges to align them properly. He slammed the tray back in, punched a couple buttons and then pressed Start with a flourish.

At first nothing happened, but after a few seconds a loud, unpleasant machine gun style ka-chung, ka-chung, ka-chung sounded, and the paper rolls squeaked until Haley cut the power. "What did you do?!" she growled at him.

"Me? I'm trying to fix it. I didn't spill a cup of coffee all down the side of it."

"It was only a third of a cup and it spilled over the edges and side. It didn't go into the mechanical part of it, and wet coffee wouldn't cause that kind of noise." Her voice became higher and louder as it became obvious she might've broken a $5,000 copy machine.

"Oh really?" Devon teased, "Now you're a broken copier expert, too?"

Logan Dunn grabbed another paper towel to wipe the drops from the table and output tray. He powered up the machine, gently reset the buttons and pressed start. The machine gun noise quieted a notch. A document printed out on dry paper and landed in the output tray without incident. "Children, children," he scolded in a Mom voice imitation, "this is why we can't have nice things."

On the way to her office Cassandra advised, "Try calling the office supply store and get a technician out here to service that. It sounded like the paper roller went bad."

Closing the door, she rested her head on the desk for a moment. She was due at the Finance meeting in 20 minutes. In her head, she heard SpongeBob sitting at his school desk, "Can I be excused for the rest of my life?"

Chapter Twenty

High heels clicking on the gray sidewalk, Cassandra hadn't made it twenty steps before the street preacher bounded right up to her with a big, friendly grin. "Hello, Dr. Sato! What a lovely afternoon the Lord has provided for us today."

Cassandra had meant to sneak out the back door. Not that she was avoiding another social media debacle. She was very busy. The preacher fell into step beside Cassandra, who searched for a safe topic. "Hello, again. Is it normal for Nebraska to have so many cloudy days in a row?"

The preacher lady looked up to confirm the current weather pattern. "Live here long enough, my child, and you will find that in the space of one afternoon we can have all four seasons."

She seemed very familiar with the weather peculiarities, like she'd lived here a long time. Cassandra wondered where she went overnights and how long she'd make her home on Morton's sidewalks and benches. She itched to ask for her name and be more friendly.

As soon as Cassandra had made it past her zone, the woman pivoted back towards the students shuffling to their next class. She transformed from quiet philosopher to fiery preacher mode. "I know what you do on the weekends! Drunks and whores! Repent or lose your financial aid! You don't repay student loans in Heaven!!"

The preacher's voice faded as Cassandra approached the Music Hall on the Eastern edge of campus. Down the path, she saw a familiar man walking towards her. His dark brown leather flight jacket with a sheepskin collar was unzipped over khaki pants, a button-down shirt and hiking shoes. He didn't saunter, bounce, or strut. His steps were efficient and quick reminding her of the many clean-cut, handsome military guys she'd seen on the Honolulu streets. Embarrassed by the amount of attention to detail she'd noticed about his approach, she fixed a natural smile on her face as Marcus Fischer got close enough to say hello. "Hey, I was on my way to your office to talk to you. Glad I caught you."

"I'm going to a Finance Committee meeting in there," she said, indicating the Music Building.

He glanced at the time on his fancy sports watch. "Oh. Bad timing, then. I told Professor Zimmerman in the Ag Sciences department that he could ride along with us this afternoon. Is three still a good time today?"

Her smile froze in place while her brain raced through her mental calendar for details on a three o'clock meeting. Several awkward moments passed before she admitted she couldn't remember. "Um ... remind me again where we're going at three?"

"The site visit for the housing services contract ... strictly a formality. Dr. Nielson asked me to go with you since it'll be your first visit to a cattle farm . . . Remember the email he sent us last week?"

She opened the slim leather portfolio containing her journal and iPad. She'd been included on so many extra emails the last few days. How had she forgotten this important one? The answer, of course, was that they were all important. Dr. Nielson was big on partnering with nearby resources in any way possible. Her first cattle farm? Not at the top of her Nebraska bucket list items, especially this week.

Fischer frowned like she should've already known this. "The farmer provides very lean, good quality beef for our residence halls and Greek houses. I've seen the budget, and we're getting a good price, too. If today's not going to work, I can reschedule for next week."

She was spending more time in meetings than with students. How many balls could she juggle until they started falling to the ground? She looked down at her blue light wool pencil skirt and matching suit top. Her navy pumps had 3-inch heels and a decorative gold buckle across the toe. "No rescheduling. I'll make it work."

Fischer shrugged. "We're somewhat flexible. Let me know when your meeting is done, or if you can't make it, we'll go without you this time."

When she'd traveled to Lincoln in September, the farm smells had assaulted her nostrils long before her eyes saw the barns, fences, and animals. Although Hawai'i's economy was largely supported by agriculture, Cassandra was a city girl at heart. She'd grown up on a 44-mile diameter island inhabited by nearly 1 million souls. Island crops were mostly pineapple, sugar cane, or locally grown produce for the markets. Maui and the Big Island had dairy farms, cattle, and fishing. None of them were as smelly as the operations she'd driven past between Omaha or Lincoln and Carson. "Thanks for being flexible. I'll do my best to be done in time."

Sitting in the conference room before the finance meeting began, she realized that seeing the farm first-hand might answer the mystery about why Austin had saved the contract with Nielson's signature. Who was hiding what from whom?

As luck would have it, the main chairperson was out sick and Dr. Schneider was also a no-show. Absent key leaders, those present discussed the projected timeline, but no one wanted to make big decisions. The meeting was cut short and Cassandra found herself back in the office early.

She passed the copier technician on the way in and gave the thumbs up sign to Lance sitting at one of the student worker desks. He smiled back and waved hello. Rachel, Haley, and Logan stuffed envelopes for a mailing. Haley held up pink message slips that Cassandra scooped up as she walked past the reception desk and into her office.

She grabbed her navy Morton College plastic bottle off the desk and went back into the main office for a water refill near the corner snack table. Surveying the food in the baskets, she noticed someone had brought Halloween candy fun-size bars and Skittles that'd already been picked over. The other basket someone had stocked with healthy granola bars, cereal bars and peanut butter cracker packets. She wondered who brought in the goodies for the students and staff to eat, and made a mental note to pick up some treats the next time she went to the food market. Most of these kids were far away from homemade treats and nurturing parents.

Tuning into their conversation, she realized the students were discussing the upcoming Obstacle Course races planned as a study break after dinner. Students formed into teams of 6 with their fraternity or sorority houses, dorm room floors or friend groups, and dressed in Halloween costumes. Rachel said, "Alrighty, then. Here's the deal. My friends are zombies. We're going to wear our regular ratty clothes and put on gross makeup. We'll look sick."

Lance stood up and showed off his zombie walk and scary face while the girls cringed in mock terror at him. Logan lived off-campus and was on a team with friends from his PoliSci class. "We're going to be superheroes. I think I'll just dress as myself."

Haley rolled her chair closer to his and smacked him on the shoulder. She teased him, "Very original. What's your superpower?"

Logan made a classic weightlifter muscle pose and boasted. "Go out with me Friday night, and I'll show you my superpower."

Rachel laughed. "Yeah, I don't think Atomic Farts count."

Haley said, "Our team is doing a beach theme. I guess I'll just wear flip flops and a sundress. Maybe carry a towel? I don't really have any more."

The event's excitement was contagious and gave Cassandra an idea about something she'd thrown into a file cabinet drawer on move-in day. She rifled through the miscellaneous junk from her old office at Oahu State. Must be something in here for a beach theme. She discarded a straw hat, large white plastic sunglasses and a cheesy Tropical Vacations, Inc. vinyl tote bag. Maybe a grass skirt?

Rachel scooted her chair closer to the others and held up her phone. "Hey Logan help me send a SnapChat to Devon with a picture of your face while you're using your superpowers. Here, make a face. Ready?"

They all crowded in front of the camera and took a selfie. "Wait . . . that was no good. Try again."

At the exact moment Rachel snapped the photo, Cassandra returned from her office holding up a coconut shaped bikini by the strings. "Haley, I can't remember who gave me this, but—"

Rachel flipped the phone around and showed the photo . . . including Cassandra stepping out of her office, the bikini in front of her chest, her face lit up by a helpful smile. Her cheeks turned a deep red. "I swear if that ends up online somewhere, you guys are all fired!"

Logan turned to the room and held up a finger, scolding them in a fake Mom voice. "You all should leave now, and think about what you've done."

Everyone except Lance grabbed their bags and scattered. Cassandra shook her head, dropped the coconuts on the desk, and went back to her office.

Her office clock showed 2:30 and Cassandra stared at the foot-high pile of student folders on her desk awaiting her attention. She also had reading to do for her grad students' theses. Well, this was a bit of a dilemma. Probably Fischer and the professor could handle the farm visit without her. She recalled President Nielson's admonishment to get out, meet people, and make herself more visible. Perhaps there was a little teeny part of her that wouldn't mind getting to know Fischer a bit better, and a car ride is a great way to converse without pressure.

She'd nearly talked herself into calling him back, when she looked up from her desk and jumped. Marcus Fischer stood in her doorway, arms casually folded across his chest. "I saw you walking back to the office."

Yeesh! Was he stalking her? Fischer's head tilted towards the main street. "Professor Zimmerman is out front in the car. We're just leaving now. This cattle feedlot supplies about 22,000 hamburgers' worth of beef annually. How cool is that?"

She stood, put on her jacket, grabbed her bag, and followed him out. "You really need to work on your sales pitch."

She pantomimed to Lance using the few signs she knew. "I'll be back here around 6. Please lock the door when you close the office. Thanks."

He gave her the thumbs up back.

Maybe they could stop on the way to buy nose plugs?

Chapter Twenty-One

Fischer dropped Cassandra at her house on the way back from the farm, then returned the college's car to the motor pool with Professor Zimmerman. She swore the men were laughing at her as they drove away, but their heads faced the street, so she wasn't 100% sure.

With great relief, she saw no neighbors when she dropped her Michael Kors pumps outside the back door. They were a total loss, caked in an inch of smelly, dried mud. A few minutes into scrubbing her feet and legs under the outdoor spigot, her stomach rumbled as a reminder that lunch's soup and salad were distant memories.

Once inside, she paused to empty the water from her bottle into her Plumeria plant that lived on the end table she passed on the way to her bedroom. She gently stroked the long green leaves for a moment and inhaled the fragrant scent of the solitary yellow bloom. The smell instantly reminded her of leis and home, however not enough to disguise the farm stench she'd tracked inside. In her bedroom, she quickly changed into loose-fitting running shorts, a gray t-shirt, University of Hawai'i zip-up hoodie, and comfortable Brooks cross trainers. She stuffed her muddy suit into a trash bag. She'd let the dry cleaner decide later whether her outfit was worth salvaging. Her face burned with embarrassment at the afternoon's memory.

The farm had turned out to be a short twenty minutes west of Carson. Fischer drove the white Chevy Malibu and chatted mostly with Professor Zimmerman in the passenger seat. The radio was turned down low, the windows rolled up to prevent field dust from covering the car's cloth interior. Cassandra listened to them talk about select grade beef, and whether it was worth paying more for certified meat in the dining halls. The two-lane highway wound over gently rolling hills. Every couple of miles they passed small family farms surrounded by acres of harvested fields that left behind clumps of broken, golden cornstalks in haphazard rows. The only water in sight was a pond every few miles.

When there was silence in the front seat, Cassandra leaned forward and asked, "Can you tell me more about the partnership the college has to buy locally sourced beef?"

Professor Zimmerman turned to face her. "It's a great example of private and public interests merging to benefit all of us. Dr. Nielson grew up in this area and introduced us to Brian Hopkins who raises cattle and runs a small feedlot here. We contract to purchase our beef from him, exclusively. He gets a good customer; and we get lean beef from a known source."

"In the future, will you do something similar for the other foods you purchase for the college? Like chicken and vegetables, too?"

"We already have a large garden and greenhouses that supply vegetables in season. We also opened community garden space to the public to plant their own produce. Last month the garden overflowed with zucchini and tomatoes." Zimmerman smiled at the memory. "Our food service cooks' creativity was stretched to the limits to design recipes using those ingredients for every meal possible. Even I got tired of BLTs this year."

She was surprised to hear Morton was on the cutting edge of food supply trends. "In Hawai'i, we had plenty of local fruits, and my family had a small garden. Nebraskans eat way more steak than we did though."

"I'm on Luke Peterson's dissertation committee, and we saw this opportunity to incorporate research into the business partnership. When we realized that the enzyme was naturally produced by human physiology, we made a protein concentrate additive to give to Brian Hopkins. Now he uses that feed additive with his cattle to boost enzyme production in the meat. Then he turns around and sells the beef to us. When our students eat the beef, it naturally raises their enzyme levels, giving them further disease protection."

Luckily this wasn't the first time Cassandra had heard about the cancer research enzyme. She thought she understood most of the science.

Zimmerman said, "Luke is the second or third student who's been involved. Earlier they identified the enzyme, developed the protein feed additive for the cattle, and isolated the enzyme for this GA's experimental treatments. Fun fact: SODs are also related to ALS (Lou Gehrig's disease) and Down Syndrome. If the team develops an injection or pills to protect people from superoxide toxicity that would be a huge breakthrough. We've noticed an increase in the enzyme among the students eating the treated beef who donate blood and plasma. So this in turn provides more of the enzyme used in our research on campus."

No wonder Nielson was so proud of this partnership. Made sense that he was anxious about negative publicity for their operations. Cassandra said, "It's pretty complicated, but if the results work the way you expect, it could have a big impact on food production and medicine."

"I'm proud to play a small role in the research process," agreed Zimmerman.

Soon they turned off the main highway and onto a dirt road, then a nearby driveway in front of a 1980s-style yellow one-story house with an attached two car garage nestled into a good-sized yard of green grass and surrounded by a protective stand of twenty-foot-tall pine trees. The circular driveway continued past the house to the other farm buildings and a barn.

Cassandra didn't know all the buildings' purposes but identified the really tall metal one as a grain storage bin. Halfway down, an open door had a conveyor belt hooked over the edge which continued to the ground near the driveway. Two large Lab dogs, one chocolate, the other yellow, bounded over to greet the visitors as they halted in the driveway in front of the garage.

Fischer and Zimmerman opened their doors, got out of the car and stood in the driveway waiting for the farmer to see them. Fischer petted the yellow Lab who gave a couple of welcoming barks, tail wagging, tongue slobbering as he danced excitedly around the men.

Cassandra sat in the car. No way was she opening that car door and getting dusty paw prints on her clean suit or scratch marks down her bare legs. That chocolate Lab probably weighed more than she did. She peered out the window wondering how long she'd have to sit there. She heard a piercing whistle at the same time she saw a tall, broad-shouldered man leave the shadow of the barn and walk towards the car. He wore dusty jeans, cowboy boots, a plaid shirt, yellow work gloves, and a black trucker style cap. His curly blond hair stuck out along the edges of the hat, and he called the dogs to his side while he took off his gloves.

A friendly smile broke across his face, and as he got close enough, she noticed he was younger than she'd expected. When he approached the car, he turned and pointed back towards the barn, commanding the dogs, "Out!" Immediately, they both stopped their circling and galloped back to the barn. Cassandra opened the car door and climbed out carefully onto the driveway's hard-packed dirt.

Professor Zimmerman and Fischer shook the farmer's hand. "Good afternoon, Brian! How're you?"

He spoke in low, measured voice. "Too much rain last week. Flooded my storage room and messed up some fencing, but otherwise I'm good."

After introductions and a tour of the buildings, they stepped outside again and regarded the large fenced in cattle yard filled with massive 1,000+ pound animals. The increasing wind gusts came out across the yard and kicked up a sandy dust cloud along the drive. Cassandra turned her face away and wondered if her hair would end up like Medusa's by the end of the visit. Cassandra had seen cattle from the road before, but up close these beasts were larger than she expected. Smellier too.

She tried to breathe through her mouth, but couldn't completely avoid it. Brian Hopkins noted her discomfort and laughed, "My grandfather always said, 'That's the smell of money, son.' You're lucky I don't have a hundred hogs, too. That'd be worse. I grew up here, so I don't even notice. My wife Janey is from Denver though, and she gets that same look on her face that you have." He smiled again, unfazed.

Fischer and Zimmerman were turned the other way, wandering over to the tractors and equipment, not paying full attention to their conversation.

Brian's charm was infectious. She felt comfortable around him. "I'm grateful for the opportunity to see your operation in person. Helps me understand the relationship between you and Morton much better."

His tanned face had a boyish quality to it when he smiled, showing off straight white teeth and deep dimples. He was an advertisement for clean, outdoor living. "Dr. Nielson went to high school with my father so I've known him since I was a boy. I jumped at the idea of joining the protein additive trials; the pilot project provides me free feed which lets me sell the meat back to the college for a fair price. Plus, I think the meat tastes more lean and tender. After these experiments are done, I'm going to buy the feed myself and use it to market my beef to specialty stores and restaurants."

She had a hard time picturing Nielson as a high school kid. "How long does it take to get FDA approval?"

"Our feed mixture contains corn byproducts, grains or other minerals and vitamins—but not medicines—so it doesn't go through special FDA approval."

Ignorance might be the better option when it came to byproducts added into her food. She remembered Austin's test results. "Do you know if an overdose of the research enzyme could cause someone to get sick?"

"I know more about the feed side of the equation than Morton's research. The average American consumes 2 ounces of beef per day—not enough to make you ill from your hamburger. Nebraskans are proud of their 'corn-fed beef.' The feed mix affects the meat's taste and since this is a business, we do everything possible to make it taste great."

Like tender Kobe beef from Japan that was popular in steakhouses back home. "I had no idea it was legal to add things to the animal feed."

"Most consumers don't know much about how their food is made."

Both fascinated and somewhat alarmed, Cassandra slowly stepped towards the fence. "How many cows are in the pilot project?"

"In this area here we have 40—Wait! Don't go any closer, it's wet over the—" Brian stopped mid-sentence and lunged for her. Too late.

She'd been looking out at the cattle instead of down at the soft mud. Her pointy heels sank down and one came loose from her foot. Cartwheeling her arms, she wobbled a couple of times but caught herself by her hands on the wooden fence.

Cassandra had it under control. She smiled and adjusted her feet back into the shoes. Fischer covered the space in a few large steps, took her elbow, and thanked Brian. "I don't have any more questions. The contract renewal should go smoothly. You'll get the paperwork in the mail in a couple of weeks. We'd better head back to town."

After shaking hands, they walked towards the car. Cassandra nodded at Fischer and pulled her arm away from his grasp. Her skin tingled where his hand had touched her elbow. "I'm good now, thanks."

She didn't need a man's help covering a short distance. She waited for them to get ahead of her and followed. Head down, she gingerly stepped across the drive, avoiding muddy spots and what looked like round, dried chunks of sawdust. Feeling more confident, she looked back again and waved at Brian. The toe of her shoe caught on a rock. She slid sideways on a large wet cow-pie partially covered by gravel, going down in a flurry of flailing arms and legs like a scene straight out of a cartoon strip.

Brian had helped her stand up and half carried her to the car. He was genuinely concerned that she was unhurt and didn't even smirk at her dishevelment. Must be the city wife that'd made him so chivalrous.

She'd given Fischer the narrow-eyed 'don't say a word' look. He shrugged and opened the trunk, pulling out an old dusty fleece blanket that he laid across the back seat for her.

Wouldn't want to ruin the college's car, eh? Not exactly Sir Lancelot.

She had to give Fischer credit though. He didn't say one word the whole ride back. Just cranked the radio up loud and ignored the funky smell. Her eyes watered from the sand and grit that had been blown into them. At least that was her story for the moisture on her cheeks if anyone dared ask. The non-stop sneezing fit also had her fuming. Allergies and clumsiness were unwelcome lifestyle changes. She pouted. *Why do I keep getting stuck in these ridiculous situations?*

Chapter Twenty-Two

Cassandra opened the fridge and surveyed the contents. A red-lidded Rubbermaid contained a few cups of leftover rice, the crisper drawers were full of fresh fruits and veggies. Sipping sparkling water, she thought stir fry sounded good for dinner when she was interrupted by two sharp knocks on the back door. Cassandra peeked out the kitchen window into the empty driveway. Confused, she walked down the steps and saw Meg's hair through the window. She unlocked the door and Meg came in, already talking. "You forgot we were supposed to meet for supper, didn't you?"

Cassandra squinted, "Why aren't you already home? Supper . . . We just had lunch. And then I had a detour—" Cassandra stopped her excuse mid-sentence because she noticed Meg was staring at the top of her head.

Meg slowly reached up and removed a stiff clump of dried mud from Cassandra's ponytail. "Tonight's the Obstacle Course on the Quad. I work late, because some of the deaf students and staff are on teams. You promised we'd eat together before it starts. I stopped by the office, and you weren't there so I came here. Why aren't you ready . . . You're not wearing that are you?"

Cassandra yanked the mud clot from Meg's hand and stomped up to the kitchen where she threw it in the trash. Meg followed, clearly amused at this rare glimpse of Cassandra not perfectly dressed, made up, and put together. "I wasted my afternoon doing a stupid PR run to a smelly cattle farm because Dr. Nielson was gone. I totally embarrassed myself by falling into a puddle of a substance I couldn't identify. But since there were giant cows all around, I can guess what it was." Cassandra sniffed her shirt. "I desperately need a shower, but I'm hungry."

"But—"

Cassandra's hands went up to ward off whatever Meg said next. She whined, "I'm pau. Don't want to go back over da kine. I ruined a suit, trashed a good pair of work heels, and my hip . . ."

She reached around her right hip and hiked up the bottom of her shorts revealing a red scratch larger than her palm and a light bruise. She gasped, "I thought it hurt! I don't have time for this." Her eyes went full-on stink eye. "Stop laughing."

Meg couldn't hold it in. She laughed out loud and protested, "I'm laughing WITH you. What's your beef? It's funny . . . Ok, the part where you ruined the clothes and got hurt isn't funny. But the vision of you slipping into a muddy cow-pie part is hysterical."

She growled. "Not laughing. Not funny. Not going."

Meg countered. "Embarrassed, hungry, dirty and GOING. Look, it starts at seven. I have to get back over there for the opening rules and introductions."

Meg pulled the fridge open and grabbed a bottle of Chardonnay out of the door. Stepping over to the cupboard, she found a wine glass and poured a generous measure into the glass. "Take this."

Cassandra accepted the glass. Meg turned Cassandra around by her shoulders and gently nudged her towards the master bedroom. "Have a warm shower, drink some wine, change into clean comfy clothes, and come back to the Quad to watch the races. I'll order you a sub sandwich to eat when you get there. C'mon, it'll be fun."

Cassandra's instinct was to argue, but she paused to take a long drink of wine. Inhaling a deep breath, she closed her eyes. "No-Nonsense Nielson had better appreciate all the extra stuff I'm doing while he's gallivanting through China."

Forty-five minutes later, Cassandra was thankful for another warm evening. She only needed a light jacket in the 65-degree balmy air. She heard thumping bass and laughter before she rounded the student center's corner. Several food tents and tables were set up along the field's edges. Brightly costumed students gathered in teams preparing for competitions. The near end of the quad was the start line. Various obstacles were laid out on the football field sized grass. Contestants jumped through tires or hoops, caught water balloons in buckets, and completed other skills before reaching the finish line. Cassandra lingered on the sidelines trying to guess the costume themes for the team competition.

A large, homemade wooden scoreboard on the far end of the field listed six team names with a grid scoring the race standings. Logan's superhero team had jumped into an early lead while they zoomed around wearing colored tights under running shorts with headgear that included taped on lightning bolts, American flags, or robotic looking components made of cardboard. One guy wearing a black mask with antennae stuck to the front stopped on top of a wooden stand with his chest stuck out and his biceps flexed while his teammates screamed at him to stop posing and keep running. He leapt off the stand athletically and darted toward the finish line but his detour had cost him the lead in his leg of the race. Other students lined the sides of the field, many of them also wearing costumes, cheering and taking photos of his antics.

When the next heat began, a couple of students dressed in a beach theme competed against others wearing full choir robes, carrying broom handles and waving wands. One tall girl tripped over her flip flop and went down in the tire agility skill just as a guy wearing thick, dark-rimmed glasses with a red scar drawn on his forehead pointed his wand at her Hawaiian skirted teammate. "Stupefy!!" he yelled. But his spell had no effect, and she returned to help her friend stand. Removing her sandals, she carried them and continued barefoot instead. Harry Potter chased them shouting, "Expecto patronum! Impervius!" Together the girls sprinted over the finish line, plastic flower leis floating behind them like capes. Their teammates celebrated by throwing inflatable colored beach balls into the crowd.

Cassandra spotted Meg and Cinda standing by the food tents and walked around the field. Cassandra marveled, "This is so creative! I can't believe how seriously they took this whole thing."

Meg handed over a paper wrapped sandwich she'd held for Cassandra. "I love watching them. The grand prize is $500 for the team and a traveling trophy. The Superheroes won the first two years I worked here, but so far it looks like the Zombies and the Sandlot guys could catch up. Five hundred bucks would buy a pretty fun after-party."

Lance jogged over to the women. His AOO t-shirt was saturated with sweat, and he wore a baseball hat, shorts and Chuck Taylor high tops.

Meg complimented his outfit in sign and spoken English, "Looking good, Benny."

Lance beamed. "We suck, but whatever."

He shifted his body to the left and signed low and in front of his chest, "Hey this is off the wall," he glanced over his shoulder, "do you know that tall guy over by the green tent?"

Meg looked to her right and moved her hands to reply to Lance unseen from the tent's direction. "What's he wearing?"

Lance replied, "The guy by the corner with the white polo shirt and straw golf hat over by the professors."

Near the finish line, a small group of mostly younger professors and their families watched the races and ate ice cream. Next to them another cluster of several older guys with gray hair, dress slacks and polo shirts stood chatting and smiling, hands in pockets. Definitely classier than students or professors.

Meg signed and spoke. "The one with the white polo? That's Dr. Schneider. He's one of the big college leader guys. Looks like some fancy donor folks with him. Why do you ask?"

Lance signed, "He looked familiar but I couldn't think of why. I assumed he was a professor. I could swear I saw him a few weeks ago. I walked into our bedroom and Austin was signing on the video phone with someone who looked just like him."

Meg clarified, "Your fraternity house? On the VP—not through the interpreter relay service?"

"Yeah. The reason I remembered him was because he looked mad at Austin. You wanted us to tell you anything unusual that happened lately. Maybe I'm wrong, but..." He finished with a shrug. "I feel like when he looks at me signing, he's not just staring. Know what I mean? Like he understands me."

Meg shook her head and raised her palms up. "How's that possible? You must have him mixed up with someone else."

"That's right. Maybe he has a twin or something." Lance chuckled, then bounded down the field towards his team.

Cassandra turned to Meg and raised an eyebrow. "I understood about half of what you two were saying. What the heck?"

Meg explained, "He said he saw Austin talking to a man on the video phone in their fraternity room. Remember that monitor?" When Cassandra nodded, Meg continued, "But

Lance must've seen him for only a few seconds and . . . got the wrong person."

Cassandra understood the video monitor part, but not the signing parts. Cinda had the same question. "What did Lance mean about staring at him while he's signing?"

Meg held up a thumb and two fingers and ticked them off. "Basically, there's three kinds of stares. First, you have the curious people who notice us signing and stare for a few moments in a, 'Gee, that's kind of neat,' way."

She tapped her second finger. "Next, there's the rude ones who openly stare longer than 10 seconds during restaurant meals or in public. They annoy me."

Tapping her third finger, "Then, there's strangers who stare like they're eavesdropping. You gotta remember, sign is different than overhearing a conversation. You can see signs from far away. Like me, for example. I can look across the field and eavesdrop on what Lance and his friend are saying."

Cassandra put her hand up to shield her eyes from the bright lights and looked down the sideline where Lance was animatedly signing to a shorter kid. "Isn't that rude, too?"

Meg shook her head, "Not really. If someone wants to sign a private conversation, they do it low or kind of hidden. If you're out in public, it's fair game."

Cassandra gave up guessing what Lance and his friend were talking about. She really needed to take an ASL class.

Meg added with a slight shrug. "I don't do it often anyway. But I know what Lance meant. I can usually tell when someone is watching me sign and they understand me. I can't explain it to you, but I know the feeling when it happens."

Cassandra filed away that tidbit. Meg was full of interesting Deaf culture facts.

An hour later the Obstacle competition was winding down with only the championship heat remaining. Cassandra commented, "I don't think it's fair that SpongeBob got disqualified for running out on the field to help Squidward when his mask slipped down over his face."

Cinda yelled encouragement to the Zombies who hadn't been trying very hard to complete the obstacles. Several of them worked in her counseling office, and she'd helped them apply makeup and rip their thrift store costumes to the proper amount of dishevelment.

Their main goal seemed to be aimlessly bumping into the other teams and trying to knock them off course. Cinda stopped yelling and stared at Cassandra in amazement. "The lofty Dr. Cassandra Sato is a SpongeBob fan? I never would've guessed."

Cassandra held up her hands by her sides. "Who could watch the 'I'm a Goofy Goober' rock video and NOT become a fan?"

Their debate was cut short by the crowd noise as the last race began. Cassandra overheard one guy wearing a baseball shirt waiting at the starting line tell the kid next to him, "If my dog was as ugly as you, I'd shave his butt and tell him to walk backwards."

The black robed guy wore a wig of flowing gray hair and flipped Baseball Shirt off. When the starting flag dropped, Gray Wig raced towards the wooden wall alongside a curly haired girl who didn't need any makeup to resemble Hermione Granger. Dumbledore took a running leap and wedged one leg over the top. Hermione tried the same maneuver, but being a full foot shorter, even her decent jump couldn't get her close to the top. Backing up, she tried again while Dumbledore lay face down atop the wall holding an arm down to her. Her third attempt was better. She locked arms with him and scrambled up and over.

In the meantime, Lance's fraternity team used a different technique where the first guy ran up to the wall and leaned over so the second runner could use his knee and back as steps vaulting over the 9-foot-tall wall. The first guy smoothly jumped up and grabbed the top then did a pull up to join his buddy over the wall. They were already at the water balloon toss before the wizards had cleared the wall obstacle.

Cassandra tried to decode their costume mix of baseball hats, gloves, and mismatched shirts. "What team is that?"

"Sandlot. Only the best movie ever," answered Cinda. She poked a finger at Cassandra's head and taunted, "You bob for apples in the toilet! And you like it!"

Cassandra shot her an incredulous look. "Excuse me?? Oh, wait . . . Movie line, huh?"

Cinda's eyes rolled way back. "Did you really have to think about that one? Gee."

Cassandra rose on her tiptoes leaning between the people in front of her to see the finish line. The Sandlot guys had a five second lead going into the last obstacle: throwing three footballs into a target 20 feet away. One guy hit his first two shots, but missed his third. The duo couldn't cross the finish line separately.

Meanwhile Dumbledore and Hermione caught up and quickly made all three throws. The Sandlot teammates on the sideline went ballistic. "You ain't good enough to lick the dirt off our cleats!"

In a complete disregard for the rules, one of Lance's teammates moved the target so the football finally went through the hole. Too late. The Wizards had already won. They danced around like they'd just won the international Quidditch Cup.

The losers heckled their friend. "You're killing me, Smalls!" "Scab eater!" "Fart smeller!" "Shut up, idiot!" Finally, their insults receded as they wandered off to the field's far corner and probably someone's house to drown their sorrows.

Cassandra wasn't surprised to see Professor Bergstrom present the trophy to the winning Wizards team assembled in the middle of the field. The trophy—an obviously home-made concoction of a golden cup atop a gold spray-painted 2 by 4 adorned with fake gems and Happy Meal toys, previously winning teams written in black Sharpie marker along the base—was hoisted triumphantly into the air.

Cassandra laughed with the rapidly dispersing crowd. The long day finally hit her, and all she wanted was home and her soft bed.

Chapter Twenty-Three

Traditional Hawaiian music played softly in the background from the iHome on Cassandra's bookshelf, and she read a transcript printed from a Facebook page. Josh Krinke, a PhD physics student, had been referred to the Student Affairs office for "odd behavior" by his dissertation committee chair. The student had written, "Those guys from Colorado were just making a point."

Cassandra gasped in horror and sprayed coffee droplets on the notes she'd been scanning before her Wednesday morning appointment. The transcript made several references to guns and Columbine, including, "Their approach may have been a little rough, but what teenager hasn't fantasized about shooting up the place and going down in a blaze of glory?"

This very quickly had gotten the attention of his colleagues. Ambiguous comments and vague intentions aside, no college wanted to become the next Virginia Tech.

Cassandra opened her office door and stepped outside. "Mr. Krinke?" She glanced around the room looking for a PhD student, but no one moved right away. She walked farther into the office, "Mr. Krinke?" she repeated and looked to Devon, the student assistant, for help. He pointed right and towards a heavy set guy camped out on the couch with a huge backpack at his feet.

Krinke looked about 40 years old with 1/4-inch buzz cut hair. He had let his beard grow out 8 inches and she noticed what she sincerely hoped were remnants of this morning's breakfast stuck in there. He wore a gray hoodie, baggy black pants, and black combat style boots whose soles were so worn, she could see a couple places where his white athletic socks peeked through the holes on the sides. In contrast to his Unabomber-looking appearance, he wore wire-rimmed glasses over intelligent eyes and his face was open and pleasant-looking.

Headphone wires poked out of his ears and he was looking down at his smartphone, thumbing through images while his head moved to the beat of his music. Cassandra walked slowly towards him and stood in front of him waiting for him to feel her presence. He looked up, smiled and reached up to pull the headphones out. "Sorry. Are you Dr. Sato?"

She beckoned him into her office. "Yes, I am and you must be Mr. Krinke? C'mon back." Prudence told her not to close the door behind them completely.

Krinke sat his large frame into her visitor chair and arranged his belongings around him. He reached a meaty hand into the bag and came up with a blue water bottle covered in peace sign symbols.

Cassandra's back was straight, her hands folded on the wooden desk. "Mr. Krinke, your committee chair, Dr. Gries, has asked me to talk to you about your Facebook posts and comments. I've read them, and admit I'm curious about your reasons for posting them in a public forum."

She pushed the pages across the desk towards him. "Could you please tell me about these?"

Perspiration beads shined on his forehead. "Well . . . I . . . uh, I'm trying to get my name out there more. You know, get some name recognition before I graduate." He made air quotes around "name recognition" and continued, "I'll be looking for a job soon, and I want people to know who I am. Create a buzz."

People already knew who he was, or he wouldn't be facing her in this office. "So these posts are meant to 'create a buzz' and help you find a job?"

He approved of her quick understanding. "Yes, exactly!"

She stared at him a few moments, speechless. How does, "It's going to be just like Columbine, man," and, "Let's get those guns blazing," help him find a job?

She tried another tack. "What exactly is your dissertation topic, Mr. Krinke?"

"Energy transfer dynamics in closed quantum systems."

She waited a couple of seconds trying to digest that one and took a guess. "But that isn't really about shooting anything with a gun or making a bomb, correct?"

His manner was eager and friendly. "No. I wanted to generate more interest in my page. I need to go viral. If you use more provoking language, the search engines find you. Then more people add comments, and your page goes to the top of people's News Feeds. I posted some things on

Twitter too, but I only have 57 followers so those don't go very far unless you get Retweets."

Right. She really needed to study more about this whole social media thing, but at the same time she was grateful her life wasn't wasted reading this garbage every day. "Are you sure those are the best ways to get attention for your dissertation and your job search?"

"I don't know. The people in my physics class noticed me. And my committee noticed. I'm here now, right?"

"Yes, but you can get in trouble for posting inflammatory statements on social media. People might interpret them differently than how you intended them. Did you intend to scare people into thinking your research had something to do with Columbine?"

"No, but I had to set them up that way so the comments made sense back and forth."

Cassandra looked down at the transcript again. "Excuse me, I don't understand what you mean." There were 35 comments under one account profile and 47 under a second. She re-read them hoping they would offer a clue about what he meant.

He pointed towards his name at the top of the transcript. "Well, you see, I have this profile here with my name and information. Then I made a second profile page using another name. That one says I'm a biologist from Ohio. Then, I made them friends with each other."

Pride glowed in his cheeks at his marketing ingenuity. "So now I can post a status on either my profile or the other. I can post comments back and forth between the two of them like a conversation! I can Like or Share things between the two profiles. I have the privacy set to public on the Ohio one, so more people can see everything!"

Indeed, it seemed resourceful. Cassandra was no expert. Her own Facebook page connected about 30 of her family and closest friends with every privacy available and maximum security settings. She never posted anything about herself; only looked at photos of the nieces and nephews or kept up on what people back home were doing. She read her news feed maybe once a week. She was far too busy with her real life to waste time engaging with high school classmates she hadn't seen for 14 years and never intended to see again.

"Thank you Mr. Krinke for explaining your social media use. I'm recommending you also schedule an appointment with Cinda Weller from the Counseling and Career office. Because of your use of those inflammatory words and your work directly with undergraduates, we need to carefully evaluate your ability to complete your degree work here. We'll be in touch with the details of your next appointment."

"I'm weird, but harmless," he asserted. "Just a guy trying to get a job. You know, the job market is rough out there. You have to work hard to stand out from the crowd," he heaved himself out of the chair and slung his bag onto his back.

Cassandra walked him to her door. "One piece of advice, Mr. Krinke: Unless you want to attract far more attention than just a job, please refrain from mentioning Columbine and explosives in relation to Morton College, our students or our staff."

His chipper composure never dropped. "Sure no problem, Dr. Sato. If you think that's best. Maybe I'll start a blog with some original info-graphics or charts. I'm sure I can think of something worthy."

Once he left, Cassandra went back to her office, closed the door and let out a huge sigh. Even if the counseling office gave him a passing grade, she'd wonder about him anyway.

Cassandra's eyebrows knitted together as she looked more carefully at the Facebook log pages on her desk. Buried 10 comments down the transcript page about the shooting Luke Peterson had written, "Sounds like we need to go out Thursday night. My project might be off the rails, too. Just gotta survive the next few weeks without everything blowing up in my face."

Krinke and Peterson. The obvious answer—there were less than a hundred PhD students on the whole campus—they were bound to know each other. Cassandra focused on Luke's message and worries. Luke had seemed unaware of the circumstances of Austin's death, but was someone else threatening to sabotage his dissertation?

Chapter Twenty-Four

Cassandra hadn't meant to seek out Professor Mike Bergstrom's office in Bryan Hall. She had stepped out between appointments for a bathroom break when the lovely, sunny view out the window beckoned her. Just a few minutes out in the fresh air.

The bright sun made her think it was at least 70 degrees outside. What a huge disappointment it was to reach the cold bench outside the admin building only to realize the sunshine was just for show. She forced herself to sit for a few minutes and turned her face upwards. Maybe if she closed her eyes and thought of Ala Moana Beach she could trick herself into believing it was warm.

A cloud passed over the sun and a shiver ran up her spine. Opening her eyes, she jumped a bit. "Oh! Dr. Bergstrom, you are not a cloud."

His hearty laugh came from deep in his chest. "Not a cloud . . . no. However, I do have my darker moments. Were you making a wish, Dr. Sato?"

"Just wishing for a warm day like we had last week. I knew it would be colder here, but I expected it to happen in December, not October already."

"Welcome to Nebraska. If you don't like the weather today, wait a few hours. It could change," he recited with twinkling eyes. "I was just headed over to my office for some coffee. Why don't you join me?"

Normally, she would have immediately dismissed his suggestion and fled upstairs to work. Some impulse—and Dr. Nielson's reminder to get out of her office more—led her to accept his invitation. Stately brick Bryan Hall sat next to the Osborne building across a wide sidewalk. As they reached the landing step to the second-floor faculty offices, her nostrils were assailed by the pungent odor of pipe smoke.

The entire campus was a smoke-free workplace, but she suspected the drywall and ceilings would have to be completely replaced if they wanted to get rid of the residual sweet tobacco smell. Cassandra kind of liked it. Combined with the dark paneled woodwork in the hallways, the decor screamed, "Philosophy professors at work!"

Following him through the polished wooden door, she was astonished by his shoe box sized office space. This was how they treated tenured professors?

His avocado green metal desk was shoved under the room's only tiny window which hadn't been cleaned in months. Folders, papers and books occupied nearly every square inch of his desk. Cassandra perched on a dilapidated yellow flowered sofa from a bygone era. Extending her legs, she could almost touch the sturdy metal bookshelf along the opposite wall. Two large frames above the sofa held quotes in graphic lettering. One in all black had a golden outline of a bat and said, "It's not who I am underneath, but what I do that defines me. -Batman." The other, "You can't know. You can only believe—or not. —C.S. Lewis" Leather volumes by C.S. Lewis, J.R.R. Tolkien, and Thomas Aquinas held place of honor on the top shelves, while textbooks by Bergstrom himself and other less notable works were stacked haphazardly on the bottom shelves.

She studied the titles by Bergstrom and noted several Batman comic books and commentaries mixed in with the scholarly texts. Chuckling, he explained, "Those are resources for the Philosophy of Batman course—my most popular class!"

He reached over to an end table wedged into the corner between the sofa and his desk to retrieve her a clean mug. Atop the table sat the only thing in his office made in this century—a compact shiny gourmet coffee machine. He worked the knobs and switches and in only a few minutes offered her a mug of delicious smelling coffee.

Opening a little drawer, he retrieved a plaid tin of British biscuits, popped open the lid and held them out to Cassandra. She was completely charmed. "You shouldn't have shown me this place. Now that I know about this, I may become a regular here."

Nicotine stained teeth peeked out from his trim gray beard. "You know, of course, that you're welcome to my home away from home anytime you need me."

She sipped the fragrant, nutty coffee and bit into the small shortbread cookie. Savoring the combination, she could feel her shoulders relax and her breathing slow. She hadn't realized how tight her body had been before this little break.

Bergstrom quietly drank his coffee, content to wait in unhurried, comfortable silence. After what seemed like five minutes but was probably one, Cassandra realized she wanted to ask his advice about the investigation. "Remember on Monday when I told you that there was no drugs or alcohol in Austin's system? Well, that might not be completely accurate. There's evidence that he may have stuck himself with a syringe from the research lab. They found an elevated level of the treatment enzyme in his blood. They haven't begun human trials yet. No one knows how much he actually injected, so it's hard to predict how or if that enzyme contributed to his death."

He nodded, encouraging her to continue.

"His cell phone still hasn't been found, but the laptop was turned in. They're following up on some payments he received from somewhere for about $600. Maybe Austin had a side job that no one knew about? Even his own roommate."

His dark eyes fixed on hers. "What do you need to ask me, Dr. Sato?"

She didn't know how he could help her, except to listen. She stalled for time. "The problem, Dr. Bergstrom, is that something just doesn't feel right. I can see these small pieces, but they don't fit together. Austin knew something was wrong before he died. He texted his roommate for help, but didn't say why. He'd saved the contract page between Dr. Nielson and the farmer."

"Those things might be connected somehow."

"Yes, they might. Or they could just be random. I can't say anything publicly though, because President Nielson and Dr. Schneider have both emphasized that we need to avoid any negative press this week. I don't know Dr. Schneider well enough to judge his flexibility on this."

She searched for the right words to use. "Dr. Schneider seems a bit arrogant. He made some comments about deaf people that were way off base."

Bergstrom relaxed into his chair and gazed out the dirty window. "You've been around higher education long enough to know that the President and the Board Chairman wield a lot of power, even at an insignificant place such as this. If you enjoy your job as much as I think you do, you can't afford to alienate either of those men."

That's why she'd kept silent so far. She was top management now and needed to think about the college's reputation first. She frowned into the empty bottom of her coffee mug. "But what if something fishy is going on here? And what if Austin somehow knew about it? I couldn't live with myself if anyone else were hurt because we're concerned about Morton's public image more than protecting students."

He was enjoying himself entirely too much. "An excellent point. You're faced with an ethical dilemma. Do you ignore the wishes of your superiors to do what your instincts tell you is right? Do you choose the actions that do the greatest good, or create the least evil?"

His glee at inserting philosophic platitudes into every-day conversation was palpable. But this was real life, not his freshman seminar class. She'd have to evaluate which course of action to follow.

At least talking to him had relaxed and distracted her from the stressful hum in her office. Rising, Cassandra returned her mug to the table. "I appreciate you listening to my ramblings."

"Anytime, Dr. Sato. Just remember: 'It is our choices, that show what we truly are, far more than our abilities.'"

Cassandra's hand paused on the doorknob. "That's a famous quote from someone I should probably recognize . . . Is it Thoreau?"

Bergstrom winked. "Dumbledore."

* * *

"Put me in undercover!" Lance insisted to Cassandra and Meg. "I know the cancer lab needs helpers now that Austin's gone. I know all his passwords and can confirm what's on his laptop. Austin complained before that he worked too many hours; it must be worse without him there."

Cassandra's relaxed state had quickly dissolved upon returning to her office from Bryan Hall. Lance and Meg had been waiting for her, their eyes bright with anticipation. Cassandra's administrator radar immediately raised a red flag. "Wait . . . how do you know there's more on Austin's laptop? What else did you find?"

Lance held up a playing card sized portable hard drive and Meg interpreted. "I may or may not have copied Austin's laptop files onto this hard drive before I turned it over to the police."

Cassandra put on her stern face. "You did WHAT? Oh man, you're going to get us all in trouble, aren't you?"

Remembering the work-study eavesdroppers, Cassandra closed her office door for privacy. Meg grinned, "Wouldn't be the first time..." Cassandra's arms crossed and she stood near the window. Meg pointed to Lance while she spoke and signed. "What's the worst that can happen? He's a kid. Kids do stupid things for their friends." Turning to Lance, Meg asked, "What did you see on the hard drive?"

Cassandra's voice rose into the hysterical range. "Meg! You're forgetting *we* are the adults. You're a mom! This is not like that time we drank too much and you puked on the Waikiki sidewalk next to the motorcycle cop. I can't afford to screw up here. Don't you get that?"

Lance smiled at the puking story then signed, "I'm sorry, Dr. Sato. You're right. I don't want to get you in trouble. I'll keep your name out of this. I'm going to talk to Luke Peterson to see about taking Austin's place at the lab. I need to know what Austin was doing there."

Meg was already all-in. When she was supporting one of her students, she was single-minded in her loyalty. Cassandra had an entire student body to consider. "What did you see on his laptop that the police and campus security missed?"

Lance hesitated. "You sure you want to know what I found?"

Curiosity and eagerness to find answers kept tugging at Cassandra, like an undertow pulls a surfer away from the safe shore. Her mouth formed a grim line. "What did you find, Lance?"

He handed over a paper which Cassandra read while Meg interpreted his explanation. "An email to Austin with a recommendation letter for an internship at AlphaBioGlobal from Dr. Schneider."

Meg stopped interpreting and asked, "The plasma center guy?"

Cassandra confirmed, "He's the only Schneider I know."

"Schneider says in the email that he will personally speak to the CEO in Lincoln at ABG. Guy's name is Aram Baral," reported Lance.

Cassandra was unmoved. "What's weird about that? Austin worked at the lab. Dr. Schneider put in a word for him at a summer internship. Connections are how you get those good jobs."

Meg countered, "At The Home Team the other day, didn't Dr. Schneider say he hardly knew Austin Price? Here, he wrote him a glowing letter. More proof that they knew each other well."

One recommendation letter wasn't convincing. Cassandra's head shook. "Ok, so they knew each other. That doesn't prove anything sinister happened. Why do you want to work in the lab, Lance?"

Lance signed, "There's work notes on the hard drive too. Like weights and measurements. Stuff that should be on the office computers, not his personal laptop."

That indicated sloppiness, nothing more. "Maybe he brought the log home and uploaded the data to SharePoint remotely?"

Lance answered, "I never saw him do work from our room. Why would he when the lab was only five minutes from our house?" They both looked at her expectantly like children asking for a puppy.

They should leave the investigating to the professionals. "This is a horrible idea. We shouldn't be interfering."

Lance proposed, "Ok, then don't tell anyone. Let's keep it between the three of us. I'll go over this afternoon and apply. If I get accepted, I'll snoop around more plus help them finish up the research study. If nothing's wrong, I'll make a few extra bucks. If I see something suspicious, I'll tell you and you can tell the sheriff. Deal?" He held out a hand waiting for her to agree.

She felt like a mother who knew her child was making a mistake, but the only way for him to learn was by experience. As long as no one else got hurt, she reminded herself. "Deal."

They shook on it. Cassandra held up a hand like a stop sign. "BUT I reserve the right to text you to back off if I think it's not safe or productive. Understand?"

Lance and Meg quickly agreed. "Understand!"

Chapter Twenty-Five

"The state patrol has combed through Price's laptop since Lance Erickson gave us the passwords. I still think it's odd that he 'found it' in their bedroom at the fraternity. Hidden under the mattress of Austin's bed." Andy Summers' voice was skeptical as he stared pointedly at Cassandra, Fischer, and Bergstrom.

Cassandra's cheeks flushed while she mixed together salad ingredients she'd brought from home. After the status meeting, she'd drive south 45 minutes to Lincoln for her first consortium meeting with her counterparts from the Eastern Nebraska Private Colleges Association (ENePCA). She looked forward to meeting professionals she'd corresponded with since her August hire date, but was leery of leaving campus at a critical time.

Fischer avoided eye contact with her and busied himself with opening a potato chip bag to accompany his sub sandwich. Cassandra had requested Professor Bergstrom join the trio to ensure the college was doing everything necessary. He also remained hunched over the conference table quietly chewing his lunch.

When no one commented on the circumstances surrounding the 'found' laptop, Summers continued, "Isn't it interesting that his laptop turned up, but not his phone?"

Again, no response from the group. Fischer said, "After five days of investigating, they don't even know whether Austin injected himself on purpose before he fell down the stairs. Maybe you should call in more state patrol people to get this ball moving."

Caught unprepared, Cassandra's eyes widened. "Do you think the sheriff's office isn't doing enough?"

Bergstrom paused mid-bite of leftover fried chicken he'd been eating from a plastic takeout container. He wiped his mouth with a napkin. "You're reading the big city newspapers too much. They just want to blame someone and splash our name around to sell papers. The articles contend the campus is full of gossip, innuendo, and terrified students instead of a medical incident."

She agreed with Bergstrom. This wasn't a one-hour detective show where they figured it all out in a neat little package deal. Besides so far, it'd been her name mentioned most often in the paper, even though she hadn't given an official statement. Talking to reporters made her forehead so sweaty her makeup felt like it dripped down her temples, along her neck, and into her shirt collar.

Summers shook his head. "We're working closely with the sheriff and patrol. I think our problem is people aren't being completely truthful."

Fischer's normally controlled energy became tense. His lips flattened and a cheek muscle beat a little pulse along his jaw. "The problem is that some people are more worried about kissing up to alumni than finding out what happened to our student."

Cassandra didn't have time for bickering. "Let's give them a few more days to get the test results back and focus on our Homecoming events." Nielson had been crystal clear about that.

Summers referred to his notes. "Main thing is, more was going on than a lab accident. Either Price hid his phone or someone else has it. We know he was paid, but no idea for what. His death could relate to his work in the lab, the enzymes themselves, or the money. Until we know otherwise, we increase security this week. Especially with the large numbers for homecoming events."

Fischer's frustration dissolved and his shoulders straightened into military mode, ready to take orders. "We can send over some housing and maintenance staff in Morton jackets to the Student/Staff Volleyball game, the parade and carnival, and the bonfire. Just let me know where and when... Hey, normally we don't check bags at the football games, do we?"

Summers flipped through the small notepad he always carried and nodded at Fischer like they were having a private briefing. "Not normally. With only a few hundred-people attending, it's usually a non-issue."

They weren't usually all in one room together. Cassandra's eyes bounced back and forth between Summers and Fischer. Their looks were light and dark, heavier and thinner, farm and city, but both had that all-business vibe going when there was a critical goal in front of them.

Cassandra's brain snapped into focus at the sound of Bergstrom saying her name. "Dr. Sato, I'd advise some generic security announcements on the website for this week." He slowly stood up and gathered his trash.

Her watch said that she'd barely enough time to pack up and get to the consortium meeting, provided she didn't get lost in Lincoln. "Yes, we can use the website to let people know that we'll be strictly enforcing the rules and checking bags. Anything else, gentlemen?"

Summers rose and came closer to speak privately to her, while Fischer and Bergstrom walked to the hallway together. Andy was irritated. "You didn't look surprised by my update. Did Lance really find that laptop under Austin's mattress?"

She hated lying straight to his face. She wasn't good at it, either. Her palms sweat, and her voice wavered. "If that's where he told you it was, then I can't tell you anything different."

Andy's eyes were hurt and his tone unusually harsh. "So you won't tell me the truth? Maybe they were in it together. How do we know Lance doesn't have Price's phone, too? What if this is some Deaf Community thing? Ask yourself if you're helping this investigation, or wasting my time."

The anger in his voice stung. "I'm telling you everything I can think of that will help." Cassandra's first loyalty would always be the students. Summers was a grown man who could fend for himself. They'd become friends and she regretted messing that up, but she wouldn't change her stance on supporting her students.

Summers' brisk steps carried him the opposite direction down the hall from where Bergstrom and Fischer waited. Bergstrom said, "see you later," and followed Summers more slowly.

Fischer silently accompanied Cassandra back to the main office door. They hesitated a moment too long, as though he was dropping her off after an awkward first date. She searched for something simple and non-committal to say before he left, but her thoughts were interrupted.

Bridget had replaced Devon at the front desk, while Rachel made copies. "Dr. Sato, the health clinic nurse just called because three students checked in today with flu-like symptoms. They thought you'd want to warn others to be careful to wash their hands and prevent the virus from spreading."

All awkward date thoughts aside, Cassandra turned to Fischer. "Now the flu? Don't we have enough to worry about already? I guess it will be easy enough to add that to the media department's website announcements."

He shook his head. "We can't seem to catch a break this week, huh?" Those clear blue eyes held hers for a few beats. "You know Summers has it bad for you, right? You can tell that, can't you?"

Fischer's directness surprised her. Was it that obvious? Sure, she had wondered what Andy's intentions were, but she'd hoped it was friendship. He was so nice to her; a genuinely good guy.

She'd always been slow to realize when men were interested in her romantically. Previously guys had asked her to dinner, a play, or event and she misunderstood thinking it was either work-related or a platonic invitation. Because Cassandra focused on work most of the day, she assumed everyone else did too.

Her strict no-dating at work policy had served her well so far by allowing her an easy excuse to numerous men. Including the super-creepy married Vice Chancellor who once tried to scam a weekend at a San Diego resort alone with her—by faking a board meeting for a national association. Before him, subtlety, distraction, and coldness had always worked. However, when Super Creep stole a kiss and groped her in her office, she dropped all subtlety. She told him if he said one more word about them doing anything but reviewing student files together, she'd take his arm and accompany him upstairs to the EEOC office to file a harassment claim with him standing right there. He finally got the message, and then tried to make her feel like she had led him on. In what language did, "Good Morning, Vice Chancellor" equate to flirtation? Idiot.

She considered Fischer's question. When she was near Andy Summers, she felt brotherly camaraderie, no sparks or flames. Not quite what she felt when Fischer stood close and spoke to her in his deep, careful voice. She tried to ignore the fluttering in her stomach. She needed to leave for Lincoln, instead of feeling frozen to this spot in the doorway deciding whether to deny it all or not.

"Uh, um..." she stammered, "Andy's been very nice and helpful since I started working here in August... I can use all the friends I can get right now." Lame. That was such a lame thing to say. Ugh.

Fischer nodded once. "Your call. Lotta guys mistake friendliness for encouragement. Talk to you later." Before she could even think of a reply, he'd already left.

She did a mental head shake to get her scrambled brain back to business and marched into her office. Not before she heard Rachel's voice behind her, "Oh, I think someone else has it bad for you, too. And it isn't Officer Summers."

Bridget had laughed and said, "If you don't want him, he's not too old for me, is he?"

She poked her head back out of her inner office. "Really, ladies? I don't have time for this."

Bridget held up a finger and drew a little zig zag in the air. "I'd make time for him. That man is fine."

Cassandra stuffed the meeting documents, her journal, and water into her tote bag. Behind the door she grabbed her coat, wondering whether it would be colder in Lincoln. She might have to hike a few blocks from the parking lot to her meeting.

Halfway to her car, she stopped abruptly. Wait a minute. Was Rachel right? If Fischer was warning her about Summers, did Fischer see him as a rival? Could he possibly like her? She hurried forward again. Maybe she'd have some quiet time on the car ride.

Chapter Twenty-Six

Meg chattered while Cassandra steered the college's Toyota Prius down the highway past rolling cornfields. "It was easy for Lance to get the job in the research lab! He offered to take Austin's place because he knew the study ended in only a few weeks. At first Peterson was reluctant, but when he found out Lance is a computer science major, he put him in charge of entering the numbers from the log books into the database. Apparently, there's a backlog."

So much for quiet thinking time on the drive to Lincoln. Cassandra loved Meg, but really could've used a couple hours for a mental break. Meg had met Cassandra near the parking lot wearing her I've-got-a-great-idea-and-you're-going-to-love-it smile. "Lucky my afternoon class was canceled! After your meeting, we can hit the mall and shop for warmer clothes. Perfect timing!"

Cassandra wore another Ann Taylor power skirt suit ensemble today, this one in a tan color with a magenta shell peeking out from her lapels. Taupe pumps with gold buckles completed the outfit. The top of her hair was clipped up in back and she'd remembered to bring colored lip gloss to apply before the meeting. The only part of her that wasn't fancy was her fingernails. She didn't have time to manicure them herself, and she wouldn't have paid someone to do it for her. The suit fabric was medium weight wool, and she was comfortably warm in the 65 degree partly cloudy weather.

Meg held up a dog-eared copy of *My Antonia*. "I'll read this Willa Cather novel from one of my English classes while you're in the meeting. Oh . . . one problem: malls here are tiny compared to Ala Moana in Honolulu and not a Gucci or Tiffany's in a four-state area. But you'll find some sweaters and warm boots."

Cassandra didn't want to admit it to Meg, but part of her was glad she'd have a co-pilot to navigate around Lincoln. She'd been there twice, but not enough to know her way around. "As long as we're home pretty early. I need to get some sleep tonight. So . . . when does Lance start the job?"

"Luke Peterson must've been desperate for help. He let Lance start right after a short tour of the lab (which smelled like nasty disinfectant.) Where they keep the food, how to set up the water, and clean the cages. I almost gagged . . . Luke gave him the computer login and password information and a short orientation to the notebooks and database. Lance picked it up quickly. Guess who interrupted our training time, though?"

Cassandra hated playing 20 questions or those stupid guessing games. She shrugged. Just say it, already.

Meg continued, "Deputy Tate, that strapping farm boy who came in and questioned Luke. I couldn't help overhearing them while Lance was going through an online database tutorial thing. He asked general stuff like, 'how concentrated is the enzyme they give to the rats, had he noticed any negative side effects, when will the study be completed' . . . that type of thing."

Cassandra chuckled at Meg when she said "couldn't help overhearing them." Right. Meg's ears would be tuned into anything related to this investigation. "Interesting. They'd already asked him those questions when I was there with Andy and Deputy Tate the first time. So . . . he seemed concerned about the enzyme itself and its side effects?"

"That's what I thought at first, too, but then Tate changed direction and asked Luke 'when are they planning another trial using the synthetic enzyme?' Luke didn't give a firm date, but said six months at the earliest. Tate asked how much Austin was paid, and if there were other medications in the lab that Austin could've sold on the side. Luke got kind of defensive then. Next Tate asked, 'Were you asking him to do extra tasks and paying him on the side?' You should've seen the look on his face!"

When Cassandra glanced over, Meg was making an appalled expression with big eyes. "So Luke answers, 'I'm not doing anything wrong. I'm just following the research protocol. You're welcome to look at anything. I've nothing to hide.' That convinced him to back off."

Cassandra guessed, "They must be suspicious about the enzyme or those money transfers that Lance found in Austin's laptop. He won a small prize for the blood drive coordination, but no one knows where the extra $600 came from, yet."

Meg continued, "After he finished grilling Luke, Tate noticed Lance quietly working on his database tutorial and interrupted him. Good thing I was there, right? ... Then, Tate asked Lance if he'd found anything in his fraternity room that belonged to Austin."

The two-lane highway went straight South to Lincoln, and at midday there wasn't much traffic. Cassandra easily paid attention to both the road and Meg's story. "Lance said, 'No, between his parents and you, Austin's backpack, books, clothes ... everything is gone—except our video phone.'"

Cassandra remembered the phone in their bedroom like the one in Meg's office. Meg's story got faster as she got more excited. "This is totally between you and me, right? You can never say you got this from me. Tate started to leave the room then turned around and said, 'How does that video thing work? Does it have memory like a cell phone?' and Lance said, 'Well ... there's a call history saved on there. But we both used it, so I don't know if you'll find anything helpful on it.' Then Lance goes, 'You could take it and check the phone numbers and messages ... I don't have time to do it between school and this new job.'"

Meg said, "So Tate looked concerned and said, 'Is it safe for you to work here, Lance?' ... Then Luke kinda looked over at them funny. Lance's eyebrows went up like he's thinking, 'Oh great. You, too?' But then Luke defended Lance and said, 'He's a quick learner, and I could really use his help to finish my research this month.'"

Cassandra knew enough from being around Meg to know that deaf people can do nearly anything they want to do. And safety isn't an issue when your visual skills are more acute than the average person who can hear. "What is with these people?"

Meg wasn't done. "Wait! So after Tate left, Luke called someone and scooted into the storage room around the corner to talk privately. Of course, I inched over to that wall where he couldn't see me and listened while Lance kept working."

Cassandra didn't know whether to admire her friend's bravery or smack her across the shoulder for nosiness. Admiration won. "You didn't!!"

"I think I heard Luke say, 'The deputy came back and asked me more questions. I don't know what they're worried about . . . I'm starting to feel like this place is bad luck . . . If I hurry up everything, I could finish all the tests by end of next week . . . I'll try to . . . yes, I know we need to finish this.'"

So many things had happened in just a couple of hours. Cassandra had a lot more to think about now. "I wonder who he called?"

They sat silently for a couple of minutes until Cassandra said, "I wish I knew more about biology. My undergrad degree was in Secondary Education for history."

They hit the northern outskirts of Lincoln, where there were more houses and traffic when Cassandra's phone beeped with a text notification. She handed it to Meg to read for her.

"It's from Marcus Fischer." Meg teased, "Are you sure I should read it? What if it's personal?"

Cassandra rolled her eyes. "C'mon. Please. Just. Stop." Although there was one little part of her heart that made a teeny leap . . . Her brain overrode that thought. "What does it say? I hope nothing happened at Morton."

Meg read, "I'm calling a halt to the farmer's beef served in the cafeterias. Want to check on kids with flu at health clinic. Better safe than sorry."

Cassandra dictated a reply: "Could just be a virus. But safe is fine with me too."

Marcus replied immediately: "Summers arranged for extra off-duty deputies on campus."

Cassandra nodded, "Tell him 'ok, thanks for letting me know.'"

Meg smiled while her thumbs worked the screen. "I'll add a couple of kissy face emojis for you."

Cassandra didn't blink. "And then I'll break your thumbs."

Chapter Twenty-Seven

Meg's head was wedged between the reclined seat and the car door when Cassandra returned to the parking lot two hours later. Eyes closed, her mouth hung slightly open with drool on her chin, and she snored softly. Cassandra stood there for a few seconds smiling, then whipped out her phone to snap a picture. Never knew when she'd need an embarrassing photo of Meg.

A few minutes later, on the way to the shopping mall, they passed an office park to the south. On one three-story building, AlphaBioGlobal Inc. was emblazoned in huge white letters. In an uncharacteristically spontaneous move, Cassandra whipped the Prius into the next available turn and doubled back to the parking lot in front of the building. Meg's head swiveled around, and she looked puzzled for several moments after the car had stopped. "Oh . . . This must be the home office for the plasma center in Carson, huh?"

"Must be," Cassandra confirmed and checked her watch. "It's only 3:50. Remember that email recommendation letter on Austin's laptop for a summer internship here?

Since we're so close, we should check it out. Maybe I could talk to a recruiter. Find out more about the internship and what types of students they want next summer. I'd be able to network better if I'd met them in person, right? It shouldn't take very long. Ok?"

Meg nodded approval, "Good thinking, kiddo. You could take credit for building a partnership with a global pharmaceutical company. The administration will love it. Let's see who we can meet. Do you remember the guy's name on that internship letter?"

Cassandra was already thumbing through her phone; she'd sent herself a copy of the letter Lance had given them.

Twenty minutes later they were wearing visitors' badges and had talked their way past the front desk sentry by giving their official job titles and mentioning they'd like a tour for potential internships from Morton College. They'd met an HR department lackey who had shown them some conference rooms, generic offices, the Wellness center gym, and handed them several glossy brochures about the wonders of modern medicine produced by AlphaBioGlobal Pharmaceuticals. They'd also heard what a great place it was to work with state-of-the-art facilities, on-site day care, and the employee cafeteria.

After mentioning Dr. Aram Baral's name several times, they found themselves waiting in his empty office. Lined in opaque glass, it was sleek and sterile. The only personalizations were his framed diplomas hanging on the one real wall: Masters in Public Health from Creighton University and his MD from Johns Hopkins. Otherwise the desk, bookcase and modern gray molded seating looked like something from thirty years in the future. Finally he appeared, hurried yet friendly and shook their hands. "Dr. Sato, Ms. O'Brien, good to meet you. Sorry to keep you waiting. Thank you for stopping by today. How can I help you?"

Cassandra pegged the CEO at 60-ish years old. Dressed in a light gray linen suit with a narrow pink tie, he exuded money and power. His dark hair and eyes could place him in any of several races or cultures, but his name and short dark beard suggested Indian heritage. "Thank you for seeing us, Dr. Baral. I appreciate your time and apologize for dropping by unannounced. Morton College is always looking to optimize our students' opportunities in the surrounding communities. We'd like to explore ways we can work with your company to give our students more hands-on experience in the biomedical fields. I understand that you offered a summer internship to one of our students, Austin Price."

Baral's face blanked a moment, searching for a memory. "Austin Price . . . Morton College . . . The one who just died? I did read about that boy's tragic story in the newspaper. Too young. I'm sorry for your school's loss."

Cassandra acknowledged, "Thank you. It has been a long week. Since you'd been counting on him to work here next summer, and I happened to be in town for another meeting, I thought this might be a good time to stop by and offer Morton's help. We'd like to suggest another student to fill Austin's summer internship, as well as learn what types of skills you need for future internships. We'd like ABG to feel confident in recruiting our highly qualified students and graduates."

A slight frown crossed his face. "Internship? Here . . . are you certain?" he said slowly. "Oh . . . that internship. Yes, it was in the very beginning negotiations stage." His head cocked a bit to the side. "How exactly did you learn about the internship, Dr. Sato? From Arnie Schneider, up in Carson?"

Cassandra realized she had overstated, but didn't know how to backpedal. She ad-libbed, "No, I don't think he told me himself. I must've heard someone else talking about it. However, Dr. Schneider did mention to me that he'd like to partner with the college to develop more internships."

Baral's frown lingered a second, but he quickly recovered his good humor. "Certainly. We'd be happy to take on a few students next summer in our testing or research labs. Of course, they'll be doing mostly boring microbiology and lab assistant type positions, but it'll expose them to the environment here. Everyone has to pay their dues."

She had nearly blabbed about Austin's letter. A little zip of relief buzzed Cassandra's spine. "I can have our career services contact ABG to set up applications and interviews so you can choose from our top students. Thanks for your time, Dr. Baral. I appreciate you seeing us unannounced."

He shook their hands. "It was pleasant to meet you both. Have a safe trip back to Carson. Thanks for stopping by."

Back in the car, Meg spoke up, "That went pretty well. Although it seemed like that internship for Austin Price wasn't a done deal yet."

Relief gave way to excitement that she'd pulled off two successful meetings in one afternoon. "Yes, I got the same feeling. Oh well. At least we met him and now he has faces to match our names. He'll know where to find us next time he comes to Carson. He seemed open to the idea of increasing our internships."

"Definitely worth our time. Glad you took that little detour . . . And now, if you turn onto Pine Lake Road and drive a few blocks, we should be at the mall. I'm feeling lucky. We're going to find you some good deals!"

Ten pairs of jeans later, Cassandra's shopping patience was near its end. Most were too big or too long. Finally, she found one pair that suited her tiny frame—not super skinny, but a flattering fit in a dark wash. When she came out to model them in front of the mirrors, Meg exclaimed, "You look hot!"

Thirty minutes later they'd found more jeans, shirts, a heavy scarf and gloves, and had crossed the mall's courtyard on the way to the parking lot. Cassandra was puzzled. "Who builds an outdoor mall in Nebraska? Totally impractical. In Hawai'i, the malls are open air and filled with gorgeous tropical plants. Why would anyone willingly walk in and out of shops in the freezing cold of winter?"

Meg shrugged. "I never come to this one in the winter. I go to the indoor mall from December to February. Of course, then you have to fight the senior citizen mall-walking enthusiasts."

"That's a thing?"

"Just wait. You'll see."

They'd driven through Runza for dinner on the way home. Cassandra hadn't realized those breaded meat buns Nielson had served her in his office actually formed the central concept for a very popular restaurant chain. She skipped the cabbage and ordered a Swiss mushroom burger and Frings—an ingenious combination of French fries and onion rings. She'd earned the extra grease. Once they were back on the road, Cassandra recounted for Meg the moment after the meeting earlier with Fischer. "Seemed like Fischer was warning me that Summers wants to date me. At the same time, he practically accused me of leading Andy Summers on."

Meg said, "Duh. I told you so. It's obvious to anyone with eyes, Cass. It might be the wrong timing, but he's interested for sure. They both are, if you ask me."

Dating multiple men was not in the plan right now. "I don't have time for that."

On the way home, Bergstrom called. She was tempted to let it go to voicemail since it was after work hours. Her guilt got the better of her, and she answered on speaker phone so Meg could hear. He said, "Cassandra. I'm glad I caught you. The board members are concerned about the negative publicity regarding the lab and the college."

Even Meg didn't know the full extent of her tenuous position. Cassandra glanced at Meg while Bergstrom warned, "This situation is volatile. We need to reach out to our allies. Remind them that student success is our priority. Do you have time tomorrow to make some calls to board members? You need to assure them you're doing what Nielson wanted."

When she hung up a few minutes later, Meg said, "It's a good thing you have Bergstrom's support. Geesh! I just show up, do my job, and go home. Your whole academic politics rigmarole is stressful! You can keep your lofty Vice President title. I don't need that."

She had a point, agreed Cassandra. Unless that "Vice President title" was a step along your life plan. Then the politics were just another skill she needed to master to reach her end goal.

Chapter Twenty-Eight

By the time Meg dropped Cassandra at home Wednesday night, temperatures had dipped into the lower fifties; the wind had picked up to 23 mph, scraping the high branches of the back yard's large oak tree against the windows and side of the house. The first few times it'd happened she had been startled; by now she recognized the noise and didn't jump at every scratch. Hearing the wind blowing against the walls made her feel chilled. She left her shoes in the front entry and padded over to the thermostat in the hallway. She cranked it up to 74, carried her packages into the bedroom, and carefully unpacked the dress shirts neatly wrapped in white tissue paper, putting everything away.

Comfortably dressed in sweats and a long-sleeved shirt, she opened a bottle of Cabernet from the pantry and savored the wine's smooth earthy taste. Since Friday afternoon, she'd been worried some outlandish science conspiracy was endangering students. Getting away for a four-hour mini-vacation with Meg had felt relaxing and normal. Cassandra had even enjoyed trying on clothes, although she'd never admit that to Meg. On the way home, they'd turned up the radio and sang along to a couple of pop songs, chatted about her brother's family, and her mom's Mahjong club.

Always multitasking, she went down to the laundry chute opening in the basement and threw a load into the washer. That laundry chute in the hallway outside her bedroom door was the coolest feature of living in a 1920s house. She'd never seen one until Meg had demonstrated by opening the little door, throwing a towel down and then guiding her to the basement to see the towel sitting in a heap only steps from the washing machine!

Setting her wine glass on the living room end table, Cassandra relaxed into the plush gray sofa. Admiring the dark wood floors, antique doors and white brick fireplace, she appreciated the house's cozy and comfortable vibe. Maybe Nielson was right, and she should make more of an effort to invite people over for dinner parties. She served as adviser on a few masters and PhD students' committees. Maybe she should plan small student group meetings in her home. Perhaps if she were to decide when and how often people were invited, she might be more open to sharing her private sanctuary. She added it to her mental to do list after the president returned from his trip.

She'd made it through ten minutes of a Season 2 rerun of The Office, half-watching/half planning Thursday's tasks, when she focused on her wine glass sitting on the simple black end table. Something was different in the room, but she couldn't say what it was exactly. She shrugged and watched the rest of the show where Jim finally admits to Pam that he loves her.

The washing machine beeped to signal the cycle was finished. When she stood up to move it to the dryer, she grabbed her empty glass to return to the kitchen. Again, she paused and looked around the room. Really looked. What was different?

Several minutes later when she closed the dryer and pressed start, it occurred to her what was different. She ran upstairs to the main floor and rushed into the living room. Not there. Went back to her bedroom and into the bathroom. Peeked behind the shower curtain. *That's so weird!*

She didn't remember moving her Plumeria plant. Sometimes she brought it into the bathroom for water or to wipe off the leaves, but it wasn't in there. She turned on all the lights and stood in the middle of the living room looking high and low. Three steps to the small sun room area in the very front with its wicker furniture and built-in bookshelves. Honestly, she should probably move the Plumeria in there because it would get more light during the winter.

Opening the front door and turning on the porch light, she took a few steps out and looked around. Nothing. She closed and locked it up then went through to the back door

Yanking it open, she flipped the light switches and froze in the open doorway.

Illuminated by the bright spotlight over the detached garage was a black stain. Lots of smaller black chunks clung to the garage door. Her brain finally caught up to her eyes and allowed her legs to move a few feet into the middle of the driveway. Under the splattered soil was a small lump of broken red pottery and soil with a foot-high plant tipped over. Some of the tender branches were snapped off and a broken yellow flower wilted atop the mound. A small scream escaped her lips. Her hands flew up to cover her mouth, and her stomach dropped like an airplane during turbulence. Finally her legs worked again, and she ran inside the back door.

What else did they touch? What else did they break? She raced up the spiral staircase to the second floor's seldom-used two bedrooms. Her heart pounded from the running mixed with growing fear. Flipping the lights, she darted from room to room. The simple guest bedroom with its white queen bed, end table, and small reading chair were untouched. The extra room was empty save a few full boxes she hadn't gotten around to unpacking yet. She tugged at the cardboard to peek inside, but nothing had been moved. Standing, she put her hands on her hips while her breath came in short gasps.

Slowly, carefully, she descended the spiral steps, wondering if each turn would bring her face to face with an intruder. How long had she been inside? The initial adrenaline wore off, and tears flowed down her cheeks as she absorbed that someone had broken into her house and smashed her plant. She grabbed her phone from the bedside table and called Andy Summers, because she knew he lived near campus too. Did they even have 911 out in the middle of nowhere?

When Andy pulled up a few minutes later wearing jeans and a Packers sweatshirt, she was on the back step huddled into a sobbing, shivering ball. He crouched down beside her and put an arm gently around her back. "Cassandra, are you hurt? I see the broken plant. Is anyone else inside your house?" She opened her eyes, and his concerned face was very close. "I couldn't really hear you over the phone. Are you ok?"

She took a deep breath and wiped her eyes and nose on her shirt sleeve. The first time she tried to speak, her voice got stuck on the lump in her throat. Finally she got herself together. "I'm not hurt, Andy."

Although she wasn't physically hurt, her stomach ached. Words came tumbling out in a nonstop torrent. "I don't think anyone is still in the house. I looked in all the rooms already. I don't know when this happened. I was gone all day until about 7:30 tonight."

She stood on wobbly legs and led him inside where he checked the rooms again. Under the kitchen sink, he retrieved a garbage bag and carefully collected the plant, pot and dirt from her driveway. Back in her kitchen, he washed his hands in the sink. "I'll write a report on your break-in. I'll take this plant to the sheriff's office for evidence."

She stood stiffly against the counter, the arms of her sweatshirt pulled down over her fists. "Do you think this has something to do with Halloween? Someone smashed a pumpkin against the house a few days ago, but I just assumed it was kid stuff. This is crazy. Someone was inside my house. I don't think I left the door unlocked, but I guess it's possible."

Giving her a gentle brotherly hug, Andy shrugged slightly. "I'm just glad you weren't hurt. None of your electronics or valuables were stolen; luckily it was just a plant. I'll talk to Sheriff Hart tomorrow, and see if he wants to ask you more questions. Are you ok to stay alone tonight?"

After another big breath, she managed a weak smile. "I'm fine. I appreciate your help."

She watched him drive off, then double locked the doors and tested every window to ensure they were locked tight, too. She slipped into her darkened bedroom and curled into the corner armchair, the moonlight from the window casting a soft light across her legs. Reaching over into the bedside table drawer, she pulled out a framed 5x7 photo of her with a dark haired young man wearing a green and white aloha shirt; her, a modern royal blue fitted muumuu. A long green ti leaf lei was draped around his neck, while Cassandra wore a shorter version intertwined with white orchids. The photographer had caught them both mid-laugh, mouths partially open, eyes shining with happiness on the evening they had celebrated their engagement. Soul mates forever. She rested her pony-tailed head against the side of the chair and closed her eyes, not bothering to wipe the wetness from her cheeks. Tucking the frame against her chest, she eventually fell into a fitful sleep.

Chapter Twenty-Nine

Cassandra hustled into the office at 7:15 a.m.—late by her standards—to the sound of a ringing phone. No one else was there, so she automatically picked up the handset. "Student Affairs office, Cassandra Sato speaking." Dropping her large tote bag on the floor, she massaged her aching back from dozing in the armchair half the night.

A friendly male voice was chipper despite the early hour. "Just the person I wanted to reach! This is Derek Swanson from the Omaha Daily News. We spoke a few days ago. Listen, I noticed that there was a break-in last night reported at your personal residence. Is that correct?"

The chill that settled on her was worse than waking in bed earlier, her legs tangled in a fleece blanket, frozen toes exposed to the cold morning air. Stuttering noises came out of her mouth while she marshaled a response. Cassandra had heard of news traveling fast in small towns, but Swanson's awareness of overnight police reports was unsettling. Thinking as quickly as possible she replied, "Just some vandalism. A broken plant. No need to worry, Mr. Swanson."

Andy wouldn't have leaked it, so the reporter must have a source in the sheriff's office. Swanson started to ask more, but Cassandra said, "I'm late to a meeting," and hung up.

Cassandra planned to use the euphemistic "meeting" excuse all morning to carve out time for the many unchecked task boxes in her daily journal. Starting right after she downed an ocean's worth of strong Kona coffee. A sharp stabbing in her temple reminded her she hadn't eaten or drank since the night before, and she rummaged in the top desk drawer until she found ibuprofen. The week's constant interruptions were frustrating, and she felt control slipping away.

A couple hours and 400 mg of caffeine later, Cassandra was feeling much better. She'd met with Media Relations staff in person to avoid any misunderstanding over wording for the website updates. The threatened headache had subsided to a dull fogginess. Next, she needed to follow up on the sick students at the health clinic. When Marcus Fischer had contacted her yesterday about putting a hold on the cafeterias serving the beef with the feed additive, she hadn't asked why. The early morning ambush from Derek Swanson had reminded her the college's image was at stake in addition to student safety.

She texted Fischer mid-morning. "Call me please when you have time. Not emergency."

Two minutes later her cell buzzed. "Good morning, Marcus. Mahalo for calling me back."

His deep voice was quickly becoming familiar, although the slight stomach butterflies she felt were brushed off.

Fischer said, "Hello boss, what can I do for you?" The way he drew out the word "boss" was like an endearment.

She shook her head to clear the fanciful thoughts. "Can you tell me more about your decision to stop serving the Hopkin's farm beef at our campus food service sites? Is something wrong with the feed additive?"

"The health clinic told me the students who checked in yesterday tested negative for influenza. Of course they might have another stomach virus; we wouldn't know that until more students get the same symptoms . . . or we'd have to do testing."

No one wanted a health clinic full of sick students. "I understand your caution."

Fischer said, "We know Price had elevated levels of the enzyme in his blood. I'm aware of no evidence that someone else in the lab pushed him down the stairs or hurt him. So what caused his death? I just don't buy the falling part. If there's any chance that enzyme is involved, we should quit serving the beef. I suggest collecting food service samples, the sick students' blood samples, and syringes from the biology lab, and send them to an independent company for analysis."

Imagining the newspaper headlines, Cassandra said, "Let's not jump to conclusions where we have no evidence. In a few days, we'll know more about this virus. We'll stop serving the beef, but let's not do outside tests at this point."

He paused so long, she wondered if the connection had been lost. "It's your call. Let me know if you change your mind." The phone line clicked off.

Disagreeing with coworkers gave her anxiety, but she had a job to do. Being the boss wasn't easy.

* * *

When Cassandra finally got a breather at lunch time, she removed her shoes, sank into the couch, and caught up on emails. Hours had passed without broken office machinery or social media snafus with the students. Feeling content, she added Sesame Vinaigrette she stored in the mini-fridge to the cabbage, chicken, roasted veggies, and rice mixture she'd brought from home.

For the second time in as many days, Lance knocked on her office door with Meg in tow. Cassandra glared at Meg, who gave her an "I don't know what he's going to say" look back.

Lance signed, "I worked in the lab this morning and snooped around for Austin's phone or anything else weird. In the storage room, I saw maybe 20 syringes in an Igloo cooler. The rest were in the large lab fridge. I asked one of the other grad assistants, but she said they weren't hers. When I asked Peterson what to do with them, they weren't for his project either."

Either Lance had great instincts or he was masterful at covering his own deceptions. Cassandra had never known him to be dishonest, so she chose to believe him. "This is probably going to get me fired, but we need to call Andy."

When she had summarized how Lance had saved a copy of Austin's hard drive which contained a recommendation letter, had begun working in Luke Peterson's lab, and had found a cooler full of syringes that the police had previously missed, Andy replied, "Yeah . . . I'll call Tate. We'll go check it out."

He didn't sound mad exactly but Cassandra still winced. "Should we meet you over there so Lance can show you where he found them?"

Andy articulated his words very clearly. "No. You all have done quite enough. Stay away from the lab unless we tell you differently." He hung up.

Cassandra frowned at her phone. Geesh. Meg tried for a laugh, "After all we've done to help, he's not even grateful?"

Cassandra said, "I knew this would somehow backfire. Even when we do something good, it's bad."

As Meg was leaving the office she said, "Let's meet at The Home Team after work tonight."

Cassandra wasn't much of a drinker usually, but after the past couple of days a large margarita sounded appealing. She resumed her seat on the couch, eating salad while triaging emails on her tablet. Andy was right to be mad. They'd all hidden information from him. Although their karmic intentions had been positive, Cassandra suspected she'd reap the results of these actions for a long time.

Gary Nielson's name amid the list of unread emails made her cringe. Putting her salad on the table, she sat up straight and opened the message from Hangzhou.

Nielson wrote: "Cassandra, our trip has been successful. Planning to announce a new partnership agreement upon my return. FYI, Schneider has been fielding complaints from donors and faculty. The Omaha article was in my inbox this morning. I would have increased security just as you've done, but my hands are tied here. Someone is bad-mouthing you, telling them your incompetence as a leader is going to lose us the science grant. That can't happen. I know you can see this through. Stay on the sheriff to get answers. Play nice with Schneider. Listen, I've known him since we were high schoolers battling it out on the football field. He's gritty and tough. If Schneider believes he's helping the college, he won't back down. It would be worse if another student were to get hurt."

That last line sent a chill down her spine. Of course she didn't want anyone else to get hurt! That was the reason for the security, stopping the beef use, and investigating the lab. What else did these people think she should be doing? She hadn't even had time to tell anyone about the break-in at her house. Nielson was worried about the NIH grant? That was the least of her current worries.

* * *

Upon returning from the Graduate Faculty Council meeting, Cassandra was on the couch critiquing one of her thesis student's proposals. Her shoes were again off, her feet propped up on the table. The iHome's quiet, ocean wave background noises couldn't completely relax her, but her mood had improved.

The ringing phone broke her concentration, and her eyes widened when she read Andy Summers' name on the display. Without waiting for her to say hello after she picked up, he barked, "Drop what you're doing. No one was hurt.

There's been an incident at the lab, and you need to come here now."

Learning her lesson from last time, she took thirty seconds to change into the flat shoes she kept in a bottom desk drawer with extra sweaters, socks and other personal items.

Jogging over to Edgerton, Cassandra heard sirens approaching and felt a cold panic in her chest. When she crossed paths with the street preacher, she swore the woman nodded at her as if to say "I told you so."

Chapter Thirty

By the time Cassandra joined the group at The Home Team, the table was already littered with napkins, mugs and an empty beer pitcher. Cinda, Meg, and Fischer were sharing a sloppy mountain of nachos, and the nearest TV was tuned to an Omaha news station doing a report about the Morton College lab incident.

The video showed Andy's campus security car and two county sheriff cars parked outside the Edgerton Center for the second time in a week. A fire truck and ambulance bustled with activity as workers in full gear and gas masks shuttled into and out of the building. The story headline on the screen said Explosion in Carson. Cassandra slid into the booth next to Meg. "Calling it an explosion is going too far. More like a leak."

Fischer's eyebrows raised and his transparent blue eyes fixed on hers. "I'd say a liquid nitrogen tank malfunction is as close to an explosion as we ever want to get around here. We're lucky that Peterson's quick-thinking averted a disaster. How many students were in there when that thing went off? Cassandra, they could've all died."

Yes, she knew. Tate's grim expression when she'd arrived on the scene had clued her in to how serious the incident could have been. Apparently, the cylinder's pressure relief valve had popped off and shot across the workroom releasing liquid nitrogen into the air where Peterson and two other students had been working. Peterson had immediately recognized that in less than a minute or two, the leaking nitrogen gas would displace all the oxygen in the room and they would asphyxiate. The students had thrown the vent hood open, flipped the fire alarm, and escaped outside before anyone had been hurt.

Cinda asked, "Sorry, I majored in Political Science. What's the liquid nitrogen used for?"

Fischer answered, "When the rat studies are completed, they use liquid nitrogen to euthanize them and flash freeze brain sections for examination under microscopes."

Meg had been happily chewing nachos when she fully understood that they killed the rats after the experiment ended. She pushed her plate away. "Thanks, guys. I'm not hungry anymore. But please, keep talking . . ."

Cassandra noticed Meg's glass was filled with water, not beer. She was about to ask why, when she realized Meg still had a half hour drive home after leaving. She ordered a margarita and scooped nachos onto a small appetizer plate. Tuning out their chatter for a few minutes, she concentrated on getting food into her system and drinking water while she waited for her cocktail. The bar was about 2/3 full of students, faculty and staff (whose eye contact she avoided), plus the regular locals who came here for dinner several nights a week.

Cinda pointed to the TV. A reporter was standing next to Cassandra on screen, and her name was displayed underneath: Cassandra Sato, Morton College Student Affairs. The captions showed their brief interview.

Reporter: "I'm here with Cassandra Sato of Morton College. Can you tell us whether this incident is related to the death earlier this week of sophomore Austin Price right here in this same lab?"

Cassandra: "The sheriff's investigators will need time to determine that. Morton is doing everything possible to ensure the safety of students and visitors this week during classes and Homecoming events." Without waiting for more questions, Cassandra turned and walked towards the ambulance where responders were crowded around two students wearing oxygen masks and being helped aboard for transport to the nearest hospital in Wahoo.

When the news cut to a commercial, they all shifted gazes to Cassandra expectantly. Taking a large gulp of her margarita, she confessed, "There's more. I haven't had the chance to talk to you today. Last night when we came home from Lincoln, I discovered that someone had broken into my house yesterday and smashed my houseplant outside against my garage door."

Her eyes welled up with the memory. "Nothing was stolen that I can tell, but someone is definitely trying to get our attention."

Meg surprised Cassandra by reaching over and placing an arm around her back. She gave her a tender squeeze and whispered quietly, "I'm so sorry, Cass." To the table

Meg declared, "Enough. We have to figure out who is doing these things and why."

Fischer's eyebrows knotted. "Are there enough off-duty deputies that one can be assigned to your house for a few days? Even if they just drive by every couple of hours, it might deter this person from coming back."

Before she could answer, her phone buzzed with a message from Andy. "Peterson and students released from hospital. I'm dropping him at home. Talk to you tomorrow."

After reading his text aloud, she realized there were others she'd missed during the commotion. One unknown caller had sent, "You don't belong here. Go back to Japan."

She showed it to her friends. Cassandra raised her eyes to the ceiling in exasperation. "I'm from Hawai'i not Japan, for Pele's sake! Can't they even get that part right?"

Meg raised her water glass in a mock toast. "Unleash the Menehune on them! Maybe we should have a case of pineapple delivered to the next board meeting?"

The others clinked glasses with Meg, trying to lighten the mood. Cinda wasn't playing along. "How many of those texts have you gotten? They have your personal number."

Cassandra propped an elbow and rested her chin in her hand. Humorous diversion hadn't convinced them to stop looking at her like they all planned to become her personal bodyguards. She fibbed. "Only a few. My name's been in the newspaper and now on TV. Once they know my name, probably it's easy to find my number. Comes with the job; it doesn't bother me."

Cinda picked at the problem like a dog with a bone. "Who's sending the messages? We know some of the board and donors are unhappy. Schneider is arrogant, clueless about deaf people, and kind of creepy, but he's not a thug. Nielson's in Zhejiang. Are there students you've disciplined that might want revenge? What else have you done the past week to piss off someone?"

Meg added, "Even if someone is trying to force Cassandra's resignation because of bad PR, don't you agree something funky is going on in the lab? Maybe when the sheriffs test those other syringes from the cooler that Lance found, they'll connect some dots."

After another round and some hot wings, Cinda and Fischer stood to leave. "I've got to get home before bath time if I want to keep my Supermom status."

Once she left Cassandra observed, "Cinda's younger than us, but she's so . . . settled."

Meg shrugged, "She's from Iowa."

Fischer nodded once as though that was a valid explanation. Cassandra ducked into the bathroom and on the way back to the booth, Fischer met her by the hallway wall. Quietly he said, "This week is getting worse by the day."

She nodded. "Tomorrow I'll order the collection of those student blood, lab, and food service samples and send them for testing. You were right earlier."

"Right or wrong doesn't matter. Students' safety matters. You sound like Nielson when you refuse to believe it's all connected."

Bullseye. She'd felt like an idiot earlier speaking to the TV reporter and reassuring everyone that the college had it all under control. "Maybe Nielson says stuff like that because he's trying to make people feel safer."

"Being yourself would make people feel safer. Catching the creeps behind this would be even better."

He seemed like he wanted to say more. He was just looking at her eyes, her hair, her mouth. She nodded, wondering why he didn't move. He said, "Just be careful," turned, and left the bar.

When Cassandra returned to the booth, Meg said, "That looked intense."

Fischer's comparing her to Nielson stung even though she'd had the same thought already. She didn't have time to sit around worrying about his personal judgments. Cassandra needed to keep the college free from worse scandal. "I can't read his mind."

Meg turned it around on her. "Ok...we won't read Fischer's mind tonight. Let's talk about you instead. You're not getting any younger. Is there a space in your heart for someone new? At least to date even if it's not serious?"

Two months ago she would have said absolutely not. Tonight, she wasn't sure. "Happiness is an elusive, moving target."

Meg stared over Cassandra's shoulder into the past. "I thought there was nothing that would take you away from your family, friends, and home." She nibbled on popcorn. "Now that you've done the inconceivable, does that throw the gate open wide?"

Meg asked nosy questions but she was so sincere, Cassandra found herself saying more than she expected. "I'd be lying if I didn't admit I was grateful for the push from my mentors to move far away and put my past behind me. That clean slate looked very attractive."

However tonight, all Cassandra could see were the huge changes she'd already undertaken. Tears welled up. "What if moving far away from my parents was the wrong thing to do? What if they get sick, or something happens and I'm not there?"

Meg laid a hand on Cassandra's arm. "Look at Austin Price, Cass. Even in our same zip code, we couldn't prevent bad things from happening."

Cassandra conceded, "We can't prevent them from happening, but I'd like to be close enough to help pick up the pieces."

Meg lightly squeezed her arm. "I've said this before, but I'm so glad you're here."

Cassandra wasn't as sure as Meg. Doubts often kept her restless in bed. She fisted her hands on the tabletop. "What if there isn't a right plan, or a wrong plan? What if you just make your choices, walk the path, and deal with the obstacles as they present themselves? Like a grown-up Whack-a-Mole. Is that the meaning of life?"

Meg laughed, "We'd need at least one full bottle of wine to answer that."

They looked around at the crowd which grew younger by the minute. Thursday nights began the weekend for many students. "What about you?" Cassandra probed, "are you and Connor still as happy as when you were newlyweds living the dream in Honolulu?"

Meg smiled. "Wow. You go right for the hard questions, don't you?"

"Keepin it real, sistah. You no like da questions, don't ask me da kine first."

Meg chuckled when Cassandra slipped into Hawaiian creole so easily. "I forgot how much I miss hearing local people talking around me. I wish someday I could live part time here and part time there."

Cassandra knew Meg's love of people and Deaf culture were why she worked, not to get rich. "On an interpreter's salary?"

"We're good. Every couple has struggles. If Connor doesn't learn how to wash dishes, I may kill him." She drank some water and hesitated. "Well, since you asked...we might try for another baby."

That explained all the water drinking lately instead of wine. Cassandra looked more closely at Meg's light skinned, freckled face. Her eyes looked wounded, not as lightly carefree as usual. "I loved growing up in a big family...But apparently wanting is not enough..."

Cassandra's heart felt for Meg. She remembered when Tony had been born. Her brother's keiki had also been beautiful babies. "Will you be able to try again? Do you want to?"

Meg's eyebrows wiggled, and she broke into her wide smile. "The 'trying again' part is the most fun!"

Chapter Thirty-One

Cassandra asked Meg, "Do Nebraska people normally have small, private funerals? I assumed since Austin was so young, it'd be very large and public." Late Friday morning, they ate turkey sandwiches from the student center at the little table in Cassandra's office.

Meg answered around a mouthful of sandwich. "No, It's pretty strange for someone his age. Maybe his family just wants to grieve privately for now. I feel weird that Lance was the only one of us invited this morning."

Suddenly there was a loud commotion in the outer office. Meg got up with her bag of chips still in hand and stepped out to look. She smirked and tilted her head back to Cassandra like, *you gotta see this!* When Cassandra joined her in the doorway, Andy Summers and another security officer stood just inside the office. Andy had one hand on his radio and the other held a baton. They were braced for a fight, eyes darting in the office corners assessing for threats.

Logan Dunn and Haley Owens gaped wide-eyed from the reception desk and work table.

"You called us?" Summers' voice was loud and commanding. "Are you all ok?"

The students slowly shook their heads and turned towards Cassandra. "We didn't call them, did you?"

"No. We're eating lunch. There's no bad guys. There's only four of us in here." She held out her hands to encompass the empty room.

Summers dropped his head, and his shoulders relaxed. "Somebody hit the silent alarm."

Logan and Haley asked at the same time. "What silent alarm?"

Cassandra pointed under the reception desk to a little box with a red button attached to the inside left wall. "The one under that desk you're sitting at, Logan. We use it to call for backup when a student gets out of control."

Haley exclaimed, "You pushed the red button!"

"Use your indoor voice, will ya?" Logan ducked his head enough to see the box. "Ohhh, that red button. I noticed it before, but I forgot to ask . . . Good to know."

Andy and his assistant holstered their batons. They spoke quietly for a minute, and the assistant left. Andy followed the women back into Cassandra's office. "You gotta make sure all the new student-workers get the training."

Cassandra would've laughed if she wasn't already on edge. "Can someone from your office come to our next staff meeting and do a refresher?"

He typed a reminder into his phone while Meg packed up her trash and left for class.

Andy stayed to talk to Cassandra. "I heard from the Lincoln fire inspector. Someone deliberately tampered with the pressure relief valve on that nitrogen cylinder. Those canisters are inspected and certified frequently. They don't just pop off. One of the students yesterday told me that thing shot across the room like a bullet; it whizzed by Luke Peterson's head, missing him by inches."

Andy Summers turned one of the student chairs around and faced Cassandra on the couch. "The next so-called accident could be worse. We shouldn't wait until another student gets killed before we do something drastic."

Sandwich finished, Cassandra bit into a large chocolate chip cookie and offered another to Andy. "I'm not disagreeing with you, Andy. I just don't know what else to do." He waved off the treat. Which was good because it might be a two-cookie day.

She recapped the previous night's conversations with her friends for him. "Cinda Weller thinks I should look at my student appointment list to see if anyone could be disgruntled enough to harm me personally."

"Other than the broken plant against your garage, what else has happened to you?" he asked.

"I mentioned before that someone smashed a pumpkin against my window a while ago. That was probably just kids' stuff for Halloween, right? I've gotten texts telling me to go home to Hawai'i, or that I'm not welcome here."

She had written the messages off as uneducated bullying, but Andy frowned. "People have actually told you that?"

Cassandra gestured to her face, "Most people I've met here have been nice, but there are definitely some folks in town who think Asian faces don't belong. Little kids stare at me in the food market; their moms pull them away like I have some disease. Or when I'm waiting in a line to buy something, I become invisible until I'm the last person left standing. The texts are more blatant, but the subtle things are more hurtful. It's been a big culture shock to realize how much I fit in at home—"

"...And how different it is here?" Andy finished. "Let me apologize for them. We've always grown up with the same families in town. While locals know that different people and cultures are out there in the world, we've always felt insulated in our little dot on the map. Ignorance never excuses bigotry, though. That's just wrong. Do any students' names come to mind who might be after you or the college for some reason?"

She wrote a sticky note with the Facebook kid's name that she'd referred to Cinda for counseling and handed it to him. "I had one whack-a-doodle—not the correct term, I know—earlier this week who looked like the Unabomber and gave me chicken skin. He knew Luke Peterson."

Andy nodded when he read the paper slip. "Counseling already gave us this guy's name. I'll follow up with him to find out where he was yesterday."

Facebook Guy was probably harmless, but it wouldn't hurt to check him out. Events had definitely taken a wrong turn. "There's one other teensy problem though. Some of the college board and donors don't think I'm handling our side of the investigation quickly enough. Or quietly enough."

"We should get the test results back soon on those syringes from the research lab. I can't make it any quicker than that."

"I don't see any way this is all connected to one thing, do you?"

His chest puffed out a little, and he leaned back. "No, but I don't believe in coincidences either. From a safety standpoint, it doesn't matter if it's all connected or not. The lab is trouble, and you're being harassed." He stood and walked over to the window overlooking the quad. "Ok, I think we should close that lab down for the weekend. It's not safe there."

Cassandra joined him by the window. She hoped the sun would shine all afternoon while she had to be outside. "That's a no-go. Doesn't someone have to feed and water the rats? Plus, Dr. Schneider mentioned that Luke Peterson's study ends soon. He'd be first in line to complain if you shut it down."

Andy was acting all authoritative and brotherly. "That's a good point. We don't need a room full of dead rats. Ok, at the very least, you should cancel your appointments and special event appearances for a few days."

She'd taken care of herself more than ten years and didn't need a protector. Sure, her family had been nearby, but she wasn't some weakling. Cassandra's shoulders tensed from his bossy tone. "I can't! It's Homecoming. Nielson scheduled me to take his place in the parade tonight. And the big game is tomorrow. And the bonfire. I won't just hide in my office."

He backed down when he saw that the brotherly thing wasn't going to fly. "I'll use extra physical plant and maintenance guys to help with security this weekend, but I still think you're vulnerable."

He'd made his point, and she'd disagreed. Cassandra firmly believed that if students had fun this weekend, people would see Morton was safe. She had one chance to prove she was ready for more responsibility. "Don't worry about me; I'm fine. We know it's something to do with the lab. Post guys around that building, and only allow the essential workers inside. The students would be thrilled if we cancel biology classes for a couple of days."

"I'd feel better if you don't ride in the parade."

She stopped herself from blurting out that she wasn't here to make him feel better. She took a deep breath and remembered he was not her enemy. "Nielson and the board want it to look like business as usual around here. We can't take away the social highlight of the semester because of a broken plant and a freak lab accident." Even as she spoke, she cringed inwardly. Instinct told her it wasn't an accident, but she couldn't cancel a weekend's worth of events on a string of unconnected hunches.

Summers searched her face until she felt a smidge uncomfortable. She worried he'd say something personal.

"Sorry, I promised Meg I'd meet her before the parade." Cassandra stood abruptly and pointed to her watch, but softened at the puppy dog eyes staring back at her too long. "I'm tougher than I look, Andy."

* * *

Meg perched on the edge of Cassandra's vintage white claw foot bathtub. They'd squished together into her bathroom and Meg spouted advice in preparation for the

Homecoming parade. "Acceptable Midwestern Fall college fashion is this: sweater, skinny jeans with knee high boots, or yoga pants with a sweatshirt."

Cassandra shook her head. "I'm still learning the ropes about this place, but even I can see that the yoga pant thing is strictly for the 25-and-under crowd."

While Cassandra started on her makeup, Meg asked, "Do you think the yoga girls even look at their backside in the mirror before they leave the house? Would your mom have let you go out dressed like that?"

Cassandra skillfully applied foundation and concealer until her skin was dewy fresh. "My mother's wardrobe has never varied in the 34 years I've been alive. Baggy black ankle pants, loose woven top and either nice black flats for work, or rubber slippahs around the house. The shirts may change over time, but it's pretty much all looked the same. She'd have an aneurysm if I had my back side hanging out like that for all the world to see. I would've been grounded until my next birthday."

"I know, right? Mama Ruth would've locked my bedroom door if my bum wasn't covered by a long top over those tight pants. It's one thing if you're out jogging and wear that thick spandex sport fabric. Some yoga pants are so thin, I can see skin color underneath them as I'm walking across campus behind these girls! And I'm not looking on purpose! Believe me, I'm trying to avert my eyes."

Cassandra had seen them too and looked anywhere but in front of her to avoid seeing the jiggling flesh under filmy cloth. She laughed while she worked on her eyes.

Meg added, "There's another part of me that's just fascinated like, wow you really think your butt and legs are so toned that you can wear those without a trace of self-consciousness. You go, girl! You have way more body confidence than I had at twenty! But after about 40 yards, I just start thinking, could you please put on a longer top so I don't have to look at everything hanging out there while I'm walking to class?"

Meg shielded her eyes on the sides of her head like a horse wearing blinders. "And I'm just an old married woman with a 9-year-old boy. By the time he's 17, I hope baggy 80's pants are back in style."

Cassandra laughed so hard she had to stop applying mascara before she poked her eye.

Meg held up the dark jeans one more time, but Cassandra shook her head emphatically. No way was she wearing them for work. They finally compromised on some slim leg black ankle pants, a white long-sleeved t-shirt and a long navy blue cardigan. Meg found a cute gold metallic belt in a box in the back of the closet. "And you, my friend, have the very opposite problem."

"I promise I'll wear the jeans tomorrow at the football game, ok? I need to look Vice Presidential at the parade. If I'm too casual, I look like an undergrad."

"You're so petite, I can see why. But you carry yourself with a 34-year-old Vice President's confidence, not like an 18-year-old psych major. You have that classy poise thing going on. Showing it off wouldn't hurt the Big Kahuna's perceptions of you. Remember this is an opportunity to schmooze some of the fancy board donors; looking calm and controlled could work in your favor."

Cassandra could see Meg's point; she just hated that her everyday hard work wasn't enough to convince them of her competence. "Bergstrom said he'd work the donors for me. Tell them about my Young Leaders of Higher Ed award, and how I came up with the idea for the Women of Tomorrow Academy."

Meg hopped up and sorted through a bin of hair products and clips. "Maybe I'll fix your hair too, so the wind doesn't blow it around in the car."

Cassandra assessed herself in the mirror: flat walking shoes, dark solid color clothes and camera-ready makeup. "What's wrong with my bun? I like my bun. It's easy and professional."

"Yes, it is. And maybe if we keep the top part up and let the bottom part loose, you will look your age, not like your 74-year-old grandma."

Cassandra flashed her with stink eye. "Hey sistah, take it easy! You get one mean!"

Meg didn't flinch, only patted the tub's edge to indicate where Cassandra should sit so Meg could reach the top of her head. "Ok before we clip it back, let me tease the top poofy. That's how we Nebraskans roll." Meg held a comb in one hand and a big hunk of thick, silky black hair in the other. She stuck a few bobby pins in her mouth. "How close to God do you want your hair?"

Chapter Thirty-Two

Expecting a small turnout of students and faculty, Cassandra was surprised by the parade fans' enthusiasm. Although the beefy football linebacker and blonde beauty in the car behind her were notably attractive, they weren't exactly famous pop stars. Didn't seem to matter to the crowd.

Her mother would absolutely love this! Cassandra and Dr. Schneider rode in the caravan's lead car followed by four convertibles holding the couples nominated for Homecoming King and Queen. She'd been the high school nerd, never the outgoing beauty queen. Cassandra pasted on her royal smile and waved at passing families.

Behind them marched the band, loudly repeating the fight song every half mile. Next came floats decorated for the contests by the dorms and the Greek houses. High school marching bands from towns nearby followed the floats. Then the Disabled Veterans wearing berets, volunteer fireman atop glossy red trucks and several Scout troops. The "Zombies Rising," theme was popular among the floats and costumes. Even the college's band members wore zombie makeup and rags instead of their normal fancy blue uniforms.

Getting into the car before the parade began was awkward because the red Ford Mustang convertible's upper back seat provided no seat belt. Cassandra had removed her high heels to save the upholstery, anchored her legs as best she could, and told herself to enjoy the moment.

Unlike her, Dr. Arnie Schneider seemed completely comfortable in his role as Parade Marshal. Dr. Nielson had chosen him because of his large donation pledge on the physics lab renovations. Schneider charmed the crowds with natural friendliness. He reached into a plastic grocery sack between them and scooped up hard candy to throw near children along the route.

One older gentleman broke from the crowd and walked up to the side of the slow-moving car. His face was flushed, "Hey Arnie! Looking good."

Schneider leaned over to shake his hand. "Good to see you, Mike!" He then checked on Cassandra attentively and leaned in towards her ear to speak names of crowd members while he pointed and waved. "There's Professor Hamilton. He's retired now but worked at Morton for 40 years." When she'd bumped into Schneider going around a turn, he'd drawled through a wide grin, "I showered this morning. I don't bite, honey."

Cassandra held onto the seat's headrest near her knees and wondered how people like Schneider and Nielsen could find the limelight so enjoyable. She was much better with one-on-one conversations than large gatherings. She longed to go home and change into comfy pajamas.

As they drew close to the Student Center, the car slowed to move into the circular drive in front of the college's plaza entrance. Cassandra noticed the street preacher amid the crowd watching from the top steps by the entry doors. As the caravan pulled around the drive and back out onto the main street, the woman shouted, "God knows what you did! Sinner!! Liar! Vengeance is mine, says the Lord!" Her finger pointed towards their Mustang, and she looked right at Cassandra.

The people standing nearby turned, startled by the woman's shrieking outburst. Cassandra's head swiveled behind them as their vehicle moved out of range. By then the preacher had quieted and stood by the doors as though nothing had happened. Had Cassandra imagined the whole weird episode? As she faced forward again, Dr. Schneider leaned towards her ear. "How do we get rid of that distasteful woman?"

Well, at least it hadn't been her imagination. It was unsettling, but there wasn't time now to analyze it. "Freedom of speech, Dr. Schneider. As long as she's on public property, we don't get rid of her."

They continued down the street until the procession reached the parking lot by the football field. Dr. Schneider got out of the parked car and turned to reach for her. Cassandra would've liked to climb out by herself, but didn't trust her balance to not trip in front of him. She allowed him to take her arm and assist her out. She straightened her clothes and said, "Thanks for your willingness to be the Marshal. I'm glad we had such warm weather for the parade." One good thing about Nebraska was you could always use the weather for small talk.

"Riding next to an exotic beauty like you was infinitely more pleasant than it would've been with Nielson. Good afternoon, Dr. Sato. I'll see you at the carnival later, no doubt."

* * *

A rustic iron lantern drew her eye to a booth filled with upcycled home decorating accessories. The corners were reclaimed wood with iron hinges, fasteners and a swirled loop at the top for hanging. Cassandra admired the craftsmanship and browsed through the rest of the shelves while she envisioned the best spot for a lantern in her house. Her mental picture of the display she'd make on the fireplace mantel was cut short by the glimpse of a tall figure wearing a black cape, a Zorro hat and mask, standing near the carnival game booth two spaces down from her.

The hairs on the back of her neck raised first and she felt eyes on her for long moments before looking directly at him to confirm the feeling. His eyes glinted in the cutout openings of the mask. She bent over to replace the lantern on the display shelf, and when she stood again, the man was gone. Odd. Usually when random strangers openly stared at her out of curiosity, the skin on her arms didn't pucker up.

Half an hour later she, Meg, and Fischer stopped to talk to a couple of student workers they recognized. Logan and Rachel were laughing because he'd scored a direct hit to the dunk tank target with a baseball, causing Simon Harris (aka. Professor Hottie) to fall 10 feet into the water below. Rachel had taken a short video clip capturing the surprised look on his face, glasses falling off mid-air, arms flying up as his body plummeted into the cold tank.

Harris bounced up again, all smiles, his t-shirt plastered to his muscular torso. Where did such a distinguished academic find time to get ripped like that? The students drifted off, and Cassandra's group moved on to the food tents. Sure she had a fun evening, but as an administrator she was constantly "working." Her game face was always on.

Activities like an inflatable sumo wrestler and mechanical bull games, photo booths, crafts, face painting, cotton candy, artist vendors and musicians attracted the entire community and surrounding area, including a Kiddie Zone for the youngest children. Cassandra was impressed by both the attendance and organization of small town social life in action.

Pausing at a photography booth displaying high quality Plains landscape and wildlife posters, she considered buying a breathtaking sunset over rock bluffs or birds in flight piece as a souvenir for her parents. Her previous experience with beautiful views usually involved the ocean. This relatively flat, mostly treeless scenery was growing on her.

Cassandra felt his gaze before she saw him. He stood alone behind the cotton candy station where a laughing staff person covered in sticky cotton fibers handed a large rainbow cone to a small boy's outstretched hand. Zorro wasn't laughing and didn't seem to be trying to blend in.

Behind her Meg, Connor, and Fischer were cheering Tony as he threw softballs at three bowling pins. One pin lay sideways, but the other two stood tall while the ball narrowly missed them. Connor offered, "Wanna try again, Buddy?"

Cassandra turned around and took one step back leaning closer to Meg. "Is the guy at the cotton candy booth to my right dressed like Zorro staring at me, or is it just my imagination?"

Meg looked over Cassandra's shoulder and then shifted to get a better view. "What Zorro guy? I see a Batman, Hulk, and the cutest little boy who in fifteen minutes will be bonkers on a sugar high. No Zorro."

Whipping around, Cassandra shook her head. "He was right there, I swear!"

She turned 360 degrees and still didn't spot him. "Ok, never mind." She needed to rein in the drama. Sure, there'd been mysterious accidents on campus. People were dressed in costumes because of Halloween. The carnival was a public place. *Get a grip.*

She forced herself to smile and pay attention to her friends and Tony. His favorite blue SpongeBob shirt already had a chocolate stain from the dripping ice cream cone he'd eaten earlier.

After he'd missed the third try at the bowling pins, and Connor had taken over—determined to win him a choice of stuffed animals—Cassandra nudged Tony with an elbow. "Hey. Do you smell that? That smell. A kind of smelly smell. The smelly smell that smells..."

"SMELLY!!" Tony finished loudly. His parents' heads turned simultaneously, questioning.

Cassandra sang, "Who lives in a pineapple under the sea?" then burst into giggles. She couldn't believe how lucky she was to be Auntie to a 4th grader who loved SpongeBob almost as much as she did. Maybe someday she'd have the opportunity to warp her own children.

Later Cassandra noticed Dr. Schneider and a tall thin, well-dressed lady she assumed was his wife seated at a folding plastic table in a fenced-off beer garden with several other couples. All had plastic drink cups and small plates of food in front of them. Cassandra asked Meg if she could lip-read their conversation.

Meg was game. "Hey, why not? Might as well put my skills to work, right?"

No more than 15 feet away, Schneider was facing them and talking to another man and a standing student whose back was to them. Cassandra thought it was Luke Peterson, but she couldn't be sure. Their discussion was animated. Schneider's intense face and finger pointing made her wonder why he was so agitated. The obvious answer was the lab student workers' health and their rat study. Sure, she was being nosy, but she needed to know.

Connor, Tony, and Fischer had gone off to visit the port-a-potties.

Meg watched the group for several long moments. "One more week...no more screw ups..." Meg leaned in towards Cassandra's ear and relayed the conversation while Cassandra looked away, appearing to be interested in the face painting booth while they waited for the guys.

"This is harder than you think... Staff... will be fine. Do your job."

Lip-reading was such a cool skill. Meg was like Cassandra's personal spy! Probably Connor used her to tell him what the NFL coaches were saying on the sidelines during Monday night football.

After a few more silent moments Meg said, "I'm leaving you for that hot babe... parade car... with me... I never loved you."

Cassandra's breath stopped. Schneider could be talking about her! They'd shared a car during the parade! He wouldn't... His wife wouldn't let him get away with that! She peeked super quick behind her to see their conversation while Meg read their lips.

The group had already stood and cleared the trash from their table. Schneider held the pile in one hand while his other went solicitously to his wife's back to guide her through the tables and out of the beer garden enclosure. Cassandra's eyes met Meg's in confusion.

Until she saw Meg's eyes crinkle in laughter, and she let loose with a huge laugh at Cassandra's gullibility.

Meg had made up that last part! Cassandra said, "Oh, nice. Very classy. Thanks, friend."

When the men returned, Cassandra and Meg were still laughing. Connor said, "What'd we miss?"

Meg raised her hand for a high five. "I'm so good."

Connor slapped her palm then kissed the top of her head. "Always known it!"

Cassandra shook her head while they turned off towards the inflatable bounce house for Tony. She had deserved that.

Chapter Thirty-Three

The four-block ride home in Fischer's dark gray Audi coupe was short and uneventful. Cassandra said, "I appreciate the lift, but I didn't ask you to be my chauffeur tonight. I'm fine."

"I can see that you're fine. Connor asked me to tag along tonight so he didn't have to deal with all of you alone." Fischer's face was serious, but his tone was light. Her first instinct was to tell him to back off. But after the last couple of days and the staring stranger, she couldn't deny she was grateful for his competent presence. Connor had his own family to worry about.

Fischer acted flexible and laid back, but he and Connor's eyes always scanned the area for threats. Maybe it was just a way of life for them after being deployed. Hawai'i was crawling with military people—nearly 40,000—and Cassandra was accustomed to that look. Fischer put the car in park in her driveway. "I'm glad I went with your group tonight and saw the carnival games through a kid's eyes. Tony throws himself into everything he does 100%. He has so much energy."

"Yeah. I love Tony . . . but he also makes me appreciate my quiet house."

Cassandra opened her car door in the driveway. She avoided lingering like a real date. Fischer asked, "I'm going to the football game tomorrow, are you?"

"I've been assigned in Nielson's absence."

"You make it sound as appealing as a root canal. You haven't gone to the other games?"

After throwing herself into work all week, she treasured her lazy Saturday routines. Cassandra shrugged. "Tomorrow will be my first."

Fischer smiled, wished her good night and drove away. Cassandra waited until his taillights headed down the street before she returned to the end of the darkened driveway to get the mail. Headlights bathed her in light as she reached into her mailbox, and a black sedan drove slowly down her street. In the retreating car's lights, she noticed a figure farther down the sidewalk coming slowly towards her. Cassandra's danger radar was on high alert; her heart beat so hard in her chest it felt like an exaggerated cartoon depiction.

Cassandra stood frozen, her hand on the mailbox flap, her legs unmoving, waiting. When the figure passed under the nearest low voltage street lamp, Cassandra recognized the long skirt, shabby trench coat and little cart belonging to the street preacher. She exhaled a long breath and shivered in the cool night air. Cassandra's North Face fleece zipper jacket had been fine before sunset, but the temperature had dropped 10 degrees in thirty minutes.

The preacher greeted Cassandra from two houses away. "Good evening, my child! You're out late tonight. Have you no guard?"

What a strange thing to say. A guard? They faced each other on the driveway. Cassandra couldn't continue to bump into her and not even use her name. "I'm sorry . . . I've never heard your name . . ."

"I'm called Esther, Dr. Cassandra Sato."

All this time she'd known Cassandra's name. At this hour, no one would snap embarrassing photos of them. Cassandra smiled warmly. "Where are you heading . . .?"

Esther pointed North. "The Methodist church on the edge of town. Pastor Talbot lets me sleep in the church basement. Surely, he lives the Truth: 'For I was hungry and you gave Me something to eat; I was thirsty and you gave Me something to drink; I was a stranger and you took Me in.'"

Cassandra felt relieved to know she wasn't sleeping on a park bench during the frigid nights. In Hawai'i, homeless people had their choice of safe, warm places to sleep. In fact, it was too welcoming at times, and care of the homeless folks was a large burden on the state's social service system. In this climate, being homeless must be dangerous.

She couldn't resist asking Esther about the parade. "Earlier this afternoon . . . when you called me a sinner and a liar? Why did you say that? What have I done to offend you?"

Her penetrating stare lasted several moments until Cassandra wondered whether she'd answer at all. "I saw the evil one. After." Then Esther reached behind her for the cart handle and continued down the sidewalk towards the Methodist Church.

"After what?..." called Cassandra as Esther walked away either unhearing or ignoring her. Cassandra could've sworn Esther had pointed right at her during the parade. She might not be the most reliable witness though. Esther had issues.

Cassandra entered her house through the back door carrying the mail and her large messenger bag. She abandoned the wish that there was time tonight for reading. She just needed to clean up a bit and get to bed.

Within ten minutes, she'd emptied the dishwasher's clean dishes, carried a laundry load up from the basement dryer, double-checked the locks on the front and back doors, and turned off the lights. She paused on the way towards her bedroom and stared gloomily at the empty end table where her Plumeria had lived. Cassandra still didn't understand how someone had gotten the plant out of her house, or why that had been the only thing disturbed. Obtaining a new cutting of the big tree still safe in her mother's Waipahu house was tricky. Her mom would ask what had happened. Cassandra would lie that it had been death by brown thumb—completely plausible.

Cassandra plopped the laundry basket on the bedroom floor and rummaged for a long-sleeved t-shirt and fleece pajama pants. Goosebumps remained on her arms and legs from the chilly driveway conversation while she organized clothes and gear for Saturday morning. She switched on her night table lamp before turning down the Hawaiian quilt bedspread.

"Wha—" she gasped. A key fob sized object lay centered on her white cotton pillowcase. Moving closer, she confirmed it was a plastic thumb drive. Not hers.

A loud voice in her brain shouted, *Don't touch it! Who put it there? Get out of the house!* Ignoring the warning, she robotically moved to the corner table, opened her MacBook Pro and inserted the thumb drive. Seconds later a video popped onto the full screen and loaded. With growing horror, she saw a person come into focus. It was herself. In her kitchen. This morning. While she brewed a cup of coffee and grabbed a Greek yogurt out of the fridge. She watched herself lean against the counter and eat the whole cup in less than a minute. She'd been in a hurry.

Where had the camera been? Why hadn't she noticed it? She peered at the screen more carefully and saw the window reflection. Blowing out a sigh of relief, she realized the camera had been outside. Her relief lasted only moments when the screen switched to a bulky guy silhouetted in a dark room wearing a black Zorro mask whose disguised voice threatened, "Next time, I won't just watch."

The tremors started in her knees. A cry escaped, she clapped a hand over her open mouth, and rushed into the bathroom. Carnival junk food spewed out violently while she gasped and coughed. Tears streamed down her cheeks. Zorro. That Zorro guy really had been following her tonight at the carnival. It hadn't been her imagination. How many days had he watched her?

It took a few minutes to wipe her face and wash her mouth. Back in the bedroom, she stared at the black screen. She whispered, "Namu Amida Butsu." For extra protection, she invoked the phrase she'd heard Meg plead many times, "Lord, have mercy!" Help was welcome from any available prophets or deities at this point.

She scooped up her phone from the night stand and fumbled through the contacts until she found Fischer's number. Without thinking about college politics or the rules, she held her breath until he answered.

"Fischer. What's wrong?"

"Someone. Was in my house . . . again," she stammered. "Please c-come back. Now!" She couldn't control the neediness in her voice. She was way beyond chicken skin. Probably she should've called 911, but she figured Fischer would get there faster.

Fifteen minutes later, Cassandra heard pounding on the back door. She slid her feet into warm crocheted slippers and turned on lights all the way. Yanking open the door, she lost all professional pretense and the tears flowed again. She pointed towards her bedroom. "In my room. On my pillow."

Fischer stalked through the kitchen, around the hallway and into the living room. He quickly assessed the room and moved toward the lights in her bedroom. Without touching any hard surfaces, Fischer bent down and scanned under the bed. Using his t-shirt to open the knob, he inspected inside the closet, then checked out the bathroom. He looked behind the armchair she'd slept in a couple of nights ago and where the photo frame was still lying on the cushion.

Cassandra followed him, and they nearly collided when he turned around. "Is anyone in the house now?"

She wiped her cheeks and exhaled an unsteady breath. "Not in here, the kitchen or the basement. I haven't looked upstairs."

He turned left and took the curved wooden steps two at a time, checked the bedrooms and upstairs bath. "No one up here, either."

Meeting her in the hallway, he led her to the living room couch. "Let me get you some water." He didn't wait for her answer, just headed into the kitchen. She heard cupboards opening and closing until he found glasses and the tap. Moments later he handed her a large glass of water. She drank some, surprised by how much calmer it made her feel. Or maybe it was his presence.

"You gonna be alright?" He ran a hand through his dark hair and looked around the room again, taking in the neat modern furniture, dark colors and simplicity of the space.

She nodded, suddenly aware that she sat on her couch in her pajamas with an employee. Probably this broke several rules. Too bad. She had bothered Andy last time for the plant. Fischer was the right man for this . . . incident. Must be his military experience that made him seem so controlled and competent. She placed the glass on the end table and held up a finger. "Be right back."

Returning to the couch with her laptop, she rewound the video and handed it to him. "This thumb drive was on my pillow when I came home."

She made it through half the video before lurching into the bathroom again. That jerk had stood outside her house, filming her this morning. Had any neighbors noticed him? Then he'd broken in. Again. And touched her pillow while he placed the memory stick there. Staring at her reddened eyes streaked with mascara in the mirror above the pedestal sink, she splashed cold water on her face and spoke to the reflection. "Get it together."

When she returned to the living room, Fischer's face was an expressionless mask. She sat on the couch and pointed at the guy on the video. "I saw Zorro. Everywhere I looked tonight. Him."

She pulled her legs up to her chest and hugged her shins. Then the trembling began. She couldn't stop. First Austin, then the plant. Then the nitrogen in the lab. Now this. What else had this creep done?

Her skin prickled with imaginary bugs crawling down her arms, and she started hyperventilating again with the thought of Zorro in her bedroom.

Fischer reached a hand into his jeans front pocket. Pulling out a small zipper bag, he opened it and fished out a little yellow pill. Reaching for her right hand, he turned it over and gently opened her fingers. He placed the pill on her palm. "Valium. It'll help you stop shaking."

For a millisecond, she hesitated. Fischer seemed so composed, but carried his own personal stock of anxiety medicine. She didn't know him much outside of work, but this was no time for scruples. Popping it in her mouth, she gulped some water to wash it down then held out her hand. "I think I need two."

Frowning, he said, "I don't know. These are pretty strong. They'll help you relax."

Her hand didn't waver, and after a few seconds he added a second pill. She would remember to ask him about the pills later. Easing into the couch, she let it swallow her up and hugged a pillow in front of her stomach.

Fischer moved to the armchair flanking the fireplace and sunk into its wide brown leather seat. Silence settled over them, the only noise was the furnace cycling on from the basement and blowing warm air through the vents.

"We need to call the sheriff. They'll want to file a report and check for evidence, if there's any left. You should've left the house and called me right away. What if that creep had still been inside?" His words scolded, but his voice had a note of respect. "You're pretty fearless. Lotta people would be more freaked out."

Cassandra drank more water. "Seems like if he wanted to hurt me, he could've done that already."

She didn't look at him closely or study his responses. They just sat, thinking and occasionally kept the conversational strings loosely tied together. "If he's trying to scare me, it worked." She addressed the floor and the coffee table. "Maybe I should make 'em all happy and just quit."

"The texts and the politics seem to be personal. That creep . . . is after you." Fischer paused a long time. "The stuff in the lab with Austin and the nitrogen don't connect."

"That's where I got stuck too. There's more. We just haven't put it together, yet."

After twenty minutes, Cassandra felt her shoulders relax and the cramping in her stomach subside. Like she'd drank a large glass of wine. She crossed her slippered feet on the coffee table, and tossed the small pillow aside. Resting her head back against the couch, she sighed.

Fischer said, "I like your house. It's cozy. Especially this chair. I need a chair like this in my place."

Turning her head, she admired his profile. The messy dark hair, shadowed chin, narrow nose. He filled the chair like a king on his throne. A relaxed king, his long legs stretched out in front of him. Legs wrapped in denim, but she could see the muscle definition under the fabric.

Whoa, where did that thought come from? Why was she staring at his legs?

She was a little too comfortable... He'd asked about her chair. She laughed a little.

"Found it at an estate sale the week after I moved in. The leather's all broken in and buttery soft. It's an expensive brand, so I figured it'd last a while longer... My dad had one like it at home, and it reminded me of him."

When she was quiet for a long time, he whispered. "You still awake?"

She smiled at the intimacy of his soft voice. "Yep. But I could sleep here."

She reached over the couch for a fuzzy fleece blanket, but struggled to pull it onto herself. The corner was stuck; she tugged a few times ineffectively. Giggling, she gave up, placing the free part over her right shoulder. Giggling wasn't dignified. She didn't hear him stand up.

Suddenly he leaned over her, freeing the whole blanket and gently tucking it around her shoulders. He smoothed it out over her legs and studied her a long moment. His woodsy, leathery scent hovered in the air between them. "You have some issues."

"Not right now, I don't. Well. Maybe I have issues, but I don't care... anymore... Will you stay tonight, please? I... don't..."

Fischer stood up and shook his head, smiling. She couldn't tell if that was a smiling-AT-her or a smiling-WITH-her kind of smile, but she was beyond caring. Those pills had definitely done the trick.

"I'm not leaving you alone tonight. In the morning, we'll call the sheriff and go from there."

He used the bathroom, turned off the house lights, positioned himself in the large leather chair and removed his shoes. Moonlight filtered onto the wood floor from the windows on either side of the fireplace. Her limbs felt heavy, her muscles like putty. Her eyelids had been closed for some time when she heard him ask, "That photo... on your bedside chair? Of you and that guy? You looked... radiant."

She considered how much to tell him. "My smile that night went all the way through me. I was very happy, then."

When she didn't add more, he prompted, "But..."

"Paul Watanabe and I were engaged the weekend after I graduated with my Master's. He'd worked as an Ocean Engineer... My parents loved him nearly as much as I—"

Everyone back home already knew this story, and she rarely had to tell it. The Valium had taken the edge off her anxiety, but couldn't mask the lump in her throat. "Two months after our engagement, Paul got a virus. First we thought he had a cold, then maybe the flu. By the time he realized something was terribly wrong and went to the hospital, it was too late. He slipped into a coma. They tested and treated him for four days, but he never woke again. He was 26 years old."

Her cheeks were damp. You'd think after eight years that wound would be scarred over.

"I'm sorry for you and both your families...That must've been...hard."

She sniffled. Her voice quieted to barely above a whisper. "The Plumeria plant the creep smashed against my garage door...was a cutting from one that I got at his funeral. I hand-carried it on the plane when I moved here."

The last image that flashed in her mind before she drifted off to sleep was Marcus Fischer dressed like an old-fashioned British gentleman, chivalrous and gallant. She smiled because the real Marcus Fischer had hard edges to him. She didn't know which version she liked more.

Chapter Thirty-Four

"What'd you do—sleep on da kine couch?" Michiko Sato's loud voice scolded from the MacBook screen on Cassandra's desk in the dining room/den. She stilled. Her mother couldn't possibly know that, right?

"Mom, I've been up for hours. Why would you say that?"

"Your eyes look tired. Why aren't you sleeping? Sleeping on the couch pillows give you wrinkles."

Cassandra might switch up the weekly call home by using a telephone instead of video if this lecturing kept up. She was old enough to sleep where she wanted without explaining herself to her mother. Maybe that was too grouchy. "Work has been hectic this week. We've had some problems with students, and I've been busy with evening Homecoming events. Next week should be easier."

The online chat had already lasted half an hour, and she needed to head to the football game soon. She forced a cheery tone into her voice. "I'm going to a football game today. Morton's Homecoming day. Meg and Connor will be there, too."

"That sounds fun, dear! Good for you getting some fresh air. Bring your heavy coat. Your dad checked the weather in Omaha. Can you believe the high will be 65-degrees? Aiyee, that's chilly!"

"Meg took me shopping in Lincoln Wednesday, and I bought a new hat and some gloves. I'm all ready . . . Actually, Mom, I have to go now. Time to head to the game soon . . . I love you. Kiss Dad and Gran for me."

"Have fun today. Get some sleep! Love you!" The chat window closed and Cassandra's eyes watered up. She was beginning to have a love/hate feeling about these calls. She loved talking to her parents and seeing their faces. When Mom turned the iPad screen and showed her blooming garden or the window view, she loved the vibrant colors of the water and flowers. She hated the tightness in her chest, the physical longing for a place so far away. She snapped the laptop shut.

* * *

Cassandra's back and behind were numb after sitting on the cold metal bleachers for two hours watching the Morton Maples Homecoming game against the Iowa Christian Crusaders. The home team was down 24-14 in the fourth quarter, but they had the ball and had switched to short running plays with some success. Cassandra, wearing a Navy-Blue Maples fleece jacket and the jeans Meg had goaded her into purchasing at the Buckle, felt toasty warm sandwiched by Meg and Connor on one side and Lance Erickson's parents on the other. Meg had advised her there was no way to prepare herself mentally for Nebraska winters so she should resign herself to wearing three layers, a hat and gloves from November until April.

"We're glad to know Lance has supportive ties here at school, Dr. Sato," Lance's mother told her in between plays. "We feel so bad for Austin's family; we've known them since the boys were in junior high."

Cassandra replied, "I can't imagine what they're going through, either. I only hope we can get answers for them soon. We're doing our best."

Mrs. Erickson patted her knee. "I'm sure you are, dear."

She must have been old when Lance had been born because she looked around 60.

Mrs. Erickson said, "Although it'd be nice if we could get email updates. Are you sure the campus is safe? That lab explosion sounded dangerous."

Her voice was kindly, but Cassandra caught the underlying tone that she was concerned for her son, too. "It was a leak, not an explosion," she corrected automatically. "The staff person in charge knew what to do, and no students were harmed. We don't want to cause undue worry by constantly contacting parents until we have definitive information. Believe me, we're doing everything possible to find who's responsible."

Connor had insisted on escorting Cassandra on the field at half-time, even against Meg's stink eye stare. He and Fischer must've talked about the break-in. Connor had gone full bodyguard on her fifteen minutes after they met at the ticket entrance. Cassandra couldn't even go to the rest room alone. She'd caught Meg up to speed on the video, the sheriff taking her statement, the deputies dusting for fingerprints and questioning the neighbors. Her inner feminist felt offended that Fischer had set a watch on her, but the practical part of her brain was grateful for the extra protection. She couldn't get that creeper's synthesized voice out of her head.

Standing on the 50-yard line during half-time, she and Dr. Bergstrom handed out commemorative plaques and shook hands with the returning Mid-Plains Conference champion football team from 1975. When she became university president someday, the half-time presentations, reporter interviews and donor special events would be frequent requirements of the job. She should be relaxed and happy as she stared into the grandstands. Instead every dark, hooded figure made her want to hide, and she felt more queasy than excited.

During the fourth quarter, Meg pointed to a skinny wide receiver and leaned in to whisper, "He's in a Statistics class I work in. Kid sleeps through class unless the teacher calls on him. Waste of a scholarship. Why don't these kids realize how lucky they are to be in college?"

Cassandra nodded; her own student loans wouldn't be paid off for another five years. Funny how when you're a student you try to get away with stuff. When you're an adult you do the math, and calculate cost per class meeting.

Meg gasped, "Did I say that out loud? Oh my God! I sound like my mother! It's happening. I'm only 33, and I sound like my mother." She slapped her leg for emphasis then turned to Cassandra. "Yesterday I found a gray hair. Make it stop!"

As they laughed together, the crowd hushed. The players on the field walked away from a big pile at the end of a play except one lineman, Frank Thompson. A trainer and a coach trotted out to help him. A few minutes turned into ten while they decided how to handle him. He moved his legs, but he wasn't getting up.

Craning her neck, Meg asked Connor, "Can you see where he's hurt?" Finally someone brought the little golf cart over, five workers surrounded him and hoisted him into the back. The delay was a buzzkill on both sides of the ball, but the remaining players finished the game. The crowd was mostly out of it by that point anyway, and the game finished without further scoring or injuries.

Connor and Meg had parked in Cassandra's driveway to avoid the crowded campus lots. Inside, she grabbed Connor a beer and herself some chardonnay. While Meg texted Tony's babysitter to update her on their estimated arrival time at home, she declined the wine offer by holding up her unfinished water bottle. Filling a bowl with pretzels, Cassandra carried it outside to the back deck where they sat around her plastic table.

Cassandra's small yard featured a smooth grass expanse stretching from the deck to the green boxwood hedge that fenced in two sides, with the third side being the garage. She apologized for her barely furnished deck. "Sorry the back is so bland; I hardly ever sit out here."

She looked forward to planting flowers in container pots come Spring. By the time she'd moved in August, the grass already had a brown tinge to it. Luckily, the underground sprinklers operated on a timer so her only chore was paying a neighbor kid to mow weekly.

An hour later, a car door slammed in the driveway and Fischer appeared between the garage and house, following the pathway to the deck. Surprised, Cassandra raised an eyebrow at Meg. She tilted her head towards Connor and made a texting sign to show that he'd told Fischer where to find them. Cassandra stood up to greet him. "Aloha!"

Fischer said hello, shook Connor's hand, and joined them at the table.

Cassandra replayed that moment in her head just after dawn when her eyes had opened to him sound asleep draped all over her leather chair. His head had tilted left, and light snoring came from his slightly open mouth. At rest, his face had looked younger than the rugged, purposeful expression he usually wore at work.

She recalled hurrying into the bathroom to brush her teeth and comb her hair, noting the deep pillow lines across her cheek. Changing into baggy sweats and a hoodie, she pulled her hair into a ponytail and padded into the kitchen. Soon after the smell of fresh Kona coffee filled the room, she heard him in the bathroom. Minutes later she had handed him a travel mug. Her face flushed. "Good morning."

She didn't make a habit of sleepovers. Especially not with co-workers. Fischer had eyed the travel mug and raised his eyebrows. "I can take a hint."

"I didn't mean you ... right now—"

"I was teasing, Cassandra." He smiled. Water droplets clung to the front of his hair where he had run wet fingers through to tame the rumples. "I do have to get going though. I've called Sheriff Hart and he'll be over within the hour. I'll see you later?"

She'd stepped toward him. "I . . . uh, appreciate your help last night. Really . . . A lot." Three college degrees and that was the best she could do? She told herself to stop talking.

Her consciousness snapped into the present time on her patio when she realized Meg was giving her the big eyes. "Hey! Cassandra, do you have more beer?"

Meg rose and took her elbow, leading Cassandra around to the side door. "I think Connor and Marcus could use some!"

Cassandra whispered when they got inside the kitchen. "I don't know what's wrong with me."

"I don't have time to list it all, but I think getting your house broken into TWICE qualifies as valid reason to act like an airhead. For a couple days. After that, you'll need better excuses."

When the women came back outside, the guys were talking about the lineman who'd been carted off the football field. Fischer reported, "I stopped at the hospital to see him. He'd thrown up quite a bit and was very weak. Thompson told me he'd won a hamburger eating contest Thursday night. Ate six burgers with the works." Meg and Cassandra exchanged disgusted grimaces. "I asked the doctor to test his blood for that enzyme from the research lab. That much meat, maybe it's related."

Six burgers was a lot by any standards. Cassandra frowned, "I thought you'd ordered a hold on serving the beef?"

"I asked around, and it was a fraternity fundraising contest. They'd purchased the ingredients beforehand so they served the beef from Hopkins' farm."

Connor remarked, "If six burgers put Thompson—that huge lineman—in the hospital, what amount did it take for Austin Price to get as sick as he did . . . assuming they both overdid the beef and the enzyme. Did Price throw up before he fell down the stairs?"

Marcus shrugged. "I read the police report, and no one mentioned vomiting. They found blood on the glove so they assume he injected himself. The coroner said he had a seizure before he fell down the stairs outside. Was that from the injection?"

Meg summarized, "So exactly how much enzyme did Thompson have compared to Austin? What about the kids in the clinic? Were they vomiting too?" She grabbed a handful of pretzels and popped a few in her mouth. "Doesn't make sense that Austin gets a lower amount of the enzyme, but he's the one who's dead."

Connor hadn't been present for most of the investigation, but his mind made the connections quickly. "Did Price's fraternity serve the beef, too?"

Another side of Marcus unfolded before her eyes. Tonight, he matched Connor's analytical succinctness. "All the food services used it per our contract. It's served on campus and in all the Greek houses, too. That's how we got such a good price." At work, he was confident, easygoing, but all business. Last night, he'd been powerful, protective, yet gentle.

Meg wondered, "Did we ever find out about those syringes that Lance found in the lab? The ones in the cooler that none of the grad assistants knew about. Am I the only person who thinks that's weird?"

Cassandra shrugged. "I haven't heard results yet. Honestly, that lab seemed pretty messy to me. Those assistants could easily have forgotten to put away a cooler of syringes. Maybe no one wants to own up to leaving them out. Don't want to get in trouble."

After more college football talk, the conversation circled around again to the lab.

"So, who exactly is in charge of the Edgerton lab? The grad assistants run their experiments, but who's the director?" asked Connor.

Marcus and Cassandra frowned at each other. She answered, "Well, each assistant has a PhD committee who helps them design and oversee the experiments. For Luke Peterson, his chair is Dr. Schneider from the AlphaBioGlobal center. I don't know which Faculty Chairpersons are on the other two GAs' committees. Why?"

Connor shifted in his chair and crossed his leg over his other knee. "Seems like the Committee Chair oughta know the most about the tests, right? He should know if eating too much meat could make the students sick?" He took a drink from his beer. "Have any of the rats gotten sick?"

Cassandra replied, "I can't remember exactly what he said, but Luke mentioned that there are side effects to the enzyme. Some aggression and biting. I don't know how many rats get them."

Connor said, "Maybe Dr. Schneider can help you understand what's going on with the students. Do you guys need to abandon this food service thing, or is it all just a big coincidence?"

Cassandra cringed, "Nielson and the board don't want anything to happen to that food contract. Or the research lab. They've made that very clear. If Morton loses the NIH grant, some Peeping Tom outside my kitchen will be minor compared to the trouble they will cause. Also, Luke and those other grad assistants are finishing their research and writing their dissertations. If the lab closes, their degrees will be in limbo."

Meg folded her arms across her chest. "Which brings us back to the nitrogen tank valve. Two accidents in one week in the same lab? The cops should be talking to Dr. Schneider. Before anyone else gets hurt."

Chapter Thirty-Five

Cassandra's phone's home screen flashed a message from Andy. "Hi Cassandra. Are you still awake? I want to show you something."

After the O'Briens and Fischer had left, she'd been reassured to see the county sheriff car roll past her house while she retrieved the mail at the end of the driveway. The rest of the afternoon had been thankfully uneventful. She'd tacked up a towel over the small kitchen window, too.

They'd better catch the video creep/Zorro guy soon. What could Andy want to show her at 9 o'clock at night? She responded, "Yep. I'm awake. Watching The Office reruns. Come to the side door." She flipped on the overhead light to brighten the gloomy living room where she had closed all the curtains.

Minutes later, Andy was inside and she was offering him a drink. He pointed a thumb towards the driveway. "I'm good, thanks. I've got my water bottle in the car . . . The Office, huh? I figured you for a Gilmore Girls fan."

She thought of her SpongeBob fixation. "You'd be surprised what I like to watch. I needed some laughs tonight. Can't handle anything serious."

Andy grimaced. It must be serious or he wouldn't be here. "Sorry to come by so late. I wanted to update you, but I didn't know if you'd go into work tomorrow."

Cassandra leaned against the kitchen counter sipping hot chamomile tea, hoping it would relax her. She warmed her hands around the mug. "Tomorrow might be my second Sunday in a row at work. I should go in for a few hours to get some stuff done before Dr. Nielson comes back on Tuesday."

Placing an official looking medical document on the countertop, he explained, "Thompson, the football player, had elevated levels of the enzyme in his blood. Monday we're sending everything to a forensic lab in Omaha. Including the samples from the students at the health clinic. Who are slowly getting better, by the way."

Setting her cup on the counter, Cassandra nodded slightly. "So...Price and Thompson tested for elevated levels of SODs. We stopped serving the beef in case that is causing a few students to get sick. What a relief they're getting better. Slight progress, right?"

Andy laid down another paper and pointed at two sections with chemical symbols and long medical biology terminology. "This is where it gets interesting. The Omaha lab tech told me that those syringes from the cooler that Lance Erickson showed us are not the same as the lab refrigerator's supplies. We tested syringes from all three studies, and none are an exact match for those."

Raising her phone to snap pictures of both documents, she paused a millisecond to meet Andy's eyes. "Are photos necessary?" He asked.

"Maybe I'll study it later." She held up a finger. "Be right back." She riffled through the messenger bag in her bedroom for the file folder where she'd collected the papers from Lance, her notes, and autopsy information.

When she returned, Andy was flipping through his small notebook. "Tate and another deputy checked the video phone history from the device in Lance and Austin's fraternity room. I haven't seen the records myself, but Tate told me the calls are predictable. Messages from both of their parents, other deaf students. They're following up with the unlisted contact directory."

Andy slowly paged through the file she had handed him. "I thought Dr. Schneider told us last week that he didn't know Austin Price? Why did he write a recommendation letter for someone he didn't know?"

She and Meg had already covered this topic. Cassandra's eyebrows lifted a little and she nodded. "True. I've written letters for kids I didn't know very well before. It happens. Usually those letters are mostly generic."

"This letter isn't generic. It's glowing. Schneider says, 'In the six months he has worked in a lab I supervise, he has been a valuable asset for our research team. Austin Price is a hard-working student whom I highly recommend for this internship.' Why did he say he doesn't know him?"

Cassandra put her hands out in the classic "I don't know" shrug. "Obviously, he knew Price better than he implied."

Andy was quiet for a minute, processing the information. "I'll talk to Tate tomorrow. We can follow up with Dr. Schneider about our questions."

A thrill of anticipation zipped through her body. Maybe they'd get some answers finally.

She pressed him, "Meg, Fischer, and I were talking earlier today and we think someone should ask Dr. Schneider more questions about the lab, too. Did they have all the safety certifications? Did the students have the proper training? What can we do to prevent future accidents? Considering your lab results, maybe he knows why there's extra syringes lying around? Could Austin have been doing something on his own?"

At first, Andy nodded in agreement with her analysis, but when she fired off questions he and the deputy should be asking, his expression chilled. "Look. I appreciate your help. We already have questions about how the lab is run."

He stacked the pages back in her file folder and closed it. When he handed it to her, she looked up at him through her eyelashes. "If I promise to just watch and not say one word, can I please go with you tomorrow to see Dr. Schneider? Someone representing the college should be there to make sure our interests are served and to know the extent of his role in all of this. He's the chairman of the board."

Andy raised his voice. "I'm the campus security director. I'm the college representative working with the sheriff's department." When she opened her mouth to talk again, he held up a hand. "You worry about your job, and let us do security. I don't tell you how to discipline students, do I?"

She squinched her eyes a little and her face reddened. He had a good point. So did she. She braced her hands on her hips and waited him out. Neither of them relented for a full 60 seconds.

He broke first, wiping his hand down his face. "You. Are. Impossible. You can come with us to ABG tomorrow. We could use an administrator's face to communicate the seriousness of this mess. But leave the questions to us, agreed?"

She tried not to gloat at winning the argument. She couldn't control the spark in her eyes knowing she'd be able to make sure all her questions were answered. "Agreed."

His stern face softened and a stab of guilt hit her heart when she recognized the longing in his eyes. She'd used his personal feelings to get what she wanted.

He moved a step closer. "I'm worried about your safety. I heard about that video and your break-in last night. I've assigned an off-duty deputy to drive by here every few hours. Please call me if you hear any strange noises or need me. I only live five minutes away, and I won't mind checking it out."

He didn't ask why she'd called Fischer to help with the video creep's break-in instead of him. His eyes showed the hurt without needing to say it aloud. No time for second-guessing her motives. The students' safety and the college's reputation were more important than Andy's feelings right now. "Ok, I will. I appreciate your help."

"You're going to get me fired too, aren't you?" His lips formed a helpless smile while he shook his head. Oh. He knew about her tenuous relationship with the powerful people?

She gave him a big, cheesy grin. "If we both get fired, you can move back to Hawai'i with me."

Whoops! She instantly regretted her rash words. Instead of the joking, friendly tone she'd aimed for, she may have invited him to move in with her in Hawai'i.

Chapter Thirty-Six

Like most small-town businesses on a Sunday, ABG was closed. Dr. Schneider himself met Cassandra, Andy, and Deputy Tate at the door, unlocked it and let them inside. Although Schneider must have wondered why Tate had requested this meeting, he showed no outer signs of irritation. He warmly shook their hands, offered them coffees from the Keurig in the lobby, and greeted the security guard who passed them in the hallway. "Good morning Jacob, we'll be meeting in my office."

Once they were seated around a small conference table in his office, Tate led off the conversation. "We won't keep you long Dr. Schneider. We just have a few questions you could clear up before we close the investigation into Austin Price's death and the accident in the Morton lab."

Schneider smiled slightly, "We'd appreciate that, deputy. This phase of research is nearly completed and we need to move on. I'm not involved in the day to day operation of the lab, but I'll tell you what I can."

Tate clarified, "You're not? I got the impression you helped design and oversee the research study. You have key card access to the lab. The security logs show you frequently go over there."

He nodded. "To meet with Luke Peterson, my doctoral student. I'm a businessman, not a full-time academic. I have plenty on my plate already, what with my duties here at ABG and on the Morton board. This past week has really taxed my time while I've put out fires with the board and donors during President Nielson's absence." He paused to stare pointedly at Cassandra.

She kept the passive smile mask on her face and didn't say a word. No way was she getting kicked out of this meeting.

"You mentioned last week that if Austin Price had mistakenly injected himself with a syringe from the study, he should not have had any side effects, correct?" Tate asked.

"That's true. Like I told you the SOD enzyme occurs naturally in our bodies."

"Ok. Can you explain the science behind why some students appeared to experience side effects from eating the enzyme-fed beef?"

Dr. Schneider sat back in his chair and crossed his arms, his index finger tapping his mouth. "I'm glad you asked me that. I've been thinking about it all week. I believe Dr. Sato is going overboard with the announcements about stopping the enzyme enhanced beef service for the college cafeterias." Again he looked in her direction. "However, Nielson and I do understand that you're trying to protect the students' welfare. I just don't believe the concentration is high enough to cause any meaningful side effects. Those students probably caught the stomach flu or overindulged at a party."

Summers interjected, "We are sending samples to a lab in Omaha tomorrow. They'll compare the concentrations from the beef samples, sick students, Austin Price, and the football player."

Schneider frowned, but nodded. Tate opened his windbreaker and slid out a folded paper. Opening it, he placed it on the table in front of Dr. Schneider. "Did you write this recommendation letter for Austin Price to get an internship at your main clinic in Lincoln next summer?"

Schneider's eyes narrowed and he adjusted his wire-rimmed glasses to read the document. "Yes, I write many recommendations for students. He came to ABG frequently as a donor; he was a recruiter for us and he worked in the lab. He's been a valuable member of our team. His accident was tragic. Untimely."

Cassandra asked, "Why did you tell us you didn't know him? When you stopped by my table at The Home Team you said you didn't know him, and you questioned whether any deaf students should be working in a lab environment."

Schneider glared at her. She also felt Summers' head swing right and give her an eyebrow. So much for that promise to keep quiet.

After a chilly few seconds, Schneider answered, "You might not understand this with your inexperience, but I don't remember every single student's name I come across. And yes, I do have reservations about whether the deaf can safely work in the labs. Obviously, it was a problem for

Mr. . . . ah . . ." He referred to the recommendation letter and pointed to his name. "um . . . Price."

Cassandra resisted the big eye roll she wanted to make. He wasn't convincing anyone. Schneider shifted in his chair. His confident demeanor was slowly melting.

Tate switched tactics. "Do you know of anything in the lab that Austin Price could've been selling on the side to make money?"

Schneider sat up and his eyes grew wide. "What?"

"On his laptop we found $600 worth of payments to him. His parents confirmed they didn't send it. We're trying to find out what he could have done to earn that much cash. Any ideas?" Cassandra realized that Tate had done a lot more work on the case than the parts she knew about.

"Of course not!" Schneider blustered. "Where are you going with this? I thought you just needed to know a few things about ABG and the Morton lab. Why are you asking me so many questions about the dead student?" His eyes shifted between Tate's and Summers' stoic faces. "Do I need a lawyer?"

Tate didn't break eye contact. "Not if you've done nothing wrong."

Schneider's chest puffed out. "I'm a well-respected physician and researcher. I work for a global corporation and serve on two boards of directors. I don't have time for this nonsense." He stood up and brought his cup to the corner water station to refill it. The bubbles made a loud glug, glug sound and the other three exchanged solemn looks while his back was turned.

Facing them again he argued, "Your interference in this research is baffling. We're working to save children's lives, and you people are obstructing one of the best projects in Morton's history. Do you have any idea how lucky we were to win this grant? Now ... Your unrelated tangents have wasted enough of my Sunday afternoon."

Tense pinpricks radiated across Cassandra's neck and upper back. Gotta remember to breathe.

"Just doing our jobs, Doctor. Like you." Tate squared his broad shoulders. "Here's an interesting coincidence. We checked the phone call history on Austin's and Lance's room video phone. Among the calls we investigated from unsaved numbers several were from Omaha. One of the numbers belonged to a deaf woman who denied knowing either Austin or Lance."

Schneider had seemed on the verge of dismissing them, but his face changed from indignation to stone while Tate continued. "The person's name is Debra Timm." Schneider's torso slowly rotated toward the window. "When asked if Ms. Timm knew anyone in Carson, she answered, 'Yes, my brother ... Arnie Schneider, lives there.'"

A surprised gasp escaped Cassandra's lips.

Schneider sunk into his leather chair and let out a loud sigh. "I'm going to level with you. I called Price's dorm room from my sister's house a few times. I gave him the $600. As a recruiting bonus. We needed more blood products to extract enough SOD to complete our research. We would've lost the NIH grant if we missed the deadline. We were at a critical juncture in the study."

His arrogant demeanor softened, and he shoved a hand through his hair. "Look, I'm sorry I said those things about his deafness causing the lab accident. Truth is, he was a good worker, but he made minimum wage in the lab."

Well, this was an about face. Cassandra's mouth opened, and she exchanged incredulous looks with Andy.

Schneider's voice was impassioned, his right fist pounded the arm of his chair. "Deaf people work harder than hearing people because side conversations don't distract them. Hell, my deaf sister Debra has worked more than 25 years at the Post Office. She's their best employee because she pays attention to the job—not that anyone thanks her for her loyalty. Austin's family didn't have much to help him out, and I didn't want to see him quit school. He did an excellent job getting more donors here at ABG. I didn't want anyone to find out. I only meant to help him."

Cassandra was stunned. So, that whole rant at The Home Team had been for show? She related to his fierce loyalty to his sister, but he didn't need to hide his help to Austin. Some people might interpret it as crossing an ethical boundary or favoritism, but she could understand his reasons. Schneider was letting Austin succeed on his own merits instead of waving his deafness around as a cause for sympathy.

After another ten minutes of uneventful questions, Tate and Summers exchanged some telepathic signal and both men stood to end the meeting. "Thanks for your time Dr. Schneider and for meeting us. We'll be in touch."

They were about to leave the office when a thought occurred to Cassandra. "When I asked Dr. Baral about the internship for Austin Price, he didn't seem to know what I was talking about. Hadn't you arranged for that with him? Wasn't that why you wrote the recommendation letter?"

It was Schneider's turn to be startled. "When did you talk to Dr. Baral?"

She was still missing a connection. "When I stopped at the main ABG office in Lincoln last Wednesday. I was in town for a meeting. I saw the headquarters building and remembered you'd mentioned setting up more internships. I used the opportunity to meet Dr. Baral and tell him about our career services..."

She frowned when he straightened in his chair. Schneider went from calm to red-faced angry in three seconds flat. "Now you've done it. Your big mouth has finally gotten you into trouble. Nielson insisted we hire a woman and this is what we got."

Her jaw fell open. She didn't know which insult to address first.

Tate had stilled. "What trouble?"

Schneider bent down in the chair covering his face with his hands. Tate leaned down right by Schneider's ear and repeated, "What trouble, Doc? Did you know her house has been broken into twice this week?"

His head flew up and he pointed at Cassandra who hadn't moved. "Her house?"

She took the whole scene in like watching a movie. This didn't seem real.

Schneider's head shook. "I...I...Baral called me Wednesday. He complained about the interruptions in the research study. ABG has invested a lot of money in this.

They dislike delays and police investigations. I told him we were rushing the end of the study as much as possible." He rose again and walked to the window. "I didn't know...I didn't think. Baral asked me if I'd told anyone about the internship. Of course I haven't."

Schneider's hands pushed his hair around both sides of his head, giving his casual Sunday attire a rumpled, beaten appearance. He faced Cassandra and accused, "How did you find out about Price's internship?"

Tate picked up the recommendation document from the desk. "It was saved on Price's laptop."

"Baral asked me if I knew you. He asked me if a Cassandra Sato worked for Morton College. I told him yes, but I didn't ask why he wanted to know...I figured he saw your name on TV." His eyes looked left and right, pleading. Scared. He blew out a breath. "If those people think you hampered their cancer research, you...are in danger."

Summers crowded up to him, too. "What kind of danger? What people would hurt her?"

Schneider dropped his eyes, head still shaking as he confessed. "My college fraternity roommate was Dr. Baral's son. I knew his family well. We were good friends for a couple years. Until he...snapped. He was kicked out of school when an ex-girlfriend accused him of putting her pet cat in the oven. She thought it was lost and didn't find it for days until she went to put in a pizza." He drank more water. "I haven't seen him in 20 years, but he's still around. He does odd jobs for anyone who pays him. If Baral sent his son after you, he will hurt you. No one will be able to stop him or catch him."

"What's this guy's name?" Tate asked.

He did a palms up shrug. "Last I knew, he went by Roy Barnett."

Summers took Cassandra's elbow and half-carried her out of the plasma center. Her legs moved stiffly and her brain processed the sights like watching actors in a film: the sheriff and college security cars parked in the lot, sitting in the passenger seat riding down tree-lined streets to her home.

Andy even guided her to the front door. After she fumbled with the key several times, he gently took it from her grasp and opened the door. She hated feeling helpless and weak. She was a strong, independent woman. She'd stood up to plenty of doubters to get this far. Now some pharmaceutical company's private creep was stalking her? In Nebraska?

"I'll have one of my guys park in your driveway. All the rest of today and tonight. We won't leave you alone. Tate and I will figure this out, Cassandra."

She was scared and angry in equal measures. "How can you say that? This jerk's apparently a professional. You can't protect me forever." Her neck and shoulders were sore from two hours of tension, but arguing with him wouldn't help. "I'm going to lie down, Andy. Call me later if you find anything."

"Tate's already on it. We're small but we do have resources at our disposal. We'll call in out of town help if needed." He squeezed her arm in reassurance and quietly left her house.

Chapter Thirty-Seven

The ringing office phone echoed through the deserted rooms and jarred Cassandra away from her early morning paperwork. She picked up the handset without thinking. "Before you hang up, you might want to know that Dr. Arnie Schneider stands to gain piles of money from the cancer research lab at Morton."

Squinting hard, she fought the instinct to slam the handset back in the cradle. "Hello, Mr. Swanson. You're up early."

Nielson's cultural exchange group was expected within twenty-four hours, and she'd spent too much of last week doing his job to focus on her own work. Normally neat, her desktop was covered in files, flyers, and books while she completed written reports about the successful Homecoming activities.

Unable to resist her curiosity about Dr. Schneider, she said, "You're not working on another story about Morton, are you?" If Nielson arrived in Omaha to front page headlines about his college, he might burst a blood vessel. "What makes you believe that Dr. Schneider will earn money from our lab?"

Derek Swanson summarized, "Schneider has worked at ABG since he graduated med school twenty years ago, although the name has changed twice in corporate takeovers. Until six months ago, he was a big fish in a small town. He made good money by Carson standards, but had lackluster prospects. He's rich on paper: lives in a big house, leases expensive cars, belongs to a couple of private clubs. Even though he's an adviser for doctoral students, he did the bare minimum of his own research."

Her eyes popped open. "Has that changed?"

"Six months ago he bought a condo in Vail and booked a European river cruise for January. I'm following up on leads that I think prove he's having an affair. He kept his title as Carson Clinic Director and ABG added him as Assistant Chief Medical Officer. My source says that's contingent on the success of an experimental cancer treatment and dietary supplement he's working on."

Despite her distaste for gossip, she wrote notes on her legal pad while he spoke. "Why're you telling me all of this?"

"When the article is ready to submit, I'm going to need a reaction from Morton administration. Is Morton getting a cut from these pharmaceutical profits?"

She frowned. "Human trials are far into the future. Nothing that advanced is happening now at the college. Look, please wait until Dr. Nielson returns before you print anything. You'd get more accurate information if you speak to him directly."

"Is Nielson personally involved? My article isn't ready. Yet. But if Schneider gets arrested in the next few days, I'll print what I already have."

Her eyebrows shot skyward. "What makes you think he'll be arrested?"

"I saw the security and sheriff cars at ABG yesterday. I know you were there too. Something's going on, and I'm gonna find out what it is."

Cassandra coughed into her shoulder. How many people were following her around, anyway? "I have no comments. Please don't use my name in connection to any of this."

She hung up. Monday had barely begun, and already she was in hot water. Cassandra tried to return to the reports, but there were too many thoughts zipping around her head.

She picked up her phone looking for a distraction and texted Meg. "Aloha. News flash. Arnie Schneider has a deaf sister in Omaha. Also, HE paid Austin the $600. Called it a recruiting bonus. A deputy has been house sitting me for 2 days. Plus, that Omaha reporter is stalking me. Maybe I'll get lucky. He'll see Zorro lurking around and catch HIM."

Meg responded quickly, "Typical Monday morning, eh? Most people eat a donut and read the paper. Not you. Even on bad days you overachieve."

Meg's sarcasm had few boundaries. Cassandra laughed. "Your moral support is unlimited."

Meg sent a happy face and thumbs up emojis. "Mahalo."

* * *

Three hours later, a knock sounded on her door. She'd been completely in the zone typing the Homecoming reports. Looking up from her desktop screen, she was surprised to realize an hour had passed since she'd refilled her coffee. Her neck cracked when she looked up at the ceiling, and her back was numb from leaning over the desk. She took the opportunity to stand and personally open the door so she could stretch her legs.

"Hey Andy," she greeted him as he entered the office and closed the door behind himself. She walked over to the corner Keurig and brewed herself another cup. "I hope you brought some more of those yummy bagels. I rushed this morning and forgot to bring a snack."

She sat behind her desk, crossed her legs and regarded him with a smile. It slipped a notch when he remained in place by the door. Unmoving. Holding no bakery bags or travel cups.

His gray uniform pants and navy Morton Security polo were freshly pressed, but his expression looked ... uncomfortable. Frowning, she set down her drink. "That's ok. I can get something from the work-study stash ..." She gestured towards the main office. Maybe she should let him speak.

His hands turned out at his sides. "Cassandra, ... I ... need to—"

Why was he stammering? She snapped, more sharply than she wanted. "What, already—"

Two steps brought him closer to her desk. His cheeks flushed red, and a few sweat beads shined on his temples. Had he run upstairs? "I've been sent to escort you off campus. The Board of Directors met this morning and placed you on suspension. You don't have to clean out your office, because you're only suspended. The student workers will cancel your meetings and reschedule your student appointments with other staff. You have five minutes to gather your personal belongings, and I'm to drive you home."

It was her turn to stare at him, unmoving. She replayed the words he'd just spilled out. Escort. Suspension. Cancel. Five minutes. Her eyes flashed and her lips formed a stiff line. He was not her enemy. Clearly, he was miserable being the chosen messenger. Which coward had sent him instead of delivering the news personally?

To him, she nodded—not trusting herself to speak politely. She calmly stood, stacking the papers and files on her desk. Pulling her lined navy trench coat over her shoulders, she grabbed her coffee mug and her purse. Head held high, she sailed into the main office ahead of Andy.

With concerned eyes and hushed tones, Rachel, Devon, and Lance watched their short procession. Before she cleared the outer door, Lance made a thumbs up sign and a little wink to Cassandra. Her reassuring smile supply was tapped out.

Twenty minutes later, her key was steady as she opened the front door and let herself inside, Andy following. The car ride home had been silent. She had many questions, but she didn't ask them on campus. Andy had barely shut the front door and stepped into the living room when she rounded on him. "Alright. Give it to me straight. What do you know?"

His eyebrows raised and he chuckled. "Not everything. Someone found out that we questioned Dr. Schneider yesterday—I don't know how. The Board met this morning and appointed Dr. Bergstrom as interim until Nielson comes back to work."

She crossed her arms in front of her, nodding. "Derek Swanson from the Omaha Daily News called me this morning with some crazy conjecture about Schneider doing experiments in the Morton lab. Probably I wasn't the first person he called fishing for details."

He searched her face. "You're still an employee, and we're still responsible for your safety. I'm going to keep a security officer parked in your driveway for a least a couple more days. We're concerned about this psycho stalking you. Deputy Tate looked up Roy Barnett, but Barnett's not a big internet user. He couldn't even find a current address or driver's license for him. I'll let you know when we hear back from the Omaha lab on all the enzyme samples. It'll probably take a couple days."

"Mahalo for the ride. I'm glad it was you who told me instead of some pompous board person." She took a big breath. "You can go back to work. I'll be fine here."

He put a hand up as though he'd touch her, but thought better and dropped it. "I'll check in with you later."

The door snapped shut, she let out a huge sigh and her proud shoulders slumped. Pulling on sweats, a t-shirt and a ponytail, she made a ham sandwich and settled into the couch. She thumbed the TV remote and wondered aloud, "What do people watch during the day?"

Her phone lit up with messages from Meg, Cinda, Marcus and even Connor who typed variations on the same theme: Old Bastards.

She copy-pasted the same response to all of them: "I'll be ok. Gonna rest a while. Talk to you later."

Dr. Bergstrom left two voicemails, but she didn't listen to them. She had no animosity towards him. He was the logical choice to make decisions until Nielson returned. She knew he'd stand up for her, given the chance.

A while later, she returned to the kitchen and rooted in the pantry until she found a bag of unopened wavy potato chips. Squinting at the expiration date—yesterday—she decided they'd still work and brought the whole bag back to her nest on the couch. A perky woman on a food preparation show demonstrated how to make salsa three ways, but Cassandra's focus wandered from the screen.

For the umpteenth time since last Friday, Cassandra replayed the anticipation and excitement she'd felt upon moving. She'd stopped at Ala Moana Beach with her brother on the way to the airport and walked barefoot near the water's edge. Slowly sinking onto the warm, powdery sand, she lifted her face toward the hot circle of the sun. The waves crashed rhythmically in and out, and the salt water smell mixed with flowers fallen from plumeria trees. Teens played volleyball behind her on the park's green grass, and families held potlucks on the surrounding picnic tables, grilling teriyaki chicken over charcoal. Tearing herself away at the last possible moment, she'd risen, dusted the sand off her slacks, and returned to the car. Her brother for once had understood that this moment needed silence.

People had advised her for years that if she wanted to advance her academic career, the surest path was to go out into the world and work at other institutions. She needed exposure to new experiences and to branch out from the people who had supported her through her schooling. That longing tug: to do something bigger and move up the career ladder had seemed like a great reason to move 3,000 miles away, but she had completely miscalculated the depth of loneliness she would feel.

What a stupid idea this was. Because of her job title, she had naively expected people would embrace her instantly. She'd underestimated how tiresome cultivating new student and faculty relationships would be. People she never saw evaluated her every move.

Local Hawaiian style could feel like a small town sometimes where everyone knew each other, your family and your business. But that was nothing compared to small town life here. In Carson, people did know your intimate details: when you went to the store, out to eat, what you ordered, whether you paid your bills on time, what time your car left and arrived. People back home noticed their neighbors' habits, but it wasn't a source of conversation at work or the grocery store.

She loved Hawai'i with all her heart. Her family was everything to her. Some people imagine that living your whole life on an island with the same group of colleagues, friends, and relatives would be constraining. To Cassandra—the comfort, reliability, and pride she felt at knowing that her family had moved to the islands over one hundred years ago with nothing; working and sacrificing to get to where she was now—was worth the occasional claustrophobia of a life lived in close proximity to a large family. She pictured her parents' faces, middle-aged, slightly wrinkled, yet always gazing at her and her siblings with love and pride.

Cassandra would've happily remained at home as Dean of Students forever. But when this opportunity had appeared, her father took her into the backyard one afternoon. Resting under the wooden trellis interwoven with bright pink bougainvillea, the fragrant blossoms were so heady she could smell them even in her memory.

He'd grasped her palms between his warm, callused hands. "Cassandra, your mother and I plan to be around for a long time. You need to have your time, your adventures. We'll still be here when you get back. You can take care of us in our old age. But we don't need you to be here for us every day, yet. We'll take care of Gran and your brother and sisters. You'd make us very proud if you go to the mainland. You will carry our culture, our lifestyle, our spirit with you always, wherever you live."

At that moment, she knew she would leave Oahu, for a while. She'd return someday armed with her many accomplishments.

* * *

Cassandra rubbed away the crusty salt crystals in the corner of her eyes, momentarily disoriented to find herself drooling on a couch cushion, potato chip crumbs on her shirt front and an enthusiastic cleaning commercial blaring from the television. Shaking her head, she realized this day was not a dream. Teetering on the edge of fitting into this place or losing everything made her realize how much she liked Morton and Carson.

Admittedly, the last few weeks contained few brag-worthy moments. Warm heat burned her cheeks while she ticked off her recent failings: the awkward photo, Austin's death, the break-ins, the students getting sick, and now her own suspension. Suspension! In her long student history, she'd never earned even one demerit, let alone a suspension. Now she was precariously employed, in the middle of nowhere, being stalked by a thug.

Brushing off her shirt, she cleaned up her spot and moved to the desk with her laptop and phone. Morton had to address the potential gossip about Dr. Schneider's personal dirty laundry and his misguided attempt to help Austin Price. Would cutting ties with him be enough to repair the college's reputation and save their NIH grant? She wanted a plan ready upon Nielson's return.

She could emphasize Schneider's desire to cure a childhood disease or his mentoring relationship as Luke Peterson's committee chair. First, she needed to know the extent of his involvement in the lab. His comments about deaf people being unqualified to work in science didn't help either.

Her eyes focused on the calendar notation for her Women of Tomorrow leadership group's inaugural meeting next week. The whole point of becoming a female university president was to do better for more students. To salvage her career, she needed to work her contacts before the connections imploded. Her finger tapped the phone screen, and she listened for the line to open. When Swanson's voice answered, she skipped the polite formalities. "Hi this is Cassandra. You seem to have a lot of local contacts. Do you have time to meet me for coffee this afternoon? ... Is there somewhere nearby that people wouldn't see us together?"

Loud laughter hurt her ear, and she held the phone's speaker at arm's length until the noise quieted. Listening briefly, she wrote an address on a scratchpad and hung up. A frown creased her forehead as her GPS app showed a location just outside of town on a gravel road.

Time to stop wallowing. She was tired of being the mouse in this game.

Chapter Thirty-Eight

Cassandra was chopping stir-fry vegetables for an early supper when Meg called. "Lance has a theory about the lab he wants to test out. Only Connor won't let me go over there with him."

Pouring oil into a hot frying pan, Cassandra hit speaker phone so she could do hands-free. "Andy said we wouldn't get the results back for a couple more days. What does Lance need to see over there in person?"

"He's been combing through Austin's laptop database files. He sent me photos of the work notes. Something's off."

Lance seemed to find more answers than the police. At least what she knew from the police anyway. A frisson of excitement formed in Cassandra's stomach. "You know . . . I've always wondered why Austin asked Lance to hide his laptop. He must've known important files were on there, and trusted Lance to protect it. Andy told me the enzyme in the cooler syringes wasn't the same as those in Peterson's research study or the other studies there."

Meg said, "Lance told me the custodians leave by 9:00 p.m. He'll sneak over there after hours to check it out. Connor told me I can't go with him."

Her voice had a strange note to it that Cassandra couldn't identify. She added diced chicken, peppers, onions, squash and cabbage to the pan, stirring quickly. "I can call Andy or Deputy Tate. They can go check out the lab with Lance."

"What if Lance is wrong? This is just his hunch. What if Austin was doing something illegal? Lance doesn't want to make his friend look bad or dredge up old news. His parents would be crushed. I would go . . . but we live half an hour away."

It finally dawned on her where Meg was leading. She held up the wooden spoon she'd been using and frowned at her phone incredulously as though Meg could see her face. "You want me to go to Edgerton with Lance? Are you lolo? I'm already suspended. Why would I risk getting caught?"

"It's the only way! You could be the person who finds proof to solve this whole thing. You wouldn't be suspended . . . you'd be the hero!"

"I can't believe you'd ask me that, Meg. I gotta eat . . . Wow." Cassandra punched the hang-up button with her pinky and added soy sauce, ginger and spice into the pan. She flicked off the burner, dumped the mixture into a bowl over sticky rice and plopped into a chair. Her normally delicious meal tasted like chunky paste as she simmered in silence.

What kind of respectable research lab had unused syringes stashed in a random cooler? Remembering the student workers' substandard housekeeping, she wasn't surprised Austin's notes were unknown to the police. Dr. Schneider and the department chair weren't involved enough in Luke Peterson's work. The administration didn't seem motivated to committing the resources to ensure their hallowed NIH grant's success. The whole study was in jeopardy if they weren't properly documenting all the data.

Once the initial anger wore off, she replayed Meg's appeal. "You could be the person who solves this whole thing."

They'd hunted for any connection between the cafeteria's enzyme enhanced beef and the donated blood enzymes used for the rat research. The police said the football player, the sick students, and Austin Price had elevated enzyme levels. Was that only from eating food service beef? Suppose they found a link between the sick students and the research lab? What if Swanson the reporter was right and there were human trials happening on campus?

Surely No-Nonsense Nielson wasn't involved in illegal human pharmaceutical testing. Assuming he didn't know, it'd still be a huge scandal for Morton. If Lance found evidence proving the reporter's theory, Cassandra had to speak up. Even if revealing the truth meant losing the government grant and administrative chaos. Her suspension would likely become permanent. Career-ending. No one hires a whistle-blower.

The memory of Zorro's masked face induced stomach-clenching dread. It'd be so easy to resign and move home. She'd grab her surfboard stored in Gran's garage, paddle out off Diamond Head, and forget this nightmare.

Lance believed in Austin enough to risk his standing at Morton. Could she enjoy the sun and surf back home if she abandoned Lance and more students got sick? Tempting, but not how her parents raised her. Ohana, first. The students were the closest thing to family she had here besides the O'Briens. University president had been a glamourous dream, but she'd rather be an entry-level academic advisor at an obscure island college and keep her dignity.

She checked the weather app on her phone while considering this ridiculous idea. Rolling her eyes, she shook her head while she tapped a message to Meg. "I'm in. Give Lance my phone number. I'll meet him over by Edgerton at 10 p.m. I hope they haven't disabled my key card. Latahz."

Meg responded only a few minutes later. "I love you! Promise you'll keep me posted. If I don't hear from you by 11, I'm calling police."

Cassandra changed into black clothes and exchanged a few texts with Lance to get their game plan settled. She promised herself, "If I wipe-out on this job, I might as well make it epic."

* * *

Cassandra crouched near the Edgerton center at 9:55 wearing a dark hoodie, a new stocking hat, and black gloves. Her hoodie pocket held folded up papers from her investigation file at home. The temperature had dipped into the low 50s and her cheeks were already chilled when Lance arrived five minutes later.

She typed a note into her phone and showed it to Lance. "I don't know if my key card is still authorized." She shrugged and he nodded. She added, "If we get stopped by anyone, let's say that you forgot your backpack in the lab and I'm helping you pick it up."

Lance tapped the side of his head in a "Good idea" gesture and gave her the thumbs up.

They moved to the bottom floor door under the stairwell and quickly swiped her card. A green light flashed on the display and the door clicked unlocked. She heaved it open and they moved inside. He pointed towards the far steps and they climbed four flights up to the lab. Lance typed in the security code near the door and they entered the lab's front room, their eyes adjusting to the dim lights.

When she inhaled pungent disinfectant mixed with urine and wood chips, her nose crinkled reflexively. In the quiet back room, Lance pulled a sheaf of Austin's printed data pages from a small backpack. He also fired up a laptop and logged on with Austin's user name. Cassandra snooped in the storage and main workrooms, feeling excited after the afternoon's gloom. Lance used a thumb drive to copy the suspicious files. She compared the numbers on the rat cages' bar codes, the treatment syringes from the medical documents, and Austin's data spreadsheet, counting as she went. Cassandra re-checked a row of cages that weren't included in the official bar codes. There seemed to be more rats than the three studies had recorded. That might explain the extra syringes Tate had sent to Omaha for analysis.

They'd been inside for maybe fifteen minutes when Cassandra heard buttons beeping outside on the door's security keypad. She ran to Lance and poked him on the shoulder. Her frantic eyes urged him as she did a "Cut! Cut!" finger-across-her-neck gesture, grabbed his arm, and ran towards the storage room. He folded the laptop and followed her inside. They'd barely closed the door without latching it when the main lab door opened.

Chapter Thirty-Nine

Cassandra peeked through the doorway crack at a tall man who carried a white Styrofoam cooler directly around to the back room. When he hit the overhead light switch, she recognized Dr. Schneider and her chest constricted. He set a small metal cylinder, his cooler, and some supplies on a steel work table then pulled a rat cage from the wall. Opening the Styrofoam cooler lid, a fog billowed out like the dry ice in haunted houses. She watched him use long metal tongs to fish out a rat and stick it in the cooler. Replacing the lid and waiting some seconds, he removed the rat, placed it on a metal tray, and dripped a liquid onto the stiff rat.

Cassandra assumed he was using liquid nitrogen to euthanize them. He returned the rat to the Styrofoam cooler for a few more seconds, then dropped it into a zipper bag. He followed the same procedure, quite haphazardly, on several more rats. Repulsion hiccupped in her esophagus.

Turning to Lance, she moved over so he could spy through the crack. She couldn't decide whether to hide in safety or confront Schneider.

When Lance stepped aside, she poked her head out a little farther. The rats Schneider had frozen were from the same row of cages that didn't belong to an official group. She mimed the question to Lance, "In here? Or out there? Which?"

His finger jabbed towards the work area. "Out there!"

Cassandra's sweaty hand eased the door open. She and Lance emerged into the room as Schneider zipped a baggie containing a frozen rat.

"You again!" he shouted. The other rats vocalized and scratched at their cages. With the lights, noises and dry ice in the air, they sensed a change. The bottom row of cages were nearly empty.

Not a biology major, the whole process with the cooler didn't make sense. Her heart still thumped from his surprise intrusion. "Dr. Schneider! Why are you freezing the rats?"

He gathered up the remaining three rats from cages and dropped them into the cooler, his hands resting on the lid. In contrast to Cassandra, his voice was emotionless. "These test subjects aren't necessary to the grant project."

He seemed much more involved in the daily research operations than he'd let on the day before. Cassandra challenged him. "This is Morton College property, not your personal workspace. Did the grad assistant ask you to remove these rats?"

She stilled her trembling knees and edged closer. He aimed the nitrogen tank's hose nozzle towards Cassandra and Lance. "That's close enough. Stay there; it'd be a shame to hurt such a pretty face. I so enjoyed our ride together in the parade. Do you know what happens when liquid nitrogen is sprayed into a room?"

Since the faulty valve incident on Thursday, yes she was perfectly aware what that would do. Cassandra slowly stepped closer and held up her hands. "Why are you doing all this?"

"I'm saving the children from cancer. I may have gotten ahead of myself in the rush to bring the treatment to market more quickly, but I can fix that. These rats don't exist."

Lance slowly turned his back towards Schneider and fingerspelled something down by his hip. By the time she realized what he was doing, she'd completely missed his message.

She shook her head slightly in frustration. He moved his fingers again. Staring harder, she concentrated. "A-U-S-T-Austin H-A-V-E have." Lance nodded once in affirmation. Then he twirled his index finger in a "Keep stalling" motion.

Austin had something. She should keep Schneider talking while Lance finished downloading data. "We can't let you take those rats. You said you'd 'gotten ahead of yourself'? Maybe we can help. What have you done?"

Just then the lab door lock pad beeped. Cassandra's and Schneider's heads turned while an unseen person punched in the security code. Cassandra met Lance's confused expression and pointed to the front door.

Seconds later, Luke Peterson came around the wall and took in the scene with Dr. Schneider holding the other two at bay with the nitrogen canister. Luke's head bobbed back and forth between them and Schneider. "What the heck?"

For the first time since Schneider had arrived, Cassandra had a flash of hope that she and Lance would survive unscathed. "Luke! Uh . . . why did you come here?"

Peterson's rumpled hair and stained t-shirt hinted that he'd recently been lying on a couch. He looked unfazed by the nitrogen canister threat. "You're in the lab after-hours which set off an alarm on my phone. I came to see what was wrong."

Cassandra's heart raced. What if Peterson had been lying the whole time? She didn't think they could stop both of them.

Schneider's hands wobbled and his face shone with perspiration. "Sorry, Luke. I'm going away for a while. You'll have to ask someone else to finish your doctoral committee work."

Shaking his head in denial, Luke's forehead crinkled and his shoulders bunched up. "You're totally screwing up my life!"

Schneider's eyes flitted between the cages, his cooler, and them. "I'm not going to be punished for something I didn't do."

Cassandra thought of the newspaper reporter's investigation into Schneider's history and finances. "Punished for . . .?"

"The subjects I'm taking were my own side project. Our third treatment was my synthetic version of the SOD enzyme in a higher concentration. Next time I make a new version, I'll have to lower the concentration. It was too potent for humans."

Was that confirmation that he had performed unauthorized human trials? She needed more time to piece it all together.

While Schneider fiddled with the cooler, Lance signed to her, "I'll tackle him, you run. We'll escape."

Surprisingly, Cassandra understood his signs and nodded once. Her knees bent, and her hands slowly moved towards a small cardboard box she planned to throw at Schneider before running. Lance's body tightened like a spring ready to uncoil.

Peterson had quietly backed up towards the dividing wall. He'd better not stop them when they ran out the door. She might be small, but she had years of experience wrestling with her older brother and she wasn't giving up.

In the moment before Lance moved, Schneider used his left hand to aim the nitrogen hose at Lance's face only 6 feet away. A direct spray would be disfiguring, if not deadly. With his right hand, Schneider signed and spoke at the same time. "Stop! You can't tackle me, and she's not going anywhere . . . Your roommate ruined everything."

Recognition animated Lance's face and his eyes widened. Taking a step towards Schneider, in a raw, gravelly voice he yelled and signed. "I saw you signing on our video phone. Austin was helping you. I knew you could understand me signing."

That night at the obstacle course when Lance had asked Meg about Schneider . . . he'd been right about Schneider being able to understand ASL.

Lance's face screwed up into rage and he accused, "I knew it! You killed him!"

Cassandra thought Schneider looked shaky, and worried Lance might spook him worse. She couldn't get Lance's attention. His eyes were fixed on Schneider.

Schneider shook his head no. "He did that himself when he poked his hand Thursday night. We had 10 extra rats that Austin tracked separately. I couldn't believe it when he texted me Friday that he felt sick. How unfortunate. I got here as fast as I could . . . but it was too late."

The puzzle pieces slid into place and Cassandra understood. That's what the street preacher had meant when she'd yelled at them during the parade! She'd seen Dr. Schneider when he came to Edgerton. He was the evil one. "YOU took his phone? You came to the stairs after he fell, and you took his phone?"

"He was beyond help when I arrived." His chin jerked in Lance's direction. "I didn't know you had his laptop." He shrugged again, and Cassandra's back teeth ground together. She wanted to smack the self-absorbed expression off his face with a vehemence that surprised her.

Peterson's attention had quietly shifted between Schneider and Lance until he erupted. "I'll never finish my dissertation because of all this crap. The IRB isn't gonna just let this go!"

His arms flew out wide to his sides. "There's no protocol for this. I did everything you asked. I rewrote the procedure. I analyzed the data. I even hurried things up so we'd finish on time." He slapped one palm in the other to emphasize each point. "I've dedicated the last year of my miserable life working on this project. The government is going to pull their freaking funding! You crazy bastard!"

The hose in Schneider's hand shook slightly. Cassandra tried to catch Peterson's eye. If all three of them worked together, they could overpower Schneider.

Peterson's voice climbed into a high whine, and he laced his hands together placing them on his head. "I thought we were going to develop the synthetic SOD enzyme together after I graduated. We were going to make supplements and beef snacks!"

Cassandra saw movement in the darkened hallway behind Peterson. She hadn't heard the keypad again; the door must have been left open.

When a figure took two more silent steps into the light next to Peterson, she saw him clearly. He was tall, heavy-set with dark hair, wearing a black fleece jacket and jeans. His face was covered by the same eye mask she'd seen him wearing Friday night.

In an instant, her anger turned to panic. She screamed loudly and grabbed Lance's arm. Zorro raised his black-gloved hand and pointed a gun at the group.

A deep, scratchy voice came from the masked man. "Good thing I followed her. Sounds like you were going to double-cross us. Dad isn't going to like that, Arnie. You always were an arrogant windbag. Enough yakking. Let's go." He waved Schneider forward while the gun remained trained on them. Zorro's head jerked towards Lance. "Tell that kid to freeze so I don't have to shoot him."

Schneider hoisted the cooler and headed towards the exit. "A gun pointed at your chest is like flipping someone the bird, Roy. A universal language."

The menacing Zorro was Roy? Cassandra's jaw dropped. Roy stepped backwards after Schneider, keeping the gun raised. "You'd better keep this quiet. Take the hint this time. I already know where you live. Better yet, go back to wherever you came from."

His hand shifted right, and two shots exploded across the 15-foot distance. Cassandra screamed as glass shattered on a shelf full of beakers. Cassandra and Lance both hit the deck and the breath was knocked from her lungs. She struggled to suck in a full inhale.

After a few heartbeats of echoed ringing, air filled her lungs again. Luke was crouched under the broken shelf. Lance and Cassandra crawled to him, avoiding glass shards that blanketed every nearby surface. "Luke! Are you hurt?"

Debris fell from his head like dandruff flakes and a temple gash dripped blood onto his jacket collar. His expression was dazed, but upon checking him over he seemed uninjured. Lance grabbed a paper towel wad for pressure while Cassandra called 911.

Andy and the sheriff arrived within ten minutes followed later by Meg, Connor, and Fischer. The three witnesses gave their statements to the sheriff. Meg interpreted for Lance and then Fischer dropped him off at the fraternity to meet up with his parents. Cassandra caught a ride home from the O'Briens.

* * *

Cassandra emerged from a warm shower wearing her long fleece pajama pants and University of Hawai'i hoodie to find Meg and Connor sitting on her couch sipping hot tea. Meg handed her a mug too, and she collapsed in the big leather armchair Fischer had slept in Friday night.

Meg beamed proudly. "You and Lance figured it out, Cass. You're heroes."

"We figured it out, but Schneider and Barnett still got away. Heroes don't let the bad guys escape unscathed."

"I'm sorry we didn't get there earlier. We had to wait for Tony's sitter to come to the house. I had no idea you were going into such a serious mess."

A few minutes later, Connor stood and offered a hand to Meg. "Unless you want us to stick around, it's time to leave you to rest and tuck my favorite wahine in bed. Andy is parked in your driveway in case there's more trouble tonight. I bet those two are long gone."

After they left, Cassandra felt too wired to go right to sleep. Pulling on shoes and a heavy coat, she went out the back door to bring Andy a travel cup.

His face lit up when she held up the cup near his driver side window. "Hi Cassandra! I'm wide awake already but thanks for the coffee."

"Nah, this is hot chocolate. I put in extra marshmallows. It's too late for coffee." She passed it to him.

"Well in that case, thanks very much. Appreciate the thought. I saw your friends leave and thought you'd go right to sleep."

The temperature had already dipped past what she'd expected for overnight in October. She wrapped her arms in front of her chest. "Sorry you're stuck out here tonight. I hope Dr. Schneider and Zorro are far, far away, but I can't help worrying they might come back."

"There's statewide and regional bulletins out for them. I promise we'll keep your house covered until they're caught."

That Roy guy was terrifying. She'd never had a gun pointed at her before. "I hope Luke and Lance are doing ok. I really made a mess of this whole thing. I should have listened to you and stayed home."

Andy did a little shrug. "Easy to say now, but at the time you must have had a feeling it was right."

Nope. Her brain had known that sneaking into the lab late at night was a bad idea, but she'd done it anyway. She shivered and said, "Thanks again for everything you've done. I might not see you again if they fire me."

"What you did was impulsive and dangerous, but you figured out what happened to Austin and with the lab experiments. That has to count for something."

She hoped that Nielson and the board would agree with Andy and her friends. She nodded slightly. "I'd better get back inside. Stay warm."

"Will do," he answered, more chipper than she felt. He made a toothy smile, "If you do get fired, we can always move back to Hawai'i, right?"

He rolled up his window, chuckling while she returned to the house. No idea how she'd explain that one to her mom.

Chapter Forty

President Nielson stepped to the media room's podium and paused in front of the microphones and cameras. For someone who had eschewed publicity the last two weeks, his confident smile came easily.

Opening his speech papers, he cleared his throat before addressing the staff, invited guests, and reporters gathered for his press conference. "Ladies and gentlemen, as you are surely aware, Morton College has recently focused on relationship building with the global community. During my trip to Hangzhou in the Zhejiang province of China, we built solid connections with the prestigious Hangzhou Commerce College. In the new year, we will host a visit from their administrative team in preparation for a more formal agreement between our institutions. Our students will have increased opportunities to study abroad, and we look forward to welcoming their students here as well."

Cassandra, tottering on her highest platform heels and wearing a serious black skirted suit, dutifully flanked Nielson onstage together with Bergstrom. Normally the shoes were strictly for short time periods, and after 90 minutes of coffee-plus-meet-and-greet, they pinched her little toes. She grudgingly admitted she was impressed by Nielson's accurate pronunciation of the city names. Maybe Nielson had learned something on his trip after all.

Glancing to the side, she watched Meg interpreting Nielson's announcement.

Nielson scanned the small crowd. "Would sophomore Computer Science major, Lance Erickson, come forward please."

Cassandra's smile became more genuine as Lance drew up next to the podium. Then she noticed Fischer standing against the back wall, his arms crossed over his chest, a pleased expression on his handsome face. Since the night in the lab, Cassandra hadn't even talked to Fischer.

"Lance played a crucial role in identifying those responsible for the student's death on campus a couple of weeks ago. In recognition of your bravery and action in difficult circumstances, I present you with a Morton Maples Distinguished Student Award and a $1000 scholarship." He handed Lance an engraved bronze maple leaf along with an envelope. They shook hands for posed photos while Meg and Cassandra shifted out of the way to give them space.

"We are grateful to Mr. Erickson as well as the campus security and other staff tasked with keeping our campus a safe learning environment. That's all I have for you at this time. Thank you for your attention." Nielson bowed slightly and exited the media room.

Cassandra, Bergstrom, the other VPs and Meg filed behind him into the private conference room next door.

Nielson turned, "Thank you all for your time this morning. Dr. Sato, I'd like to meet you in my office in five minutes."

Although willing to accept whatever consequences came from her actions, her heart still skipped a beat. Cassandra whispered to Meg. "What's that about? He's already read the police statements. I told him everything I know."

Meg shrugged, "Only way to find out is to go talk to him. I'll tell Fischer he'll have to wait in line." She wiggled her eyebrows, and Cassandra rolled her eyes.

Cassandra discreetly rubbed sore toes while she waited in the wooden armchair facing Nielson's desk. His gracious award presentation to Lance had been deserved, but there'd been no mention of her name during the media session. Not that she needed public affirmation for doing her job. Her stomach flip-flopped and she regretted the extra coffee burning a hole in her digestive tract. If the board wasn't satisfied with her version of events, it might be too late to rescind her suspension.

Nielson entered, closed the door, and quickly sat in his leather chair. His hair had been neatly combed for the press conference and he looked confident in his navy suit. Placing his folded hands on his desk, Nielson's mouth arranged into an expression between grimace and simper. "I want to tell you again how grateful I am that you figured out what was happening."

Was she being let go? He sounded sincere, but not as encouraging as she'd hoped. Cassandra had risked her life for her students and the job. If he wanted more from her, she had nothing else to give. "Thank you. The investigation was very complex. Many people worked to piece it together. Lance Erickson was very dedicated to his friend's memory."

"In light of these developments, I want to amend your contract."

If Morton needed a scapegoat, so be it. She'd choose students over career again, given the choice. Her only regret was how long it'd taken to realize what her priority should have been all along. She frowned, "Amend it . . . how?"

He produced several crisp pages from a file on the credenza and signed the last. "This contract changes your status to permanent employee, effective immediately. You have proven trustworthy to handle all the duties of your position. And more." Handing her his gold pen, he turned the papers in her direction. "That is . . . if you want to stay in Carson?"

She'd get to keep her dream job. On her terms. "Permanent . . . Wh- yes! I would like to stay. Thank you for your confidence." Adding her name under his, she sat up straight. She'd call her parents when she got home later. They'd be thrilled.

"This press release will be distributed to the media today. Excuse my presumptuousness, but I'd hoped you'd accept my offer." He handed her a copy of the announcement.

Cassandra breathed slowly out her nose while she read. "Several years ago, during a strategic planning process, the Board of Directors identified improving diversity on campus as a priority for the students, faculty and Carson community. Our recent hiring of Dr. Cassandra Sato as Vice President for Student Affairs was a key first step in that process. The Morton community cannot thank her enough for her recent crisis management and persistence in holding those in power to the highest standards of integrity. We proudly welcome her as our newest permanent administrator and hope she will continue her career for many years in Carson."

Well. She stared at the page extra moments to allow time for her watery eyes to dry.

Nielson leaned towards her. "This whole business has been scandalous. I'm greatly relieved that the police and faculty senate agree that my personal actions regarding the beef contract were justified. The Hopkins farm will reduce the feed additive concentration to follow daily recommended serving sizes." His blue eyes scanned the framed awards and memorabilia honoring his academic tenure that lined the walls and bookshelves. "I worked with Arnie Schneider for ten years. I had no idea about his 'mysterious treatment.' I'm selecting a task force to make recommendations to enhance transparency and reliability in all our facilities."

A knock sounded on his office door and Julie poked her head around the opening. "Sheriff Hart is here for you, sir."

"Please send him in."

Nielson rose to shake Hart's hand. "You have further information?"

Hart remained standing, turning his hat slowly in his hands. "The state patrol pulled over a speeding car in Western Nebraska. The driver shot at the state trooper, who returned fire and killed the driver. The driver had several IDs on him—one was for Roy Barnett—and a black mask. We're confident that we'll be able to match the gun to the one used in the lab, and the mask to the video evidence from Ms. Sato's home. Dr. Arnold Schneider, the passenger, was arrested unharmed and gave an extensive statement. We later interviewed Dr. Baral from the ABG corporate office in Lincoln. He claimed to be unaware of Schneider's synthetic treatment, and so far, we have no direct proof linking the company and Austin Price's data. Personally, I believe ABG sent Roy Barnett to Carson. There must be evidence linking him to Ms. Sato and the lab accident. We'll continue our investigation, but I wanted to keep you informed of the current status."

Nielson sat back, his shoulders lowered in obvious relief while Cassandra considered the implications. If Schneider quietly confessed his role, the whole sordid situation would disappear soon from the news cycle. Despite everything she'd personally been through—from Morton's perspective—that would be the best-case scenario.

Instead of leaving when Sheriff Hart finished his report, he remained silently standing. Clearing his throat, he produced a folded document and said, "Dr. Nielson, I'm also here to give you this." Laying it on the desk, Hart explained, "It's a subpoena for details about the contract between Morton College, Brian Hopkins, and the pharmaceutical company."

Nielson's relief vanished and his lips formed a tight line while he opened the papers and skimmed the first page. "Someone complained to the attorney general's office that illegal student experiments were being conducted on campus." His knees cracked when he stood and placed his palms on the desk. "That's simply untrue and you know it, Larry!"

Hart backed up two steps towards the door. "I'm just the messenger. Of course, I know you wouldn't be involved in using students as guinea pigs. Those Lincoln bureaucrats got nothing better to do than..."

Cassandra interrupted, "I don't think that investigation will get very far, Dr. Nielson." She pulled her cream leather tote bag onto her lap and felt inside at the bottom. When her fingers grasped a thumb drive, she paused long enough to consider the ramifications of sharing the information at this moment. Her gravel road "meeting" with Derek Swanson had been less than 48 hours ago, but felt longer. When he'd given her the thumb drive, she hadn't been sure how, or even if, she'd use the contents. Now seemed a timely opportunity to show her support for Nielson and the college. She offered the thumb drive to Sheriff Hart. "Once the Omaha news reporter prints his complete expose on Dr. Schneider's undergraduate transgressions coupled with his financial records, Morton's beef contract will be cleared."

Both men turned to her hopefully. "I talked to Derek Swanson on Monday. His investigation into Dr. Schneider's background, finances, and professional relationships started over a month ago. He has copies of our contract, the farmer's records, and even statistics about the number of students who donated plasma to ABG. When the whole truth comes out, it will show that Morton is serving healthy beef to our students and contributing to medical research."

No-Nonsense Nielson wasn't big on affectionate displays at work, but the fatherly look of pride on his face made her know she'd made the right move by working with the reporter.

* * *

Cassandra marched into the Student Affairs office, greeting Rachel and Devon with the confident smile of a newly permanent employee. Opening her office door, she heard voices chattering and laughing. Meg, Cinda and Fischer were seated on the couch and chairs around the low table where frosted mini cupcakes with sprinkles waited in a small plastic container.

She laughed, "Making yourselves at home, I see? Don't you all have work to do?"

Grinning, Fischer handed her a white business envelope. "Actually, I'm delivering my resignation."

Cassandra's smile faltered, and she tilted her head. Today's emotional roller coaster ride was getting old. She wanted off. None of these twists and turns were part of her plan. And she strongly disliked twists and turns. Her eyebrow raised. "Excuse me . . . you're leaving?" Wasn't this a back-to-work celebration?

"Dave Gonzales over at Facilities and Maintenance is retiring, and they've asked me to take over."

Her hand slowly reached out for the envelope. "Oh . . . ok then . . . I will accept this. Congratulations." A few seconds later, the implication hit her . . . that would make him an administrator too, and no longer her employee!

Meg leaned over and chose a chocolate frosted mini cupcake. She held it up like a champagne glass. "I have an announcement, too."

Cassandra went in for the other chocolate cupcake, Cinda chose a red velvet, and Fischer took a vanilla.

"Connor and I are going to have another baby!"

"Oh wow, that's wonderful!" said Cinda with red frosting on her teeth and lips.

"Congratulations!" said Fischer.

Cassandra's eyes dropped to Meg's flat stomach. "When are you due?"

Meg's smile animated her whole face. "In March. Cheers!" She raised her cupcake and took a big bite.

The others followed suit. Cinda pulled Meg into a hug. "One more thing. I saw an email announcement that Lance is running for student government next month. How cool would that be?" She stood up and stepped towards the door. "Congrats again to y'all. I gotta get back to work. Thanks for the cupcake break."

"I have class across campus soon." Meg scooped up the plastic tray and closed the lid. "But I'm taking the leftovers. If I'm going to gain 25 pounds, some of it may as well be cupcakes."

Suddenly uncomfortable alone with Fischer, Cassandra brushed the crumbs from the table top into her hand and reached over to shake them into the trash. She was eager to get back to work now that she didn't have to worry about backstabbing donors or stalkers following her home. Fischer reached under his chair and pulled out a twelve-inch wide white ceramic pot with a painted yellow flower on the side.

Nestled in loose dirt and potting soil was an eight-inch grayish green stick with little knots spaced inches apart along the sides and one green pointed leaf on top.

Despite recognizing the type of plant, Cassandra was confused and frowned slightly.

Fischer set the pot in front of her on the table. "After that night at your house, I asked Andy Summers if the deputies still had your Plumeria plant in evidence. They did, and I got it back. The campus greenhouse staff helped me re-pot what was left. It's pretty small, but hopefully you can make it grow again."

They had carefully placed new gravel around the edges. Her eyes welled up with tears and she whispered in awe. "This . . . is the sweetest thing you could have done."

She was leaking. He grabbed a couple tissues from the box on her desk and moved to sit beside her on the couch. "I didn't want you to lose this, too."

Cassandra wiped her eyes and hugged him. "Thank you. Just . . . Thank you."

When he left a few minutes later, she stood sniffling in her office and admired her artwork and mementos. The window behind her desk revealed vibrant orange and yellow leaves covering the trees surrounding the quad. The little survivor plant glowed in the warm sunlight. Carson was nothing like Hawai'i, but for the first time she felt at home.

Next in the
Cassandra Sato Mystery Series

Dead Week, **Book 2**

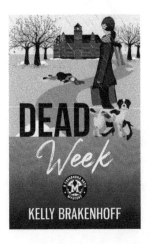

Reach Kelly at her website at **kellybrakenhoff.com**

Like Kelly's Facebook Page to get the latest updates:
https://www.facebook.com/kellybrakenhoffauthor/

Sign up for periodic emails with Kelly's special offers, recipes, and book recommendations here:
http://eepurl.com/ggOkvP

DEAD *Week*

BOOK 2 IN THE *CASSANDRA SATO MYSTERY* SERIES

Chapter One

If Cassandra Sato had to pinpoint the moment enthusiasm for her dream job faltered, it was when her weather app displayed a morning temperature of thirty-eight degrees with a predicted high of forty-two. Morton College in mid-November had more in common with the arctic tundra than a tropical paradise.

No one in her native state of Hawai'i would consider forty-two degrees a high temperature. Ever.

After three months, Cassandra had grown accustomed to Nebraska and the college, if not the frosty weather. Hard work and a good plan had gotten her to this point in her higher education career so quickly: a thirty-four-year-old Vice President of Student Affairs. A student's tragic death in October had been unsettling, but with the help of friends she'd passed her first professional test.

Fast walking from the Faculty Senate meeting back to the Osborne Administration Building, Cassandra slid Professor Zimmerman's printed memo into her leather portfolio and drew her numb hands inside her coat sleeves for protection. Only two weeks earlier, her boss, President Nielson, had announced his retirement then left on an extended vacation with his wife. In his absence, Cassandra felt added pressure to prevent shenanigans or disorderly behavior during the remaining weeks until the holiday break.

Inside the gloriously warm lobby, she climbed three flights of stairs to her office suite and paused to check her reflection in the elevator's mirrored steel surround.

Winter hadn't officially begun, yet Cassandra's red cheeks stung with cold. Her watery eyes had loosed a small mascara trail near her nose that she wiped away before entering her office suite.

Facing the doorway, four student workers deep in animated discussion crowded around a laptop screen on the reception desk. Since the September budget cuts and hiring freeze, Cassandra's secretarial needs had been cobbled together by part-time work study students whose primary concerns were passing Chemistry and getting dates for Saturday nights. She longed for a permanent assistant someday soon.

Logan Dunn, a dark-haired senior, quickly typed while the others dictated.

Rachel Nagle's voice rose above the hubbub. "I think a hunger strike is way better than blasting really loud heavy-metal music!" Then she slowly signed in American Sign

Language to Lance Erickson, the deaf student standing near Logan's desk.

"I was gonna suggest a smoke grenade," said Logan, "but I love the irony that loud music irritates hearing people and the deaf people don't care. Weaponized sound . . . now *that's* style."

"Skipping meals makes my blood sugar drop." Bridget's French-manicured hand daintily rested over her heart. "I think we should nix the hunger strike and just have people sign a petition."

Logan leaned away from the keyboard, allowing Lance to read their ideas on the laptop screen. "Petition drives are too easy. No one pays attention to them. We could always just boycott class. Preferably on Tuesday during my European History test at 11:30." He acknowledged Cassandra's entrance with a charming smile.

"What are you future felons up to now?" Cassandra crossed her hands in front of her chest. "Please tell me this is for a class?" Normally their amusing antics involved breaking office machinery or mixing up appointment times, not planning terroristic threats.

Rachel nodded, "Yeah, my Deaf Studies class has been working on an advocacy project. We've recruited students to support our cause, and we have to follow through with one of our ideas. Lance took the class last Spring so he's helping me decide our final tactic."

Lance put his two palms face out at Cassandra and shook his head no. Then he made a bomb gesture and his cheeks mimed an explosion. His head shook again.

The "no grenades" denial didn't reassure Cassandra. Professor Zimmerman's memo hadn't mentioned the Deaf Studies class by name, but hunger strikes, smoke grenades, and boycotts sounded like *alleged* demonstrations.

Rachel's eyes shone with excitement. "Professor Bryant told us that if we wanted things to change on campus, we had to advocate for them. Like back in the 80s. Another freshman in my class complained that Morton isn't accessible for us deaf people. So, we're going to protest and get them to change it."

Since Cassandra was likely the "them" who'd deal with their student misconduct charges if they crossed the line, she needed to set them straight from the beginning. Cassandra knew deaf students could have a classroom interpreter from talking to her friend Meg O'Brien. What more did they need?

"Wait." Laying her portfolio on the reception desk, Cassandra held up a hand. "Let's back up. Did you say, 'us deaf people,' Rachel? What do you mean?"

Rachel raised the left side of her long blonde hair, showing Cassandra a hearing aid behind her ear.

Cassandra's eyes widened. "I've never noticed that before. I thought you could hear."

Rachel nodded, "I could until tenth grade. Over six months, I completely lost my hearing on the right side, but my left still has a little bit. I started learning some signs my senior year because if I'm going to be deaf the rest of my life, I might as well use ASL. I've been trying an interpreter in my classes, but I don't understand enough yet to really learn that way."

"If you don't understand ASL well yet, how do you keep up in your Deaf Studies class? Does an interpreter tell you what Dr. Bryant is signing?" asked Cassandra.

Rachel said, "Everyone in my class is learning ASL. Our professor uses sign, his PowerPoint, and gestures to communicate with us."

"Is any of your family deaf?" Logan asked.

"I wish I knew. My dad's family can all hear, but my mother was adopted. I want to research her birth parents, but it's kind of a sensitive subject for my mom."

Bridget frowned. "Your mom doesn't know her birth parents' names?"

"When I asked in high school, Mom said she believed her birth mother had made the best decision she could. She didn't want me to search for her birth parents, but I need to know about their genetic history."

"Nothing about adoption is easy. I understand why your mom is sensitive about it," said Cassandra.

"We studied about causes of deafness in my class with Dr. Bryant." Rachel bit her fingernail. "There's even one called Usher Syndrome 3 where people lose their hearing in their teens and twenties. Like me! Then when they're 40 or 50 years old, they also go blind."

Cassandra knew enough from Meg to know that being deaf didn't have to be a barrier to a great job and family and life. Adding blindness would definitely be harder though.

Rachel fought back tears. "What if I have that? Or what if I carry a gene that means my future children will become deaf, too?"

"Surely the odds of you having that specific type of syndrome are very, very small, Rachel," Cassandra reassured. "Let's not get ahead of yourself in worrying."

"I'm going to convince my mother to let me take a DNA test over semester break to check for the genetic syndrome." Rachel added, "I found my mom's birth certificate and searched my birth grandmother's name. She was a student here at Morton in the 1970s."

"What a coincidence," said Cassandra.

Rachel's eyes flickered off to the side before meeting Cassandra's. "Not really. One reason I chose Morton was to find out more about my birth grandparents' families. My grandmother is dead. I saw her online obituary from 1976."

Cassandra had heard of students choosing a college because it was near the beach or they'd been offered a good scholarship. Following your dead grandmother's footsteps was unusual, at best.

"Promise you won't tell my mother I know all this!" Rachel pleaded, "I may have snooped for that birth certificate."

Cassandra didn't want to tangle with anyone's mother. "I won't tell your mom."

Rachel blew out a sigh. "Thanks, Dr. Sato."

"No worries, Rachel. But what if she finds out you went behind her back?"

"She'll be mad for a little while." Rachel shrugged off the warning.

"Now, for the rest of you lot," Raising a finger, Cassandra made eye contact with each of them in turn. "Smoke grenades are not a joke. The college frowns upon blowing up stuff."

Lance showed Cassandra his phone screen where he'd typed a list for the class advocacy project titled: "Things on campus that aren't accessible. Public TVs not captioned, public announcements spoken in English only, classroom videos not captioned, no emergency alert or 9-1-1 text system."

If they presented their concerns appropriately, Cassandra would be happy to help. "I look forward to seeing your advocacy proposal when it's finished." She stopped short in her inner office doorway. "And Logan, you'd better study for your history test, because no way is a class boycott going to happen."

Rachel said, "It worked before at Gallaudet University in Washington, DC. They got out of classes for a week, got the president fired, and pressured the Board to appoint the first Deaf President in school history."

Cassandra advised, "In any negotiation, it's better to make your requests privately first before you escalate to more serious and public moves."

"That's not what Professor Bryant told us. He was at Gallaudet in 1988, and he says deaf people are tired of fighting this battle."

Professor Bryant's student advocacy project had the bones of a great learning experience, but campus anarchy was not how Cassandra planned to end her first semester. Demonstrations and boycotts were the last thing the college needed after the difficulties of last month. With Nielson's exit, it fell to her to keep the peace. She'd have to keep a close eye on this project.

Acknowledgments

Dear reader, thank you for making it to the end with me! I hope we get to ride many more book adventures together.

So many people have helped me during the past four years: I'm grateful to the NaNoWriMo community for believing that stories matter and in the power of creativity to transform people's lives. Without their roadmap, my childhood dream of becoming an author would never have happened. Thanks to the Book Doctors, David Sterry and Arielle Eckstut, for the coaching opportunity I won after being voted the 2016 Pitchapalooza Fan Favorite. You helped shape my first NaNoWriMo project into something readable.

Thanks to Sione Aeschliman for her insightful guidance, her love of good stories, and her willingness to teach me, all with a smile. Michelle Argyle, thanks for the stunning cover that fits this story so well.

Tammy Gries and Scott Mueller, thanks for your willingness to explain complex biology and farming concepts to me again (and again). Roxanne Styskal from Nebraska Wesleyan University, for campus security expertise. Any technical errors are entirely mine.

Lori Ideta, who sends me beach photos when it's snowing here, thanks for showing me the meaning of Aloha and ohana.

Thank you to Abbey Buettgenbach, Peggy Scherling, Dave Balcom, Chris Timm, and Jean Hinton for reading early versions of this book. I know there were others I'm forgetting to name, but it's been four years and we all know my memory isn't getting any better. Mom and Dad for reading multiple drafts and your superior spellchecking.

This journey has introduced me to many new writing friends, both online and in person like Macie, Mandy, Patty, Shane, Susan, and Fr. Winter, and especially Laura Chapman for her patient publishing advice and spoiling us with delicious food. Gotham Writers teacher Greg Fallis and the mystery class, thanks for your honest criticism and advice. Jessica Sinsheimer and Julie Falatko at the Manuscript Academy for giving so generously of their time and talents to bring good books into the world. Shoutout to the FB Pitch Wars YA group for your encouragement, advice, and holding me accountable. (Looking at you, Morgan Hazelwood.) Tim Collins and Rusty Marcum who keep us all laughing.

My Book Club, which began as an excuse to leave our babies for a night out and a glass of wine. Thanks for the past 19 years and counting; you have become my closest friends and cheerleaders.

Speaking of cheerleaders, thanks to my PPH sisters and their husbands, Diane & Doug, Tammy & Brian, Sheri & John, Gail & Blaine, Donna & Mike, Jodi & Shawn, Laura & Jesus, Peggy & Ken. I'm so grateful to know you all. Jodi, thanks for our long Saturday runs together through rain, snow, and sweat.

Thanks to Joe, Jon, Kate, James, Claire, and Colton for putting up with my running, healthy cooking phases, and five years of Novembers with infrequent hot meals and clean clothes. They say having a weird mom (and mother-in-law) builds character, so you all should be set for a while.

Dave, thanks for giving me quiet time to follow my dreams while you mowed grass, washed cars, did laundry, shoveled snow, walked the dog, cooked dinner, and a million other things to show us how much you love us. Our thirty(!) years together have been one long exercise in willing the good of the other. I love you.

Thanks to Kirstin, Nathan, Duane, Tim, Terri, Mary Jane, and everyone in heaven who has lifted me up and pointed the way when I asked. I'm most grateful to God for his loving mercy. Every life is a worthy story.

About the Author

Kelly Brakenhoff is an American Sign Language Interpreter whose motivation for learning ASL began in high school when she wanted to converse with her deaf friends. Her children's picture book series featuring Duke the deaf dog is coming later in 2019, beginning with *Never Mind*. She serves on the Board of Editors for the Registry of Interpreters for the Deaf publication, *VIEWs*. The mother of four young adults, a cranky old dog, and a rambunctious puppy, Kelly and her husband call Nebraska home.

3 1901 10064 9427

CPSIA information can be obtained
at www.ICGtesting.com
Printed in the USA
LVHW031722261121
704539LV00007B/741

9 781733 742405